PROOF

Books by Fern Michaels

The Wild Side
On the Line
Fear Thy Neighbor
No Way Out
Fearless
Deep Harbor
Fate & Fortune
Sweet Vengeance
Fancy Dancer
No Safe Secret
About Face
Perfect Match
A Family Affair
Forget Me Not
The Blossom Sisters
Balancing Act
Tuesday's Child
Betrayal
Southern Comfort
To Taste the Wine
Sins of the Flesh
Sins of Omission
Return to Sender
Mr. and Miss Anonymous
Up Close and Personal
Fool Me Once
Picture Perfect
The Future Scrolls
Kentucky Sunrise
Kentucky Heat
Kentucky Rich
Plain Jane
Charming Lily

What You Wish For
The Guest List
Listen to Your Heart
Celebration
Yesterday
Finders Keepers
Annie's Rainbow
Sara's Song
Vegas Sunrise
Vegas Heat
Vegas Rich
Whitefire
Wish List
Dear Emily

The Lost and Found Novels:

Secrets
Hidden
Liar!

The Sisterhood Novels:

Rock Bottom
Tick Tock
19 Yellow Moon Road
Bitter Pill
Truth and Justice
Cut and Run
Safe and Sound
Need to Know
Crash and Burn
Point Blank

Books by Fern Michaels (*Cont.*)

In Plain Sight
Eyes Only
Kiss and Tell
Blindsided
Gotcha!
Home Free
Déjà Vu
Cross Roads
Game Over
Deadly Deals
Vanishing Act
Razor Sharp
Under the Radar
Final Justice
Collateral Damage
Fast Track
Hokus Pokus
Hide and Seek
Free Fall
Lethal Justice
Sweet Revenge
The Jury
Vendetta
Payback
Weekend Warriors

The Men of the
Sisterhood Novels:

Hot Shot
Truth or Dare
High Stakes

Fast and Loose
Double Down

The Godmothers Series:

Far and Away
Classified
Breaking News
Deadline
Late Edition
Exclusive
The Scoop

E-Book Exclusives:

Desperate Measures
Seasons of Her Life
To Have and To Hold
Serendipity
Captive Innocence
Captive Embraces
Captive Passions
Captive Secrets
Captive Splendors
Cinders to Satin
For All Their Lives
Texas Heat
Texas Rich
Texas Fury
Texas Sunrise

Books by Fern Michaels (*Cont.*)

Anthologies:

Tiny Blessings
In Bloom
Home Sweet Home

Holiday Novels

Santa's Secret
Santa & Company
Santa Cruise
The Brightest Star
Spirit of the Season
Holly and Ivy
Wishes for Christmas
Christmas at Timberwoods

Christmas Anthologies

A Snowy Little Christmas
Coming Home for Christmas

A Season to Celebrate
Mistletoe Magic
Winter Wishes
The Most Wonderful Time
When the Snow Falls
Secret Santa
A Winter Wonderland
I'll Be Home for Christmas
Making Spirits Bright
Holiday Magic
Snow Angels
Silver Bells
Comfort and Joy
Sugar and Spice
Let It Snow
A Gift of Joy
Five Golden Rings
Deck the Halls
Jingle All the Way

FERN MICHAELS
PROOF

ZEBRA BOOKS
Kensington Publishing Corp.
www.kensingtonbooks.com

ZEBRA BOOKS are published by

Kensington Publishing Corp.
900 Third Avenue
New York, NY 10022

All Kensington titles, imprints, and distributed lines are available at special quantity discounts for bulk purchases for sales promotion, premiums, fund-raising, and educational or institutional use.

Special book excerpts or customized printings can also be created to fit specific needs. For details, write or phone the office of the Kensington Sales Manager: Kensington Publishing Corp., 900 Third Avenue, New York, NY 10022. Attn. Sales Department. Phone: 1-800-221-2647.

First Kensington Books hardcover printing: July 2024
First Zebra Books mass market paperback printing: September 2024

ISBN-13: 978-1-4201-5561-7
ISBN-13: 978-1-4201-5564-8 (eBook)

10 9 8 7 6 5 4 3 2 1

Printed in the United States of America

This book is dedicated to all who help rescue animals.
Bless you and all God's creatures.

Prologue One

Stillwell Art Center
Buncombe County, North Carolina

Stillwell Art Center was coming up on its third anniversary. The forty-acre complex was home to a two-story lavish building where dozens of artists occupied glass-enclosed workspaces overlooking a meticulously landscaped atrium in the center. The rear of the building had large glass sliding doors that opened to a stone patio with café tables. Beyond the patio was an equally meticulous park where visitors could bring their dogs and let them run in a designated area, where they were supervised by an attendant.

The genius behind the artisan village was Ellie Stillwell, a seventy-something former art professor. It was when her husband Richard passed away that she discovered how much money her real estate, bonds, and investments were worth, and that the farm and land she'd inherited from her family spanned hundreds of acres.

Ellie and Richard had never had children. The farm,

Richard's law practice, her position at the college, and their dogs were all they needed. But Ellie wanted to leave a legacy, something for the community of artists, and for the community as a whole. It took almost two years and a lot of council meetings, surveys, revisions, building plans, and cajoling before they broke ground. Initially many of the council members were dubious about the viability of an art center outside Asheville, North Carolina. *Who would go watch people paint? Throw pottery?* Ellie had ready answers: It would be a place of interest. A destination. She explained that the atrium would be surrounded by gourmet shops, where people could purchase sandwiches, salads, pastries, cheese, wine, tea, and coffee between visits to the many artists' studios, where they could watch the artists at work—and hopefully purchase something. Strategically placed café tables in the atrium as well as on the outdoor patio would provide a place to eat and relax. In addition to the elegant food court, Ellie would allow community organizations to hold their events free of charge.

She continued to explain and defend her ideas, including Thursday nights devoted to music, when people could listen to smooth jazz or a string ensemble.

After much debate, she won over the council and began the year-long construction.

Not only was the Stillwell Center artist-friendly, but it was also dog-friendly and kid-friendly. Well, sometimes kid-friendly, depending on which entitled group of wine-slugging women showed up. Some days a particular group of women came with their undisciplined children—and no nannies—which gave Nathan Belmont, head of security, a run for his money. Literally.

One time he chased a five-year-old over three hundred yards through the well-kept gardens. The tipsy mother hadn't noticed her child was missing until Nathan carried him back into the atrium. It wasn't a daily event, and everyone knew who that little group of designer clotheshorses were, so they were prepared when the women and their offspring appeared for a version of Chuck E. Cheese.

While Ellie would never proclaim whose art she preferred, she'd developed a strong bond with Luna Bodhi Bodman, the occupant of The Namaste Café. Luna had once been employed as a social worker in child psychology, but her real passion leaned toward the metaphysical. Ever since childhood, she'd had a way of knowing things. A gift, some would say. She could read people like an open book, and she would do cold psychic readings for customers if they were so inclined. A large easel and drawing pad were her medium. When people came seeking advice, she would stand behind the easel and draw whatever images came to her. It was uncanny, as Ellie discovered when Luna told her things about Richard that no one could have known.

Luna was very low-key when it came to providing insight to customers, even though her reputation was well-known. She never solicited. They had to ask. Luna's bohemian wardrobe, granny glasses, and waist-long hair might have been a clue as to her practice, but then again, it was an art center, and many of its denizens wore unconventional clothing.

Luna's older brother Cullen took the corner spot on the first floor, next to her café. When he'd graduated from college, he was employed in an office doing office-type things. The type of things that weren't fulfilling for him. When their parents retired from their antiques business, Cullen took it over and expanded it to include restoration, then became a master craftsman, resuscitating discarded furniture.

The third person in Ellie's close-knit group was Lebici "Chi-Chi" Stone, a stunning woman whose handcrafted jewelry was an extension of her beauty. Her parents had brought her and her brother to the States when she was nine. Before moving, her father worked in Kano, Nigeria, and was employed making ceremonial bowls. Chi-Chi showed an interest in the craft at an early age. As she grew, so did her fascination with jewelry. She studied metalsmithing after high school, and during her summer breaks, she visited Nigeria and brought gemstones back to incorporate into her work. Now, at thirty-nine, she was renowned for her jewelry, which fetched anywhere from 500 up to thousands of dollars for custom pieces. Chi-Chi and Luna had become best friends, and a romance between Cullen and Chi-Chi began to grow. They often had dinner together, and when Luna's love interest, Marshal Christopher Gaines, was in town, it was always a cheerful occasion. Unless Luna was on one of her missions to solve a mystery, which usually involved one of the items in Cullen's workshop. Then it became a madcap adventure that drew all of them into Luna's world of mystery.

Prologue Two

The Caribbean

For their fifteenth anniversary, a thirty-something couple decided to make a return to St. Kitts. With its rolling green hills, fertile land, and pristine sandy beaches where the deep rich blue of the Atlantic meets the tranquil turquoise of the Caribbean, St. Kitts is a small island of 50,000 people. Just southeast of Puerto Rico, it beckons visitors to experience its beauty. At only sixty-five square miles, it's a very low-key alternative to the more popular and much larger islands, like Jamaica and Puerto Rico, which are seven and eight times its size.

With the exception of the addition of some eateries, water sports, and a golf course, the island has changed very little over the years. It has preserved its casual, slow-paced, easy, island vibe.

The couple was sitting on the veranda that overlooked Mt. Nevis, having their final breakfast of the trip.

"I'm going to miss this place," she sighed.

"Yeah. Me too," he replied as he scrolled through

his phone. "We could stay a few more days. The booking site says it's available."

"Really?"

"Yeah." He continued to read the information on his phone. "Get this, the house we're staying in is on the market."

"For real?" she asked.

He began to read aloud: "'Beautiful cottage, two bedrooms, two baths, with view of Mt. Nevis and the sea. Built two years ago. Great income property.'" He stopped. "Yeah. We're the income."

"Wait, honey. What are they asking?"

"'Call for quote.'"

"So call them, for Pete's sake."

"Why?"

"Income property. We've been talking about investing in something why not this?"

He looked up from his phone. "You're serious." It was a statement, not a question.

"Why not? If we're going to buy something for rental income, this could be perfect. I betcha it would pay for itself, and we'd have a place to spend our own vacations."

He looked at her. "Let me see what I can find out."

She gave him her best Miss Hennepin County smile and squeezed his hand. He placed the call and spoke with a realtor while writing numbers on a piece of paper. "Sounds like a worthwhile venture. Let me speak to my wife about it. I noticed it's available to rent next week, so we'd like to stay on. Give us more of an opportunity to delve into this proposal. Great. Thanks. Talk soon."

He turned to her. "If what he told me is accurate,

you're right. This place pays for itself, provided there are no hurricanes."

She giggled. "How much are they asking?"

He slid the paper over to her. "That is in the ballpark, honey. What's the difference if the property is close to home or in the Caribbean?"

Her rosy cheeks got rosier. "Everything!"

"Are you sure you want to do this? Part of the plan was that I would take care of the property, like fixing stuff. It's not going to be profitable if I have to fly here to do it."

She knew he was kidding. "Well, I'm sure there's someone who could manage it for us. Whoever is managing it now, maybe. Did the realtor say why the owners want to sell it? We're not sitting on a sinkhole, are we?"

"Nah. The husband needed medical care, which means the family needs money. I don't know if they're desperate, but if you're really sure, we can try to negotiate."

"Swell!" she cooed, with her beauty pageant smile and pink cheeks.

Two days later, they were sitting in the realtor's office, filling out the paperwork. The closing wouldn't be for a few more weeks, so they flew home and made arrangements to return when the date was set. They were both keen to "Pop the bubbly from our veranda."

Everything proceeded according to plan, and the couple made their second journey in a month. The closing went smoothly, and the couple did exactly what they'd anticipated and opened a bottle of champagne on their new veranda as they watched the sky turn from light pink to deep red to purple.

The following morning, the couple decided to rent a

small powerboat and cruise the shoreline of their new home away from home. She clung to his arm as their boat scooted around what appeared to be an old fishing boat. She noticed someone was hanging off the side and pulling up a basket of something. She thought it might be a crab trap, until a shot rang out and the person who had been leaning over fell in the water, surrounded by a pool of blood.

She started screaming, and her husband hit the throttle and hightailed it out of there until the fishing boat was no longer in sight. They felt shock and horror as they flew past the dock where they were supposed to return the boat.

"What should we do?" she yelled over the sound of the ramped-up motor. "We need to go to the police." She started shaking as he slowed down the skiff.

"I don't know if we should do that," he said. "We're in a foreign country." He cut the engine and let the boat drift.

"What does that mean?" She was in tears now.

"We don't really know who's corrupt and who isn't. We gotta be careful," he cautioned her.

"What if we call the American Embassy?"

"I think the closest one is in Barbados."

"How far is that?"

"Too far for this little dinghy."

Several days later, slivers of the couple's boat were found floating along the shoreline. There was no sign of their bodies. The newspaper simply reported:

> American couple feared dead in St. Kitts due to boating accident.
> No other details are available at this time.

Chapter One

The Namaste Café
Tuesday

It was a quiet start to the week. The center was open Wednesday through Sunday afternoon. Mondays and Tuesdays were devoted to meetings, paperwork, deliveries, and catching up. Luna opened the café for anyone in need of coffee, and The Flakey Tart delivered a basket of croissants for Luna to oversee. She fired up the De'Longhi La Specialista espresso machine and put out cups and plates. It was a self-serve situation on the days the center was closed to the public.

Luna fixed a cup for her brother and brought it into his workshop, her dog Wylie following behind her.

"Why the long face?" Cullen asked as she handed him his java.

"Huh? What do you mean?" Luna glanced up at him.

"I know that look. Something is on your mind."

She shrugged. "No. Not really." She was lying, and he knew it.

"Don't give me that, little sister. What's up?" He leaned against the long shop table.

"I can't quite put my finger on it."

"That could be a good thing or a bad thing." Cullen was well aware of his sister's *feelings*. "Things okay with Chris?"

"Yeah, fine," she said mechanically.

"You sure?"

"Oh, yeah. Sure. Of course." She furrowed her brow, then turned and went back into her café.

Cullen knew there was something bothering Luna. The problem was, if she couldn't put her finger on it, then it was impossible for him to help. He also knew she would eventually figure it out.

Luna sat down at her easel. Nothing was coming to her. It was almost as if she were numb. Physically, mentally, spiritually, and emotionally numb. She closed her eyes, took her pen, and drew a large question mark on the pad. "So? What is it?" she shouted at the inanimate object staring back at her. Wylie also sensed Luna's uneasiness and plopped his head on her knee. Luna looked down into his big brown eyes. "You got an answer, pal? 'Cause I sure don't."

She got up and made herself a cappuccino, then spotted a glorious work of art flowing across the atrium. It was Chi-Chi. She often dressed in vibrant colors that perfectly draped her five-foot-seven-inch frame. A matching head wrap held her long, black box braids in place as they cascaded down her back.

No wonder Cullen is in love with her. Luna sighed.

"E̩ káàrò̩." Chi-Chi gave her the morning greeting.

"E̩ káàrò̩," Luna replied. "Your usual?"

"Thank you. I can do it. This is your day off."

Luna got up and moved toward the counter. She gave Chi-Chi a side hug. "What's on your agenda for today?"

"I am going through all the papers my brother left behind. He is so disorganized. It is astonishing he can get back and forth from Nigeria without finding himself in Nova Scotia."

"You don't know that it hasn't already happened," Luna joked.

"You are right. He would never tell me if such a thing happened to him."

"Because you'd never let him forget it."

"Please. I cannot unsee the spectacle that was on display when I walked into my house and found him with Jennine. I do mean on display. It was a very unpleasant experience."

"The thought is horrifying." Luna giggled. "But not surprising."

"We never should have left him alone."

"He is a grown man." Luna smirked.

Chi-Chi grunted. "I do not believe those two words go together: *grown* and *man*. They are just silly boys in larger clothes with bigger feet."

Luna barely stopped coffee from escaping out of her nose. "Do you feel that way about Cullen?" Luna had a twinkle in her eye.

"He is a man. A good man. A smart man. A kind man."

"Yep. All of those. But he's still a guy." Luna rolled her eyes. "I grew up with him. I oughta know."

"By the way, who were you talking to before I came in?"

"Huh?" Luna seemed confused. "You mean Wylie?"

"No. Before. You asked, 'What is it?' Your voice was more demanding than usual." Chi-Chi winked at her.

"Oh, nothing." Luna sighed.

"My dear friend. You cannot pretend there is nothing bothering you. I do not mean to pry, but you do not seem to be yourself today."

"That's just it. I have this weird feeling, and I cannot figure it out."

"Weird in what way?" Chi-Chi pulled out a chair. "Please sit with me."

"Have you ever had the sense that something is gnawing at your subconscious, but you can't bring it into focus?" Luna asked.

"Not very often. But when I do feel that way, I go deep into my work. It brings me into a different state of consciousness. That is when many answers come to me." She patted Luna's hand. "But I am not telling you something you do not already know."

"You're right about that alpha and theta state. I just can't seem to get there today. It's as if my mind has drawn a blank. I feel edgy. Unsettled."

Chi-Chi eyed her friend curiously. "Do you think it could be that you are uneasy because of your relationship with the marshal?"

"No. Our relationship is solid. We're good," Luna insisted.

"But is it as good as you want it to be?" Chi-Chi pushed.

"What do you mean?" Luna peered at her friend over her coffee cup.

"You and Chris have been seeing each other for almost three years, am I right?"

"Well, we really can't count the first year." Luna stared back at her.

"Let me ask you: Do you want more?" Chi-Chi pried.

"More what?" Luna asked casually.

"Please, Luna. I am not a fool. Are you satisfied with the limited time you have together?"

"Okay, so he lives two hours away. We manage." She took another sip of her coffee.

"Is *managing* what you want?"

"I don't know." Luna sighed yet again. "We're very happy when we are together."

"Ah. That is my point: when you are together. How happy are you when you are not?"

"I'm busy." Luna swept her arm, indicating the café and her easel.

Chi-Chi smiled. "I can tell you are not going to discuss this with me."

"There is nothing to discuss." Luna shook her head for emphasis.

"If you say so." Chi-Chi got up. "I am going to say good morning to Cullen. Meanwhile, I suggest you continue your conversation with your sketch pad." She smiled and turned toward the door that connected the café with Cullen's showroom.

Luna remained in her seat, staring into space.

As Chi-Chi stepped into the showroom, a soft bell rang in the back, signaling someone had entered. Chi-Chi was familiar with Cullen's routine and made her way past the beautifully restored pieces of furniture, lamps, and a variety of once-discarded home goods such as old lanterns, plaques, a coatrack, and an umbrella stand. She called out, *"EẸ káàrò!"*

"EẸ káàrò," a voice in the distance replied. "Come on back."

Chi-Chi admired the most recent armoire Cullen had revitalized as she entered the workshop area. Cullen was wearing a work apron, and a face shield sat atop his head.

"Good morning!" He was grinning from ear to ear. "I'm covered in sawdust," he said apologetically as he attempted to brush some of it off.

Chi-Chi waved a hand in front of her face, fanning away any remnants from his work. "I can see that." She blew him a kiss.

"You look lovely today." He smiled at her.

"Thank you. And you? You look like you do every morning," she teased. "But I like it anyway."

"Good thing for me. So, what are your plans for the day?"

"I will be going through the paper mess my brother left for me." She paused. "May I ask you something?"

"Of course."

"When I was speaking to Luna, she seemed very distracted. Almost worried. She was not behaving like her usual self."

Cullen picked up the damp towel that he kept on the workbench and wiped his hands. "I was thinking the same thing. She seemed a little off. I mean *off* as in not her usual kind of off." He managed a grin. "She was almost sullen."

"Ah. Yes, that is a very appropriate word. Sullen." Chi-Chi tilted her head. "Do you know why she may be in a mood? And please do not say *hormones,* or I will have to slap you." Chi-Chi was serious. She'd had enough of the female moodiness/hormone stigma. If men could experience having a period just one time, they would never criticize a woman again for going through her monthly challenges. Then add paying sales tax on the necessary items. It was infuriating.

"Easy." Cullen could see the fire smoldering in Chi-Chi's eyes. "I would not dare to suggest . . ." His voice trailed off before she could get in a good punch, verbal or otherwise.

Chi-Chi folded her arms. "What did she say to you this morning?"

"Not a whole lot. I asked her if there was something bothering her, and she was vague. Something about not being able to put her finger on it. Then I asked about Chris, and she said things were fine."

"Hmm," Chi-Chi responded. "I got a similar response from her."

"It's been several weeks since they've seen each other," Cullen reflected.

"Yes. And they usually spend every other weekend together. Something is not quite right. I can feel it in my bones," Chi-Chi said.

"You're beginning to sound like her, too!" Cullen chuckled.

Chi-Chi gave him one of her *stop before you say something stupid* looks. "Maybe you should call him and invite him to a game, or whatever men do together." She looked him directly in the eye.

Cullen blinked several times before replying. "I suppose I could, but Luna might get annoyed."

"Why would she? He is your friend, too, is he not?"

"True. And we have hung out together before." He looked up at the local community calendar. "There's a classic car show in Asheville on Saturday. That could be interesting. Maybe I'll get into the car restoration business."

"That is a brilliant idea," Chi-Chi said.

"Getting into the car restoration business?" He tightened his lips. "I was kidding."

"I know you were kidding, but that could be your excuse for going. You can tell him that you have been considering classic car refurbishing and want to research the idea." Chi-Chi was normally uncomfortable with subterfuge, but this was for a good cause. Plus, she wouldn't be the one carrying it out.

"Now *that* is brilliant," Cullen responded cheerfully. "We make a good team."

"I happen to think so." Chi-Chi was almost blushing. "You have your assignment, so now get busy." She turned on her heel and waltzed out the door.

Cullen watched the colorful fabric float away. He pulled his phone from the drawer that kept it safe from flying splinters and speed-dialed Chris's number.

Chapter Two

U.S. Marshal's Field Office
Charlotte, North Carolina

U.S. Marshal Christopher Gaines looked down at his cell phone. The caller ID said Lucinda, Gaines's ex-wife. "This can't be good," he muttered to himself. "Yes, Lucinda. What's up?"

"Chris, it's Lucinda."

Yeah, duh.

"I have something important we need to discuss."

"Everything alright? Carter okay?" Gaines's thoughts sobered as they turned to his son.

"Yes, everything is fine, actually," Lucinda said matter-of-factly.

"So?"

"So, I wanted to let you know that Bruce and I are planning on moving to Chicago."

"You're what!" Gaines bellowed. "When was this decided? You can't take Carter out of the state without my permission."

"I realize that, Christopher, but Bruce has an opportunity to buy into a dental practice in Chicago."

Chris had been thrilled when Lucinda remarried. After Carter was born, she'd complained she was bored, so she started working at a dental practice when they moved to Charlotte. It didn't take long for Lucinda to have the dentist wrapped around her finger—and a few other body parts. When the affair became obvious, she blamed Chris. She said he was married to his job, and she didn't want to live her life alone. Fortunately for Chris, he didn't want to live with a whiny, spoiled woman who seemed to have forgotten what had attracted her to him in the first place: he was a U.S. Marshal. He kept long hours, often traveling for days at a time.

But, like many people, Lucinda ignored reality and hoped things would change for the better, or to what she wanted. Unfortunately, under most circumstances, they only changed for the worse. If one wanted things to get better, the changes had to be big. Really big. In Chris and Lucinda's case, the big change was her affair. With both of them getting what they wanted, it was a relatively amicable divorce. Chris was not bitter about Lucinda's transgressions. He was relieved. And then even more relieved that there would be no alimony. He had no problem with child support, but paying alimony to someone who clearly was able to work but didn't irked him to the moon and back.

"We'll have to go back to court," he said into the phone.

"I was hoping we could resolve this between the two of us."

"I don't think so, Lucinda." Gaines was in law enforcement. If there weren't any rules, then they couldn't be enforced, and he didn't want Lucinda to have the advantage of doing whatever she pleased. "We have a legal and binding joint-custody arrangement."

"I am aware of that, Chris." She softened a bit. "But do we really need to go through all that legalese stuff when we can work this out together?"

"Nope." He was adamant. Lucinda's life's work was to get her own way, but he wasn't about to let her sweet-talk, threaten, or pull whatever tricks she had planned. "Call your lawyer, and I'll call mine." He waited for a response.

"I really wish you wouldn't be so difficult," she huffed, sounding more like herself.

"Lucinda, I am not being difficult. I'm being thorough." He inhaled. "When is all of this supposed to happen?"

"Within the next six to eight months," she replied.

"Then we have time to work this out." Chris was being thoughtful, not for her sake, but for his own. And Carter's.

"Oh, I am so glad to hear you say that," she murmured.

Chris was trying to keep the lid on his steam. "Don't get so excited, Lucinda. This is not going to be easy. Listen, I have to go. I have a meeting in ten minutes."

"It's always about your job, Chris," she snarked.

"Please, Lucinda. Let's not get into that now."

"Fine. You'll be hearing from my lawyer. Bye."

Chris's mind was racing. This could not be happening. He was not going to send his son off to the other side of the country. Not with Dr. Tooth. Lucinda's husband Bruce was a good dentist, except for one thing:

he had the worst buck teeth in the state of North Carolina. Why any person would trust their mouth to someone who was oblivious to his own was a head-scratcher.

Carter was in eighth grade now. Since he was six, he'd practiced hard to develop his baseball skills with his dad. Chris had once been a professional baseball player and was an active participant in Carter's growing interest in the game. Chris trained Carter at home and on the field, where he coached Carter's team. A winning team, at that. The previous summer, Carter's Little League team went all the way to the finals. Most of the kids were in eighth grade now and were no longer eligible for Little League, so Chris had helped the school form a softball team for the students. He was determined to make sure this team was a winner, as well.

No, Lucinda was not going to break up the team, at home or on the field. Chris took a few deep breaths before he went into his meeting. Things had been going along smoothly with his job, his son, and his girlfriend. And now the monkey wrench known as Lucinda was thrown into the mix. This was going to get ugly. He picked up his phone and called his lawyer. "Houston, we have a problem." Chris always laughed at that opening line, because his lawyer's name was actually Houston.

"What's up, man?" Evan Houston laughed.

"Lucinda is moving to Chicago."

"When? Why?" Evan asked, rapid-fire.

"Six months, maybe. Dr. Tooth is buying into a practice out there."

"Have they seen his teeth?" Houston mocked.

Chris laughed. "Apparently not." He paused. "We are going to have to renegotiate the custody agreement. As in, I want full custody."

"I can understand that," Houston replied. "You know it's going to be a battle."

"Of course, it will be. We're dealing with Lucinda," Chris agreed.

"But you could make a good case for yourself. Bruce is not Carter's father, and not at all involved in Carter's activities. Correct?" Houston noted.

"True. He's basically invisible. I don't think he's been to more than one of Carter's games," Chris responded.

"Good. Start keeping track of his involvement—or lack thereof—but don't let on you're keeping score. You don't want Lucinda pulling a stunt and having Bruce suddenly become interested in Carter's life."

"Good point. I won't even ask if Bruce will be attending any of Carter's games, or his science project exhibit."

"Great. Make sure you keep notes on how often Bruce helps with his homework, too."

"That I can say with confidence is a big *never*," Chris replied. "I have a meeting in five minutes. We'll recon later. Thanks, man. I appreciate the suggestion and the advice."

"Any time. Always happy to help the U.S. Marshal service," Houston said before he ended the call.

Chris had met Evan during his first case in Charlotte. Chris's area of responsibility was missing children and human trafficking. Evan Houston practiced family law. A child had been abducted from his backyard by one of his relatives. Chris was immediately called into the investigation. Two days later, the child was fortunately found unharmed, and his uncle was arrested, charged, found guilty of child endangerment, and sentenced to five years in prison. The mother was terrified that she and her son would be in constant danger from her estranged husband's family. The family wanted her boy, and she was sure they would also want revenge. She sought Evan's help to represent her in an application for relocation, and Chris helped facilitate the request. Both men were fathers. Both men had boys the same age. There was an immediate kinship between them, as they imagined what it would be like having one of their own go missing. From that day forward, the two men were tight friends.

When Chris told Evan about Lucinda's indiscretions, Evan offered to represent Chris in his divorce, pro bono. Free of charge. Evan, too, had suffered a betrayal and knew exactly what was to come for his friend: Aggravation. Lack of cooperation. Empty threats. Blame. And a whole lot of B.S.

Chris gathered his tablet, a pad, pen, and his cell phone and strode down the hallway to the conference room. He was breathing a little easier now, thanks to Evan.

Chris's appearance could be intimidating to some. He was just over six feet tall with a well-toned body. His gait was confident. His long black eyelashes surrounded deep blue eyes that demanded one's attention. One wouldn't say his eyes were steely, or cold either. But they had the ability to pierce the veil of anyone who attempted to lie. It was one of his best weapons. Then there was his smile. Warm. Inviting, if he chose.

He had black wavy hair with a dash of gray at the temples that gave him the appearance of a man who packed a lot of experience for someone about to turn forty.

He'd first met Luna Bodhi Bodman a few years prior during a search party for a little girl. Luna wasn't the least bit daunted by his handsome looks or air of authority. He had been struck by her confidence and self-assuredness. She was quite different from anyone he had ever met, and it took a little time for him to become smitten with the quirky and eccentric free spirit. Luna had very few filters. Not that she was unkind, but if something was on her mind, or in her gut, she felt compelled to say it.

The two developed a strong friendship while they collaborated on other cases involving missing kids. He appreciated her ability to "read" people and advocate for "doing the right thing." After several assignments, Luna left her job with social services and opened a café in the Stillwell Center outside of Asheville. It was a two-hour drive away, but Gaines wanted to maintain the relationship. Perhaps even take it a step further.

The grand opening of the art center had given him the perfect opportunity to show his face, and perhaps kiss hers before the night was over, but he'd almost missed the event. He had remembered sunflowers were her favorite and combed Charlotte until he found a florist who had them. He was running late and came close to breaking every traffic law between Charlotte and Asheville. Not only was his car racing, but so was his heart.

He had handed her the flowers and profusely apologized for his tardiness, but the look in her eyes and the expression on her face made it all worthwhile. He let out the biggest exhale, realizing he might have been holding his breath the entire length of the interstate.

His recollection of that night was broken by voices coming from the conference room. There were a half dozen people gathered around the long table.

Chris's boss, Frank, was sitting at the head of the table and began to speak. "People, I have some news. There are several positions opening up in the Witness Security Program. As some of you may know, the number of people in the program has grown considerably, thanks to prosecutors increasing the number of deals they cut. Unfortunately, our staffing hasn't grown at the same rate, but we finally got more funding for more jobs. For those of you who wish to transfer, you have my utmost respect and support."

Questions were flying across the table. "Where?" "When?" "What's the pay scale?"

"Simmer down. I have the job description and details printed out." Frank passed several sheets of paper to everyone seated. "The only downside, if there is one, is that most of the positions require relocation. It's all outlined in front of you."

Chris's eyes darted to the word *Chicago*. If Lucinda moved to Chicago, he could apply for that position, but he didn't want to move. He knew Carter wouldn't want to move, either. He had his friends, activities, and school here in Charlotte. And baseball. *Chicago was no place for baseball. The Cubs winning the World Series was a fluke.* It would be too much of an adjustment for a kid Carter's age. He was on the verge of puberty. Moving would be much worse than breaking out in pimples, or trying to figure out what the rest of his body was doing.

Then Chris saw the words CHARLOTTE—PENDING. The job was with the Western Division of North Carolina, covering territory from Charlotte to Asheville. His life was in North Carolina. His son's life was in North Carolina. And what about Luna? They were getting so close. He didn't want to lose her. He thought back to his conversation with Evan. First things first. Apply for full custody. He knew he had to talk to Luna about it. Get her take on it. Emotionally, intellectually, and of course, with Luna's metaphysical superpower way of thinking.

Just as Gaines was leaving the room, his boss took him aside. "Chris, you are my most senior marshal. As much as I would miss having you on my team, the position in North Carolina WITSEC comes with a promotion and a raise."

"The info says 'pending.'" Gaines pointed to the paper in his hand.

"It does. 'Pending' whether or not *you* take the job." Frank rested his arms on the table behind him. "You've been an excellent agent. You handle people well. I won't lie—this job is a mountain of paperwork and managing people, but it will also give you a normal schedule. You'd only go into the field under extreme circumstances. But we can discuss this more after you mull it over."

"Thanks, Frank. I appreciate it." There was no mulling or thinking required. He'd ask for the job in Charlotte. If things got really ugly, and Lucinda got her way, he could negotiate a transfer. Maybe. But he wasn't getting on that bus just yet. Not without a serious fight.

Chris had started to leave when Frank called out, "I'll hold the job here until you make up your mind. But don't take too long. I'm getting pressure."

Chris made the decision right then and there. "I'll take it." The timing was actually quite perfect. More money. More stability. More ammo for his fight for custody.

Frank smiled and held out his hand. "You'll do great. There will be a lot more face time with bureaucrats, but I have no doubt you can handle it."

Chris shook Frank's hand. "Thanks. This is exactly what I needed today."

Gaines stepped quickly down the hall, shut the door of his office, and started to punch in Luna's number to see if they could get together for the weekend. It had been three weeks since he had seen her. Much too long. But before he had a chance to press *send*, a call from Cullen came through.

"Hey Cul!" Gaines answered on the second ring. "To what do I owe this unexpected call?" Then he froze. "Everything alright?"

"Yeah. Everything is fine." Cullen cleared his throat, for he was about to embark on a clandestine operation to suss out the situation between the marshal and his sister. "I've been considering expanding into classic car interior refurbishing."

"That could be cool," Gaines replied.

"Yeah, so there's a classic car show in Asheville this weekend, and I thought if you're free, maybe you'd like to go?" Cullen felt like he was back in high school, plotting against or with his sister.

"Carter has a game Saturday morning. Should be over by noon, but I wouldn't get there until after three."

Cullen quickly referred to the calendar again. "The show's open until ten. But, hey, if it's too much of a haul, I totally get it."

"No, not at all. I'm just thinking it through. Carter's mother is supposed to be at the game, and he's supposed to go back to her place. That would save me some time."

"Cool. Let's plan on grabbing a bite to eat in Asheville and then go to the exhibit. I don't think I'd want to spend more than an hour and a half there. I might buy something I shouldn't."

"That makes two of us." Chris laughed.

Cullen waited for Luna's name to come up. Nothing. Then he had to say, "I was hoping for a guy's night, but I don't want to get Luna in a tizzy."

Gaines laughed. "No worries. I'll let her know you invited me to a guy's night, and she and I can meet up later." Gaines was confident his plan would be acceptable to Luna.

Cullen didn't want Luna to hear the news of their plans from Gaines. He didn't want her to think he had gone behind her back—which he had—and then have to explain himself out of trouble. Or maybe not. Chi-Chi was correct. Gaines was his friend, too. But . . . but what if he told Luna he was just thinking of inviting Chris? That way, he would get a different reaction from the one he would receive if he told her he had already asked him. Yep, that was going to be his approach. He wiped his hands again and walked briskly into the café, hoping Chris hadn't already called Luna.

He heard her phone ringing and rushed into the shop just as he heard her say, "Hey, Chris. What's going on?"

Cullen thought he was going to throw up. Luna was going to kill him unless he could circumvent that call. "Luna! Can you come with me? Quick!"

Luna looked at her phone and then back at Cullen. "Chris, I am going to have to call you back. Cullen needs me to look at something." She ended the call.

Now Cullen had to find an excuse for hauling her into his workshop so abruptly. He hurried ahead of her.

"Cullen! What is going on?" Her dog Wylie echoed her question with a *woof.*

He decided to deviate slightly from the truth. "Listen, I'm thinking about refurbishing classic car interiors."

"And?" Luna placed her hands on her hips.

"And there's a classic car show this weekend."

"And?" She leaned forward, probably hoping she would get a clear response.

"And I was thinking of asking Chris to come out. Make it a guy's night."

Luna eyed him curiously. "Okay. And?"

"And nothing. I just wanted to run it past you first." He wondered if Luna's radar was up and she could tell he was lying. Lying about refurbishing cars, or his call to Gaines. Or both.

"Whatever. He's your friend, too." She let out an impatient sigh. "So what was so urgent?"

"That was it." The color was leaving Cullen's face.

Luna threw up her hands, spun on her heel, and marched out of the workshop. "Men! Idiots!"

Cullen quickly dialed Gaines's number before Luna had a chance to get back to her phone.

"Yo. What's up?" Chris answered. Cullen could hear a beep, indicating Chris had another call coming through. That would be Luna calling him back. "Hang on a sec." Gaines hit the call waiting button. "Hey, doll face. Can I call you back this time? Your brother is on the other line."

Luna gave her phone a strange look. *That didn't take him very long. Guys are so weird.* "Sure. No prob." Again, she ended the call.

Gaines returned to the other caller, Cullen. "Hey. Sorry about that. But it was your sister. One cannot ignore your sister." He chuckled.

"You got that right."

"What's up?" Chris repeated.

Once again, Cullen was searching for another ruse. "What are you going to wear?" Cullen hit himself in the head with his phone several times. *Now* that *was totally lame.*

"You alright, bro?" Gaines could not recall any man ever asking him what he was going to wear. But he answered, "Pants, shirt, shoes, socks. The usual." He scratched his head. "Why?"

"I didn't know if you were going to wear a blazer or not." Cullen was digging his mortification hole deeper.

"Why? Are you planning on buying me a boutonniere?" Gaines chuckled.

"As a matter of fact, I was thinking about it. What color do you prefer?" Cullen decided to go along with the joke instead of being defensive.

"How about a red rose?"

"Red rose it is," Cullen replied. "No, seriously, I didn't want to be over or underdressed."

"It's a car show. Anything goes. But, yes, I will be

wearing a blazer, since we're going to grab a bite to eat afterward. Is there anything else you would care to discuss?" Gaines was grinning.

"No. That about covers it," Cullen answered, and then let out a huge sigh of relief.

"Alrighty then. I'll see you a little after three on Saturday." Gaines ended the call.

Cullen realized he still hadn't covered the Luna part of the equation.

Gaines dialed Luna's number again. Perhaps they wouldn't be interrupted this time. He had some important information to share with her, but it required an in-person conversation. Meeting up with Cullen would be a good opportunity to make a brunch date with her.

Chapter Three

Stillwell Art Center

It took several minutes of phone chaos before Luna and Chris finally had a moment to chat.

"Lu, your brother invited me to a car show this weekend."

"Yes, he told me he was going to. But boy was he acting weird about it." Luna also thought to herself, *That was kind of fast.*

"You're not kidding. He actually asked me what I was wearing." Chris chuckled.

"Seriously? '*What are you wearing?*' How bizarre. Maybe he's been inhaling too much glue in his workshop." Luna laughed.

"I don't want to assume I'll be staying at your place, but I was already planning to call you to see if we could get together when Cullen beat me to it." He cleared his throat. For a smart, strapping man, he was jelly when it came to Luna. "Sorry. I should have checked with you first."

"Don't be ridiculous. I understand your bromance

with my bro," she teased. "Now if you said you were coming out to visit my brother and made no plans to see me, well, *then* we would have a problem," she said. "You *will* be staying with me, correct?"

He stuttered. "Yes . . . yes . . . of course."

"Unless you have a better offer?" she joked.

"No. Not at all. We may not be back until after ten, and I don't know what you have planned for the evening."

"Well, I can tell you that as of now, I have no plans, and if I did, I would most certainly change them for you." She wasn't lying or being patronizing. Any time she could spend with Chris, she would give up whatever else was on her agenda.

"You are a doll," Chris replied.

"Since you and big bro are going out, I'll check in with Chi-Chi to see if she wants to do something, and then we can all meet up later."

"Sounds good." He paused. "Thanks for being so accommodating."

"Accommodating? Isn't that a bit formal?" Luna peered at her phone. Something was up. She could feel it. But what was it?

"I don't want you to think I'm taking advantage of your good nature." Chris winced, hoping he wasn't digging himself in too deep.

"Puh-lease." Luna stretched out the word.

"Sorry. Long day, and it isn't even close to noon."

"No prob. Let's touch base after I talk to Chi-Chi, and then we can finalize our plans for a sleepover." She was almost blushing. So was he.

"Great. See you Saturday. And tell your brother I want a turquoise boutonniere."

"Huh?" Luna asked.

"Private joke. Talk later."

"Okay. Bye." She ended the call but kept staring at the phone.

After a few minutes, Luna got up, went back to the easel, and flipped her sketch pad to a clean page. She closed her eyes and began to draw. This time, it was two question marks. She stared at it. "Very strange," she said to no one. She absentmindedly played with the large John Jay College of Criminal Justice ring that was hanging on a chain around her neck. Chris had given it to her when they went to New York on a wild adventure involving kidnapping, art, and deception. She smiled. It was always an adventure with him.

Luna picked up her walkie-talkie. Every shop at the center had one so the proprietors could keep in touch without using their cell phones, and in case there was an emergency. Luna beeped Chi-Chi's line. "Hey, girlfriend. Want to have dinner with me on Saturday?"

"That would be lovely," Chi-Chi answered.

"Yeah, Cullen and Chris are going to a car show, so we are on our own. We can meet up with them later."

"Oh good—I am happy it worked out."

"What worked out?"

Chi-Chi realized she was about to expose her and Cullen's behind-the-scenes interference. "I was praying that you and I could spend some time together." She held her breath, hoping it was a good save. She hated to lie.

"Uh, okay. You know you never have to pray to spend time with me, just ask." Luna looked at the walkie-talkie with a questioning expression. *Is everyone acting weird, or is it me?*

"Thank you. I very much appreciate it." Chi-Chi was cringing. Better to end the conversation before she stuck both feet in her mouth, and she wore a size ten. "I must go. Let's speak later. Goodbye."

It wasn't unusual for Chi-Chi to be abrupt. But this time, Luna felt an undercurrent. Her friend was hiding something. She was now convinced *everyone* was acting weird. She moved back to the sketch pad and ripped off the previous drawing. She was tapping her pencil against her cheek when Cullen walked in. "Now what?" she sneered.

"Excuse me, but I just wanted to go over the weekend plans." Cullen folded his arms and gave her a look.

"Sorry. There is something bugging me, and I just can't figure it out."

"That's what you said earlier." Cullen softened a bit. "Have you tried drawing something?" he asked.

Luna picked up her first drawing.

"A question mark," Cullen noted. Then she showed him the next one. "Two question marks."

"I hope it doesn't mean we are going to have money problems." Luna sighed.

"Doubtful," Cullen said. "Our cash flow is good, and I have a lot of jobs ahead." He paused, knowing his next few words might set her off. "What if you stop obsessing about what you don't know and focus on what you do know?"

Luna tilted her head and looked up at her brother. "Have you met me?"

He grunted. "You got a point, Sis. Sure you're okay, though?"

"Yeah. It will eventually reveal itself to me." She sighed.

"See? Give it some time to percolate in that fertile brain of yours."

"Thanks, Cul." She stretched. "So tell me more about this new area you want to explore? I didn't know you had an interest in classic cars." She peered at him.

"Maybe it's my age, but I'm finding things that have been around for a long time have value." Cullen wasn't lying about that. "Furniture, lamps, sconces. Why not auto interiors?"

"Well, you've done a lot of work with leather and reupholstery. I guess it makes sense," Luna said thoughtfully. "Have any idea where you want to start?"

"Not really. I figured I'd look around. Talk to people. Find out the process, steps, do some networking. The usual." Cullen was beginning to think this actually *could* be a good idea. At least worth looking into for real.

"Chris is coming around three, right?" Luna asked.

"Yeah. We'll head over to the car show and then grab some dinner."

"A guys' night out?" Luna teased.

"You could say that. Chris and I haven't spent a lot of time together for a while. It'll be good to catch up."

"I hear ya. We haven't seen each other in three weeks."

Cullen stopped suddenly. "Oh gee, Sis, sorry. I didn't mean to impede on your time with Chris."

"No problem. I'm glad you invited him. I was going to see what he was doing this weekend anyway. Chi-Chi and I are going to have dinner together, so we can all meet up at my place afterward."

"Sounds like a good plan." He kissed her on the top of her head.

Luna touched the spot. *Odd.* He hadn't done that in a very long time. "Cul? Are you sure *you're* okay?"

"Yep. Couldn't be better." He smiled and walked toward the adjoining door to his showroom.

Then she remembered and called out, "Chris said to make it a turquoise boutonniere." She scrunched up her face.

"Stupid joke." With that, Cullen knocked on the doorjamb, turned, and left.

Luna shook her head and looked down at Wylie sitting at her feet. "What do you think, pal? Is it me, or is everyone acting a bit off?"

He lay down on the floor and put his paws over his eyes.

"Just as I thought." She bent over and ruffled the fur around his ears.

Chi-Chi nervously clicked on her walkie-talkie to speak with Cullen.

"I cannot pretend about things," she said heavily.

"What's wrong?" Cullen asked.

"I almost spilled the rice with your sister."

"Spilled the beans," Cullen corrected.

"Whatever you call it. I do not like lying to people."

"Why? What happened?"

"Nothing, really, but when she told me Christopher was coming this weekend, I said I was happy it worked out. Then she asked me 'what worked out,' so I told her I said a prayer that she and I could get together." She sighed. "I feel so foolish."

"Don't worry about it. Luna is a very spiritual person, and she advocates creative visualization. Manifestation. You know, that kind of stuff. She probably took it along those lines. You were thinking about it, and it happened." Cullen was trying to soothe Chi-Chi's angst.

"But seriously, Cullen, if you want me to be a part of any mischief, I am not going to be able to lie."

Cullen laughed. "You have the highest level of integrity. That's why everyone loves you." Then he froze. Had he ever told her he loved her? For real kind of love? Sure, there were many times when any and all of them would sign off with "love you," but had he ever looked into her eyes and told her exactly what she meant to him? Maybe what he should really be refurbishing was his ability to express his true feelings. Unlike his unfiltered sister, Cullen was always buttoned up, whether it was his shirt or his feelings. Maybe it was time for a change in wardrobe, physically and emotionally.

Chi-Chi noticed the pause in Cullen's usual chatter and realized he was considering what he'd actually said. But in her heart, she knew they all loved each other, and they were lucky to have such a strong bond of friendship. She and Cullen were romantically involved, but they'd never talked about where their relationship was going. Maybe it was time for that conversation.

Chapter Four

Stillwell Art Center
Tuesday, Late Afternoon
Luna's Dresser

Cullen felt a little creepy about going behind his sister's back with the ruse of wanting to get into classic car refurbishing in order to play matchmaker. Not that Luna and Chris needed to be matched, but Cullen was concerned about his sister's mood and the fact that she and Chris hadn't seen each other in three weeks. Cullen knew from experience that long-distance relationships were not easy to maintain.

He thought the world of Chris, but he sensed Luna's growing discomfort. She would never admit it. At least not to him. Maybe not even to herself. Cullen always wondered how she could be so brilliant when it came to reading other people, but so clueless about her own relationships with men. But Chris seemed to be the exception, though the distance and lack of commitment were worrisome. Not that Cullen should judge. He was as guilty of ignoring the elephant in the room as anyone else. If Luna and Chris had talked about a commitment, she'd never mentioned it to him. The class ring and "going steady" was cute, but it wasn't an engagement ring. He shrugged. It really wasn't any of his business, but Luna was his sister, and he adored her. What he really needed to focus on was his own relationship and what it meant to him and to Chi-Chi. But that would wait until the weekend, after he'd had time to rehearse what he was going to say to her. First, he had to figure out exactly what that was.

The buzzer from the rear loading dock rang. Cullen went to the back of the workshop and opened the door. A small pickup truck had pulled in.

"Hey, Cullen! Look at you—all grown up, with a business in this fancy place!"

"Duke! How the heck are you?" Cullen grasped the seventy-something man by the shoulders. Back when Cullen's parents had their antique business, Duke was their delivery driver. When Luna and Cullen were kids, Duke would let them ride in the flatbed of the truck and take them to a pumpkin farm or an apple orchard. No one would imagine doing that now, and it was nearly horrifying to think about what could have happened back then. *Like drinking out of the garden hose*, thought Cullen. "Come in! Come in!" He slapped Duke on the back.

"This is some setup you got here." Duke smiled, showing off his two gold molars. He took in the large workshop with its pristine workbench and wall of tools. He whistled. "Never thought you'd be in the furniture fixin' business." He shoved his hands into his overall pockets and marveled at the space.

"Yeah, well, I always had an interest, and along

came an opportunity, so I took it." Cullen nodded. "Follow me. There's someone who will be very surprised to see you."

The two men walked slowly from the workshop through the showroom, Duke stopping at almost every piece of restored furniture. "You do all this yourself?" he asked in awe.

"Yessir." Cullen pointed up to the ceiling fixtures. "Got busy with some lighting, too."

"Man-oh-man. You're some kind of wizard there, kid." Duke's head was moving in all directions. He didn't know what to look at next. "How'd you come into all this?"

"Well, you know my folks wanted to retire and had a lot of inventory. I didn't want to be solely in the antiques business, so I started with what they had on hand, then began working on my own projects. Almost everything here is my work. I only have a couple of pieces left from their business."

"Man-oh-man," Duke repeated. "They sure must be proud."

"I hope so. You know my dad. Not much for touchy-feely stuff or handing out compliments."

"Yeah, but you always knew somehow he was proud of you. And your sister. By the way, what is she up to these days?"

"Follow me." Cullen walked to the door that opened to Luna's café.

"Duke!" Luna squealed with pleasure when she spotted them. "What on earth are you doing here?" She gave him a huge hug, staying clear of his scruffy beard.

"Your brother asked me to deliver something that was in storage." He looked around Luna's place with the same awe he'd exhibited at Cullen's. "This place yours?"

"It is." Luna grinned. "Cullen figured if he kept me close by, he could make sure I stayed out of trouble. Welcome to the Namaste Café."

Duke stopped short when he looked out to the atrium. "Holy smoke! I heard about this place but never came by. Thought it might be a little too hoity-toity for me." His jaw was agape. "This here place has a bunch of artist types, food, and all that other stuff?"

Luna laughed. "Yep, and all that other stuff." Duke was not quite a hillbilly. "How about a cup of coffee?"

"I don't want to put you out."

"Duke, this is a café. This is what I do. I make coffee." She left out the psychic stuff. She didn't want to spook the man. She had done that enough times, like when she was eleven and told him things she could not possibly know, such as how his brother had stolen five hundred dollars from Duke's coffee can when he believed he had it well hidden in the back of the freezer. She'd thought he was going to have a heart attack when she asked him, "What happened to the frozen money?" He never answered her. It was hard enough for him to admit it to himself, let alone say it out loud: "My brother is a cheat." He simply turned pale, got in his truck, and drove away.

Cullen pulled out a chair. "Have a seat."

"I don't want to take you away from your work." Duke peered into the atrium and noticed the place was empty.

Luna was reading his mind again. "The center is closed on Monday and Tuesday, but I'm usually here and keep the coffee going for anyone else in the building. I'll give you a tour after our coffee. What would you like? Cappuccino? Espresso? Latte?"

"Them's too fancy fer me. Got a regular cup of java in that fancy machine?"

"Sure do. Cream and sugar?" Luna asked.

"Is there any other way? I mean besides all that other stuff?" He snorted.

"Coming right up." Luna turned toward the coffee maker and began whipping up a latte for Cullen. She also brewed a regular cup of java for Duke. While Duke was gawking at the interior landscaping and the scope of the center, she grabbed a couple of scones and brought everything to the table.

"How's the family, Duke? Still living in North Carolina?" Cullen asked.

"My daughter and her hubby moved to Georgia. He got a job in Savannah working for Gulfstream Aerospace. I'm glad I made that girl go to college so she could meet a fine man. And she did. She's a teacher, you know."

"I remember when she first went to school. You were so proud," Luna said.

"Yep. Someone in this family needed an edge-u-cation." He slapped his knee. "Still waiting for them grandbabies." He slurped his coffee and then shook his head. "But I don't think that's gonna happen. But it's okay, I guess. They're happy."

Luna patted him on the hand. "That's all that matters. And health, of course. Speaking of health, you're looking pretty fit!"

"Well, I try to walk a few miles every day. And then I help out at the local farms. It's hard to find good workers, so I lend a hand when I can. Gotta be a good neighbor."

Duke was a kind spirit. He'd worked for the Bodmans for over twenty years and was generous with his time. He charged a flat fee, even if the job took twice as long as he planned. But the Bodmans were appreciative and always gave him a liberal bonus each year. They also appreciated his babysitting skills, such as the times he would take the kids for a joyride while the Bodmans had business to tend to.

"So what did you bring for Cullen?" Luna asked.

Duke shot Cullen a look. He knew it was supposed to be a surprise, but maybe Cullen had already told her.

Cullen cleared his throat. "Just something I came across when I checked the storage unit a few weeks ago. I'm trying to clear it out little by little."

"So you're bringing stuff here," Luna teased.

"Only stuff that's salvageable. And one thing at a time." Cullen peered over his coffee mug. It was true that he'd wanted this to be a surprise—well, it still would be when Luna saw it. He'd been hoping he could refurbish it first, but knowing Luna, she would have sniffed his secret out sooner rather than later. Besides, he might do something to it that she wouldn't like. Yes, it was better to show her right away.

As they were finishing up their coffee, Luna spotted Chi-Chi in the distance and waved her over. A beautiful cloud of colors floated across the atrium.

"Lordy. Who is that?" Duke asked in awe. "Some kind of princess?"

"You could say that." Luna winked at Cullen. "She's from Nigeria. Makes beautiful jewelry." Luna got up from her chair, followed by Cullen, then Duke.

"Ẹ káàrò!" Chi-Chi nodded to everyone. Cullen got up and pulled a chair over to the table.

Cullen introduced her. "This is Lebici Stone. Chi-Chi, this is Duke, a longtime friend of the family."

She reached across the table to shake his hand.

"You are some kind of beautiful woman," Duke said as he shook her hand. He couldn't stop staring at her.

"Thank you," Chi-Chi replied with dignity, her head held high.

"Luna tells me you're from Nigeria?" Duke still hadn't blinked.

"Yes. My family came to the States when I was young. We still have some relatives there, and my brother visits several times a year."

Duke was enthralled. "And you make jewelry?" He was staring at her amethyst bracelet.

"I do. This is one of my pieces." She smiled.

"Well, alls I can say is your work is as beautiful as you are."

Cullen glanced over at Luna and grinned. He couldn't remember ever seeing Duke this enamored with anyone. It was a nice surprise.

Chi-Chi gave Duke a humble nod. "Thank you. You are very kind."

Duke slapped his leg again. "How about you take me for a tour of this place?" He stood and crooked his arm. Chi-Chi looked alarmed, but Cullen gave her a reassuring nod and whispered, "He's harmless."

The four of them paraded out the door into the sunlit atrium with Wylie in tow. Duke stopped short and let out a low whistle. "I heard lots of things about this here place, but just couldn't picture it in my mind.

Imagine a huge tree like that on the inside?" It was obvious Duke was not a worldly man. Maybe that's why the Bodman family was so fond of him. He was the opposite of pretentious and looked at most things with wonder. He wasn't a stupid man. Just far from sophisticated.

Chi-Chi immediately took to his kind nature and began to explain all the different shops and artists as they strolled around the inside perimeter. As they walked to the automatic door that led to the patio, two German shepherds came bounding toward them. Duke let out a shriek. "What in the Sam Hill is going on?"

Chi-Chi squeezed Duke's arm. "Meet Ziggy and Marley," she said. The dogs stopped abruptly and sat at attention. Cullen reached down to pet them, and Wylie gave them both a headbutt. "They belong to Ellie, the genius behind this endeavor."

"Scared the bejeezus out of me." Duke was clutching his chest.

"Sorry. We're so used to them, we forget they can be scary for people who don't know them," Luna explained. She reached down and gave both dogs a "good boy" scratch behind the ears.

Ellie wasn't far behind the two dogs. "Hi, everyone!" She waved.

"And that is Ellie Stillwell," Chi-Chi explained further.

"Hello," Ellie said immediately.

"Howdy, Miss Ellie." Duke chuckled, remembering the TV show *Dallas* from the 1980s. "So tell me, who shot J.R.?" He couldn't help voicing the compelling question that 83 million TV viewers once asked.

Ellie laughed. She had lost count of how many times people had asked her that question. "It was Kristin. And he deserved it."

Everyone laughed. Even though the show had first aired almost a decade before Cullen and Luna were born, it was a well-known pop-culture classic.

Cullen introduced Duke to Ellie, explaining his association with the Bodman family and their business.

"Nice to meet you. I see you've already met Ziggy and Marley," Ellie said.

"Sure have. Gave me a good scare, they did." He smiled as they shook hands.

"Sorry about that. They're really sweet unless someone tries to hurt anyone."

"I'm sure of that, ma'am." Duke flashed his gold teeth again.

"We were about to give Duke a tour," Cullen said.

"Excellent. I'm going to attempt to learn a new software program. Enjoy!" Ellie walked over to the large staircase that led to the second floor of the gallery, with Ziggy and Marley wagging their tails behind her.

"Seems like a nice lady," Duke remarked. "She single?"

Luna almost spit. Now *that* would be a very interesting matchup. "Sorry, Duke, she's taken."

"A lawyer," Cullen added. "You don't want to mess with those types," he joked.

"You got that right, sonny boy." Duke reinserted Chi-Chi's arm through his. "And what about you, pretty lady?"

"She's mine." Cullen made the official announcement. Very much to his own surprise. Then his hands began to sweat as he worried what Chi-Chi might think of this little outburst.

"Well, lookie here." Duke stopped and turned. "If anyone deserves someone as magnificent as this lady, I suppose it's you, Cullen Bodman."

"Glad you approve." Cullen's face was flushed. He looked over at Chi-Chi, who had the biggest smile on her face.

"It is true, Mr. Duke. We are together." Chi-Chi gave Cullen a sideways glance and smile of approval.

"I guess that leaves you and me, Luna." Duke was kidding, but his comment prompted Luna to add her own status.

"Sorry. I'm going steady." She dangled the ring that hung around her neck. "To a U.S. Marshal."

"Huh. A U.S. Marshal, eh?"

"Yep. Who woulda thunk it?" Luna cackled.

"Well, surely not me. You were always a bit of a rascal."

"That's putting it mildly," Cullen added. Luna elbowed him in the ribs. "See? She's still a rascal."

"Well maybe one of y'all can have those grandbabies for me." Duke laughed. Chi-Chi, Luna, and Cullen froze.

Once they regained their composure, the quartet roamed past the patio and the grounds behind the center as Luna pointed out the highlights.

"A dog park? Whaddya know." Duke was still in awe of everything he was experiencing. "This is kinda like Disney for grownups. And dogs."

They meandered back to the interior of the center. "This is fan-tas-tic." Duke enunciated each syllable. "I understand why you'd wanna work here."

"That's the best part. It doesn't feel like work." Cullen grinned. "Especially when you're surrounded by special people."

"Thank you, bro," Luna chimed in.

"Yeah, you too, I guess," he teased, and got another elbow in the ribs. "Keep it up and you will be on my no-fly list."

"Ha." She gave him a smack on the arm with the back of her hand.

"And this is what I have to put up with every single day." Cullen pretended to be serious.

Luna jerked her thumb in Cullen's direction. "Me, too."

The group made their way to the workshop and the back entrance. Cullen put his hands over Luna's eyes.

"What are you doing?" she protested.

"Just be quiet for a second. Can you do that?" Cullen clasped her forehead. He helped maneuver her to the door and then released his grip.

Luna looked down at the flatbed part of the truck. "Oh, my goodness!" she squealed. "My old dresser!" She jumped down from the loading dock and climbed into the back of the truck.

"Hold on there, little lady!" Duke said with concern. "Don't you go hurtin' yourself now."

"Oh, wow! Cullen! Thank you! Wow!" Luna proceeded to open the drawers. The first thing she pulled out was a copy of *Harry Potter and the Prisoner of Azkaban*, then a Backstreet Boys CD.

A copy of *One Last Time* by psychic medium John Edward was also in the drawer. She held it up. "See? I've been validated!" Luna had read the book when she was twelve and became an avid fan of Edward's show,

Crossing Over, when it aired in 2001. She begged her parents to watch it with her to prove she wasn't a loony tune. At the time, Cullen countered, "It's on the Sci-Fi Channel." She'd stuck her tongue out at him back then—and did so again now.

"Okay, Miss Smarty Pants. How about we get this into the shop, and then you can have your trip down memory lane," Cullen urged. "I am sure Duke has other things to do."

"Oh, that's alright. I got nowheres to be," Duke responded.

"Let's not encourage her, okay?" Cullen snickered. "Come on, Duke, let's unload it." Cullen pulled the lever that lowered the loading dock platform to meet the back of the truck. Then he hopped down the portable steps.

Luna wrapped her arms around the old dresser. "I am so happy to see you again." She rested her ear on the top of it. "What's that? You're happy to see me, too? That's terrific."

Cullen disengaged her arms and looked up at Chi-Chi. "Did you know she also communicates with inanimate objects?"

Chi-Chi folded her arms and grinned. "They say that is a sign of a highly intelligent person."

"Oh, geez. Now I'll never hear the end of it." He grimaced.

Luna gave him a peck on the cheek. "You are the best, Cul!" Then she scooted out of their way. "I can't wait to see what else is in this treasure trove."

"Maybe it will keep you out of trouble," Cullen joked.

"As if." Luna smirked.

Once the dresser was secure in the workshop, Duke said his goodbyes. "Give your folks my best. I sure miss workin' fer 'em."

"I'm sure I can find a few things for you to do over here." Cullen handed the man 500 dollars.

"Much appreciated," Duke said, then realized Cullen had overpaid him by 400 dollars. "Cullen, this is too much!"

"I can't hear you," Cullen said, as he hoisted the platform up. Everyone waved, and Cullen shut the door as Duke drove off.

The diversion of Duke's arrival had lightened the air. Chi-Chi was no longer feeling guilty, and Luna was feeling brighter, knowing Chris would be coming. Plus, she now had mementos to explore. And Cullen was walking on air. He'd taken the first step by proclaiming his relationship with Chi-Chi to an outsider. Now all he had to do was tell her in private.

Chapter Five

Stillwell Center
Tuesday

Luna could barely pull herself away from the keepsakes in her former bedroom dresser, but Ellie needed her help. A local college group had planned to have an awards ceremony and formal dance at a nearby hotel, but the ballroom was flooded due to a water pipe fiasco, and the only place that could accommodate one hundred people on such short notice was the atrium at the center. It was all-hands-on-deck. They had two days to work a miracle.

Luna ran up the stairs to Ellie's office, with Wylie galloping behind. Ziggy and Marley were lounging on their plush dog beds when Wylie bounded in and joined them. Luna and Ellie sat across from each other and began going over the details.

In addition to their food kiosk at the center, The Blonde Shallot specialized in catering and was able to create a simple menu—the guests were teenagers whose palates were less than demanding. The Cheese

Cave could provide charcuterie to be placed on the high-top tables, and The Flakey Tart was now responsible for one hundred tortes. Since monitoring everyone's drinking age would be impossible, Victor Deci from The Wine Cellar contacted his distributor and ordered several cases of nonalcoholic beverages, including Mockaritas in place of Margaritas, Mockapolitans in place of Cosmopolitans, a pseudo sparkling rosé, and fake beer. Nathan would keep a close eye on the partygoers to be sure there weren't any flasks or other surreptitious means of smuggling in booze. No one was leaving the center inebriated.

Suki Kyoto, owner of Between the Folds, offered to hang her origami work among the trees in the atrium to give it a festive vibe. Devon Scott from Blowin' in the Wind agreed to arrange several of his wind chimes in the garden area. Alex volunteered to wrap twinkling lights in the trees inside and out. Everyone was determined to turn the teenagers' catastrophe into a night to remember.

Luna was busy making arrangements for the band. They were already booked for the gig; now she just had to figure out where to put them. She and Ellie went over the plans. Food and beverages would be served in the atrium, and the band would be on a riser in the garden area, where the patio could serve as the dance floor.

Ellie went down the checklist. "Looks like we have everything covered."

"What about valet parking?"

"Good idea." Ellie phoned Sunset Valet and booked them for the evening. "I have them under contract, and we haven't used our maximum dates this month," she explained once she was off the phone.

"Were the students able to get their deposit back from the original location?" Luna asked.

"Not without a fight." Ellie sighed. "The venue has insurance. They can recoup what they'll lose. There's no reason they should withhold any of the money."

"True." Luna nodded.

"If it comes down to a legal battle, I am sure George will get their refund after one phone call," Ellie scoffed.

Luna laughed lightly. "He is such a mild-mannered, eloquent gentleman. It's hard to imagine him being intimidating."

"You should see him in court." Ellie gave her a devilish smile. "He can cut you into shreds, and you'd never know you were bleeding to death."

"Now that's kinda gruesome, Ellie." Luna wrinkled her nose.

"Sorry, but lawyers must be surgeons in the courtroom. Cut away the B.S. and get to the truth."

"That's a much better description!" Luna laughed.

"So have you found anything interesting in your dresser?"

"A bunch of stuff that I can barely remember collecting. Isn't it funny how everything is of the utmost importance until you look back on it and wonder why you even worried about it? Or even remember it?"

"Especially when you are a teenager."

"You're right about that. A pimple could mean the end of the world!" Luna laughed out loud. "Well, I'm glad we're able to help these kids with their soiree." She chuckled again. "Kids. It wasn't *that* long ago that I was nineteen." She halted. "Whoa. Wait. That was almost half my lifetime ago. Yikes! I guess I can officially call them kids."

Ellie was smiling. "Honey, *you* are a kid compared to me."

"Oh geez, Ellie. I didn't mean anything by that." Luna thought she had shoved her size-seven foot in her mouth.

"I know you didn't."

"I don't think of you as being older than me. Just more mature."

"It's okay, Luna. I understand where you're coming from. I think even though we're from different generations, we were raised with the same values. The same ethics. I think anyone under twenty-five struggles to find their own compass."

"Too much social media!" they said in unison.

As they began to gather the paperwork that was strewn all over Ellie's desk, Ellie brought up a new subject. "Luna, I've been thinking about adding an indigenous display to the center for Christmas. There are a few Lumbee artists who make beautiful ornaments from pinecones."

Luna stopped in her tracks. "That is an excellent idea. I know there's been a lot of controversy as to whether or not they are a real tribe."

"I've been reading up on it. It's because they are descendants of Sioux, Iroquois, and Algonquins. Many sought refuge from the fighting and colonization and retreated to the swamps along the Lumbee River for protection. As a result, there were intertribal marriages among the different groups. In 1885, the state of North Carolina recognized them, but it took another seventy-plus years for the federal government to acknowledge them with the Lumbee Act. Unfortunately, they do not receive the full benefits of federal recognition as other tribes do."

"Well, that stinks," Luna said. "Can't they open a casino?"

"That's part of the problem. The Cherokee have lobbied against them for fear it would threaten their gaming business."

Luna scrunched up her nose. "Wow. There's politics inside of politics."

"You are correct, my dear," Ellie replied. "That's why I want to showcase some of their art. Give them a little visibility. They'll get some press, and maybe it will help them with their cause to get full recognition. Nothing like embarrassing politicians in the press."

Luna laughed. "Is that even possible? Politicians, embarrassed? They have no shame."

Ellie chuckled. "Let's not get too cynical, dear. It doesn't align with your aura." She gave Luna a wink.

"Ha. You're right. I have to stop watching the news." Luna looked over at the three dogs, casually lying across each other's legs, Wylie's head on Ziggy's stomach. "Why can't we get along like them?" She smiled at the happy dogpile.

"And that is why I prefer to associate with few people but many dogs."

At the word *dogs*, all three raised their heads.

"Somebody want to go out and play?" Ellie leaned over and spoke to them. All at once, the three bounced to their paws and wagged their tails in a drumbeat rhythm.

"I'll take them down," Luna offered. "Come on, you guys." The dogs were already at the top of the stairs before Luna had left the office. The three canines were waiting at the large sliding patio doors long before Luna could catch up with them. On Monday and Tuesday, when the center was closed, the automatic door opener was not engaged. A human had to hit the button. The dogs were pacing, and Wylie gave a soft woof, urging Luna to move faster.

"I am going to have to teach you guys how to do this," Luna said, as she quickly pushed the big red button twice. The doors moved slightly, then closed. "See? This is how it's done!" She repeated the movement. The dogs were giving her the stink eye. "Oh, come on, you guys! You're smart. One of you should be able to do this." She did it one more time. "No? Well, fine." She hit the button, but this time, she let the door stay open. She swore she heard one of the dogs fart at her on their way out.

Luna went into Cullen's showroom and walked to the workshop in the back. Her dresser remained by the far wall, untouched since the day it had arrived.

"You plan on going through all of this any time soon?" Cullen asked as he rewired a midcentury ceiling fixture.

"I should probably pack everything up and take it home, but being around the dresser while I'm going through my stuff gives it that extra energy." Luna wasn't talking about cereal, or caffeine-laden beverages. She was referring to the vibration of the piece itself. "Everything is made of energy, you know," she reminded Cullen for the zillionth time.

"Did you hear me give you an argument?" Cullen said as he carefully replaced the globe.

"No. Just a friendly reminder." She chuckled. "Getting excited about your date?"

The question threw him. All day, he had been thinking about arranging a special date with Chi-Chi. It was time they had that "grown-up" conversation. He wanted it to be romantic and private. He was toying with the idea of preparing dinner for her. He thought about contacting her brother Abeo and getting a Nigerian recipe from him. Then he worried he would do a terrible job, and it would turn out inedible. But if they went to a restaurant, it wouldn't be private. Then there was the insecurity and fear that she might not feel the same way he did. Who would be more embarrassed?

He stopped abruptly. "What date?" He knew Luna was psychic, but could she be *that* good?

"Oh, do I sense something?" Luna raised her eyebrows.

Yes. She was that *good.*

Cullen immediately became defensive. "What are you talking about?"

Luna placed her hands on her hips and cocked her head. She didn't have to say a word. She knew she had him. She took a step back, pursed her lips, and began to tap her foot.

Cullen tightened the screws on the globe while Luna tightened the screws on him. "Okay. Okay." He wrapped the fixture in protective Tyvek and placed it in an equally protective box lined with sheets of foam. He turned, leaned against the workbench, crossed his ankles, and mirrored her folded arms.

Luna pointed a finger at him. "Crossed ankles. Folded arms. Up against the bench. Hmm. Interesting. You are hiding something, and your back is against the wall."

"Let's not overstate the obvious. My back is against something." Cullen's voice was serious.

Luna could feel his anxiety. "What's going on? Everything okay?"

He took a deep breath. "I'm in love with Chi-Chi."

Luna resisted the temptation to say *no kidding*, but she knew this was huge for Cullen. Mr. Buttoned-up was letting his emotional guard down.

"Cullen, I think it's wonderful." She walked over to him and gave him a big hug. "So what's wrong?"

"I haven't told her yet."

Luna pulled away, stared him in the face, and slowly repeated what she had just heard. "You haven't told her yet." It wasn't a question. She'd thought he would have told Chi-Chi by now. Maybe not tell his sister, but not tell Chi-Chi? Luna was stunned. Her brother wasn't all touchy-feely, but given his love for Chi-Chi, that they had been dating for over two years, Luna had assumed they would have verbalized their feelings for each other.

"Huh. Is there any particular reason?" Luna was sincerely perplexed.

Cullen looked down at the floor. "I guess I'm afraid of rejection."

Luna knew now was not the time to tease her brother. "Oh, Cullen, Chi-Chi adores you."

"But does she love me?" He looked up.

"It would appear she does, but as far as expressing emotions, neither of you are very good at it. I mean, you guys laugh, get angry, and all that. But verbalizing something deep? Ha. Chi-Chi maintains her dignity, and you . . . well, you are even more close-mouthed. Unless you're annoyed at me." She put her hand on his arm. "Tell her, Cul. Time—it keeps ticking. Make the most of it by letting everything flow. And I don't mean by being indifferent. I mean let your feelings flow with your words. If she feels the same, then you can dismiss all the fear you're carrying right now. If she doesn't, then you know the answer, and you can carry on. Plus, you owe it to her. Your honesty."

Once, when they were kids, a branch snapped and caught Cullen in the face. It was the only other time she'd ever seen a tear in his eye. Except for now. She gave him a big hug. "Now go do it, or I'll start calling you 'Sissy Pants.'"

He dabbed his single tear with his knuckle and then let out a big huff. "Okay, so here's my question. Should I cook dinner for her?"

"Well, wait. Are you planning on proposing?" Luna asked.

"No! I mean, not yet. I haven't gotten past the 'I love you' thing. Baby steps, baby sister."

"If you make it too romantic, she may think it's a proposal."

Cullen nodded. "Huh." His dilemma had now worsened.

"When were you planning on doing this?"

"Friday. I figure if it doesn't go well, I can drown my sorrows with Chris on Saturday."

"But the four of us are supposed to get together after the car show."

"Right. Well, if it doesn't go well, I don't think Chi-Chi will want to get together, do you?"

"What about Sunday brunch? Or a picnic?"

"I'd have to close the showroom, and Chi-Chi would have to get someone to run her shop."

"I could keep an eye out on the showroom. I'm sure Chi-Chi could get one of the pages to mind her store."

"Won't it seem strange if I ask her to take a day off? You know how she is about that."

"True. Okay, so what about Sunday dinner? After the center closes?"

Cullen finally smiled and kissed Luna on the top of her head for the second time that day. "You're a genius."

Luna touched her head again. "Dinner is not genius, but if you think so, then yes, I am brilliant."

"Don't push it, missy." He walked into the large storage closet where he kept shipping materials and then reappeared with a large brown box. "Here. Get busy."

Luna plucked the box from his hands and began to open the drawers of her dresser. She giggled at the memorabilia again. "The Backstreet Boys. They're back!" She giggled again. "In a Downy Fresh commercial."

"You can probably sell that CD on eBay," Cullen joked.

Luna clutched it to her chest. "Never!" She smiled as she began to place the books and other items into the brown box. "Oh, look at this!" She waved a Yankees' World Series Championship baseball cap at her brother. "Now this is something I would never sell."

"You are such a goofball," Cullen teased. "Yes, I know. You won it in a bet. You predicted the Yankees would win, and I said it was going to be the Mets." He grunted. "Like either of us really cared."

"It was the fun of winning bets with you." Luna grinned.

"Yeah. Tons of fun." He looked at her. "I think you have an unfair competitive advantage."

"What do you mean?" She looked up from the souvenirs of her past.

He made little circles next to his temple with his forefinger.

She slapped him on the leg. "Ha, ha. 'Kooky' is *not* a synonym for crazy."

"Well, you're half right," he teased her again.

"So, Mr. Romance, what are you going to do about dinner with Chi-Chi?"

"What if I just invite her over for dinner and a movie?"

"That sounds harmless."

"I'll tell her I would like to hang out with her. Alone." He stuck his chin out. "For a change."

"I'd be insulted by that remark, but you have a point." Luna opened the next drawer. She paused and giggled.

"What?"

"In college, Brendan and I had a science professor who looked like an alien. You know, an almond-shaped head and big eyes. She always wore bizarre earrings. During class, Brendan drew this on a napkin from the student center." She handed it to Cullen. It looked like E.T. wearing chandelier earrings.

"Funny."

"Not so funny when I burst out laughing, and Dr. Woodmere wanted to know, 'What's so funny, Ms. Bodman?' I apologized and hoped she didn't want me to share it with the rest of the class. I'd have been thrown out." Luna peered at the drawing again. "I have to say, it's a good likeness of her!" She chuckled, but then her mood abruptly changed.

"Oh my." She lifted a glossy booklet from the box.

"What?" Cullen asked.

"The program from when we went to the Kentucky Derby."

"Oh yeah. You went with that same guy Brendan . . . Nelson, was it?"

"Yeah. Brendan Nelson." Luna's voice was hushed.

"You alright?"

Luna snapped out of it and placed the program in the box. "Yep. Fine." When she reached into the drawer again, she pulled out several yellow ribbons. She sat and stared at them for a moment.

"Are you sure you're alright?"

"You remember that retreat I went on my senior year of college?"

"Yeah. It was a bunch of you from a writing class. What about it?"

"Nothing," she lied. "We all just joked that we felt like hostages, so on the last night, we went into a big box store and bought a bunch of yellow ribbons and tied them on everyone's cabin door."

Cullen looked perplexed for a moment, then remembered what yellow ribbons stood for. In the '70s, the symbol of support for a missing loved one was popularized in a song called "Tie a Yellow Ribbon Round the Ole Oak Tree" by a group called Tony Orlando and Dawn. He began to whistle the tune.

"Oh, please stop! You know neither of us will be able to get that song out of our heads for the rest of the day!" Luna slapped her hands over her ears. Cullen began to sing the lyrics just to annoy her.

"Ugh!" Luna tossed the remains of her past into the box and scurried out of the workshop, singing "La . . . La . . . La . . . I can't hear you . . . I can't hear you . . ."

Wylie followed, but not without a look of confusion in his big brown doggie eyes.

Luna made her way back to the café and set the box on the table. She had an uneasy feeling. A rush of memories came flooding through her mind. Memories of a love long lost. Or was it a crush that got crushed? She began to replay the last two years of college in her head.

Luna and Brendan met during their junior year, when they shared the same psychology class. The class was divided into groups of two in order to work together on a hypothesis, each having opposing theories. It was a debate of sorts, but on paper. They had most of the semester to work on the project, and then each team would present their summation to the rest of the class.

The purpose was to understand the mechanisms of theory. Psychology was a growing discipline, and it was important to know who the players were in its development. Carl Jung vs. Sigmund Freud represented the most notable difference of theory. One of the class requirements was that the students do their research within the university library. It was an in-person collaboration, and the students would set their own schedules. That, too, was an exercise in planning and development. Luna had hoped she would be paired up with Brendan. He was funny and smart and willing to share information with his peers, rather than hoard it like many other insecure young adults.

The two immediately clicked. It was their sense of

humor. Without saying a word, they could give each other a look and burst out laughing. After the third "shush," the librarian threatened to ban them from the building. Brendan turned on his charm and pleaded with the skinny guy whose glasses were held together with first-aid tape at the bridge. Luna kept staring at the ground. She could not imagine how Brendan kept a straight face. She felt a little guilty, because the reason they'd been laughing was because of the librarian's glasses. He appeared to accept Brendan's apology, turned on his heel, adjusted his already skewed glasses, and marched away. Luna had to keep biting her lip or else they would have been flung outside, into the quad, and permanently expelled from the building. The two made a pact they would refrain from hilarity until after their two hours of research were complete—then they could howl all they wanted at the student center.

It became a thing. They met at the library once a week, did their research, and then grabbed something to eat. It was the one night of the week Luna looked forward to. The friendship hadn't developed into anything serious, except they were seriously good buddies. Luna was quite comfortable linking her arm through his when they walked across the campus. Some people thought they were involved, yet there were never public displays of affection except for the occasional arm-bumping and leaning into each other's personal space. Luna knew there were whispers, and if she overheard anything, she always set the record straight. The dilemma arrived when Luna thought she might be developing a crush on Brendan. Not good. But what could she do? She surely wasn't going to make a move on him, but sometimes her instincts told her he might feel the same way. Still. She wasn't going to push it. There was too much at stake.

But when Brendan started dating a junior from a nearby university, Luna was crestfallen. *Why her and not me? Because you never said anything. Oh, am I having a debate with myself? No, it's an argument.* She was going to ask Cullen for advice, but he wasn't exactly Mr. Romance. No, she would have to bite the bullet, accept reality, and move on. She promised herself she would never let an opportunity pass her by again.

Regrets. They were the worst. A lack of boldness and not taking the opportunity; a felt connection and again not taking the opportunity. It was true that the biggest regrets in life weren't the things you did; they were the things you didn't do.

But being human, one often breaks promises, especially those we make to ourselves.

Luna thought about her promise to herself, and sure enough, she had broken it more than once. If nothing else, this short trip down memory lane had been a good reminder, and it gave her an appreciation for Cullen's apprehension about telling Chi-Chi how he felt.

Cullen startled her with a knock on the café's door-frame. "Find anything worth keeping?"

"I still have a bunch of stuff to look through. I'll probably throw most of it away." But did she want to? Would it erase the past? Maybe it should be erased. She put the papers away and put the lid on the box. That was enough reminiscing for one day.

"Cul? I'm glad you are going to tell Chi-Chi how you feel. It's important to let people know you care about them. Don't let your fear get in your way." She knew she was repeating herself, but thought a reminder was necessary.

"Got it, Sis." He smiled. "You sure you're okay?"

"I dunno. Maybe it's hormones."

Cullen stiffened. "Geez, if *I* suggested that, you would punch me in the face."

"True. I can say it because they are *my* hormones." Luna put the lid on the box. "Will you put this in my car, please?" She didn't wait for an answer and handed him the box.

"You closing up soon?" Cullen asked as he took ownership of the mementos.

"Yeah. I'll check with Ellie first to see if she needs anything else for the shindig on Thursday."

"You guys—I mean gals—I mean women . . ." Cullen paused, knowing some women were offended by lots of things when hormones struck. "What do you prefer I call you?"

"What do you mean?" Luna squinted at him.

"Guys? Gals?"

"You mean that play?" Luna was busting his chops.

"No, silly. How do you like to be referred to? As?"

"Luna." Now she was giving him a hard time.

"Please, Luna. Sometimes I feel I have to tiptoe around people with all this political correctness. Don't misunderstand me. I get it. I mean, I want to say the right thing."

Luna stared at him. "Boy, you are really having a meltdown, aren't you?"

Cullen shook his head. "No, but I am making an effort to choose my words carefully."

"And I appreciate that. But I'm your sister, for heaven's sake. You've referred to me with some rather unflattering names over the years."

"Ha, ha."

"Listen, I don't care if you call us guys, gals, pals, kids, team, whatever. As long as you're not trying to be derogatory."

"I would never!" Cullen raised his voice.

"Calm down, brother. You know what I think? I think we need to go get a pizza and a beer."

"Sounds good." Cullen exhaled.

"Should we invite Chi-Chi?" Luna gave him a sideways look.

"She has a late appointment, so she's not available." He seemed relieved.

"Okay. Let me give Ellie a buzz. I'll catch up with you in your workshop." Luna picked up the walkie-talkie and buzzed Ellie. "Hey, Ellie. Cullen and I are about to head out. You need anything?"

"I think we have everything under control." Ellie sounded confident.

"Super! I'll see you in the morning. Scones and cappuccino! *Ciao*!" Luna clicked the *off* button on the device, then nodded at Wylie. "Come on, pal."

She met up with Cullen at the back of his shop. "Does Three Brothers have outdoor seating during the week, or should I drop Wylie off at home?"

"I saw tables on the sidewalk when I drove in this morning."

Wylie yawned and yapped a sound of approval. Three Brothers was one of the few places that allowed dogs to be tethered to outdoor tables. If people didn't like it, they could go find pizza somewhere else, which wasn't that easy to do. At least not really good, authentic pizza.

Cullen arrived at the restaurant a few minutes before Luna and snatched up the last available café table with a market umbrella. Apparently, several other dog owners had had the same idea. *Or did the dogs telepathically communicate with their owners? Luna would surely go for that theory,* Cullen thought.

With Wiley on a leash, Luna made her way to the table, carefully sidestepping a golden retriever, a boxer, a Yorkie, and a terrier. None of the dogs seemed to be bothered by the other dogs, or the other people, for that matter.

"Must be 'Dogs Night Out' at the pizzeria." Luna grinned at the other diners as they nodded in agreement. She wrapped Wylie's leash around the leg of a chair and sat down.

Cullen snickered. "I was just wondering if they passed the idea along to their owners telepathically."

Luna cackled. "You are finally starting to get it."

"Oh, I got it, alright. I just didn't know what to do with 'it.'" He used air quotes. "I ordered a pitcher of Blue Moon."

"Great."

"You don't normally drink beer. What's the occasion?"

She shrugged. "Variety is the spice of life, I guess."

"Speaking of spices." He cleared his throat. "I don't think I'll be able to find the right ones to make an authentic Nigerian dinner for Chi-Chi."

"I wouldn't try experimenting if I were you, unless you ask her to help you prepare dinner."

Cullen rubbed his chin. "That's a thought. We could cook together."

"Yep. That way, it's still romantic, but doesn't have the 'will you marry me?' vibe," Luna replied. "So now you ask her if she'll teach you one of her favorite dishes and bring the necessary spices and give you a list of the other ingredients."

"Sometimes you are smarter than you look." Cullen beamed and teased at the same time.

"I hope you're not planning on auditioning for *America's Got Talent*, because you are no comedian."

Gorgio, the owner of the pizzeria, approached their table with a foaming pitcher of beer and two menus. "*Buonasera*, Luna," he greeted her.

"*Buonasera*, Gorgio. *Come stai*?"

"*Molto bene*!" He grinned. "You are practicing your Italian."

"Yes. That and *ciao* are my go-to phrases," Luna joked.

"*Cosa vorresti mangiare*?" he asked.

"Not fair!" Luna grinned. "The only word I kinda recognized was *mangiare*."

"*Molto bene*!" Gorgio made a slight bow. "You see? You can speak Italiana."

"Well, okay then. I shall have pizza!" She leaned in. "Is pizza 'pizza' in Italian?"

Gorgio laughed. "Yes, we invented the pizza!"

Luna laughed in return. "I kinda knew that. I think I'll have a personal pizza with some *spinaci* and extra mozzarella." She used the Italian word for spinach and pronounced mozzarella like a true Italiana: *moots-a-rell*.

Gorgio turned to Cullen. "Your sister. She learns quick."

Cullen was not going to make any attempt at a foreign language with the exception of the words, "Pizza and pepperoni."

"What about *il tuo cane*?" Gorgio nodded to Wylie.

"I try not to give him h-u-m-a-n food," Luna answered, but Wylie's ears picked up.

"Telepathy." Cullen chortled.

"Maybe a meatball? No sauce, please," Luna said. "Here's a question for you, Gorgio—is it sauce or gravy?"

Gorgio let out a huff. "It depends who you ask. Gravy is popular in New Jersey, and sauce is popular in New York." He shrugged. "But for me? Gravy has meat. Tomato sauce is tomato sauce. *Capisce*?"

Luna laughed. "So if I order marinara sauce, it's tomato sauce?"

"It's marinara," Gorgio said, rolling the *R*s. "And *si*, tomato sauce is tomato sauce. Marinara has no meat. Just tomatoes, basil, and oregano."

"Thank you for explaining and settling the long debate."

"*Piacere, mia cara*. My pleasure." Gorgio nodded. "Anything else?"

Luna and Cullen looked at each other. "Maybe some stuffed mushrooms to start?" Cullen added.

"*Va bene.*" Gorgio smiled, shuffled through the group of idle canines, and retreated into the restaurant.

Luna leaned closer to Cullen. "Back to the menu. What else do you have planned?"

"I honestly have no idea. Chi-Chi has fixed plenty of Nigerian dishes for me, but I never asked what went into them."

"Okay. So she'll give you a list of ingredients to buy. Wine? Beer? Smoothies?"

"A lot of smoothies are made with lumpy stuff."

"Lumpy stuff?"

"Grains, fruit, and I'm not sure what else. I checked online, and they all look too healthy."

Luna almost spit out her beer. "Just ask her what she'd like to drink. I think you are making it much more complicated than necessary."

"It's because I'm nervous." Cullen's face reddened a bit.

"I get it. I really do. You know, today when I was looking through some of my stuff, I realized I suffered from the same kind of rejection anxiety."

"Since when?" Cullen looked dubious.

"Since forever." Luna pulled the orange slice from the edge of her glass and tossed it into her beer.

"You? Come on. I don't believe it!"

"There are some things that I keep under wraps." Luna raised her eyebrows.

"I also find that hard to believe." Cullen leaned back into his chair.

"I know I come across as confident. And I am. About a lot of things. But when it comes to matters of the heart, I am a big chicken."

"Yeah, but you and Chris seem to have a good relationship." He pointed to the class ring she was wearing around her neck.

"It took a year before he kissed me." Luna blushed.

"He was being polite." Cullen peered over his beer mug.

"And I never gave him the green light. Not that I

didn't want him to, but I was afraid to make a move. You know, kinda like leaning in."

"That is something I can relate to." He looked her straight in the eye. "I am truly stunned. I would have thought you pushed him onto the ground and kissed him first!"

"How little you know me after all these years." Luna shook her head. "Don't think the thought didn't occur to me, though." Then she laughed.

"Okay. So I'm not that far off track, little sister."

"Nope. I just didn't have the guts to do it. Good thing Chris had more nerve than I did." She giggled. "But . . ." She giggled again. "The first attempt came to an abrupt stop, because we smashed noses and couldn't stop laughing."

"It occured to me that you and I never discuss our romantic inclinations," Cullen mused.

"Not since I told you the time when what's-her-face was cheating on you."

"Nora." Cullen placed his mug on the table and filled half his glass. "Yeah. That was a stinger, alright." He took another sip. "Isn't it funny—odd, funny—that here we are, adults. Grownups. And we act like we're still in the third grade."

Luna chuckled. "Old habits die hard. But time you changed yours. Don't be a chicken. Don't have any regrets."

Cullen smiled. "You're pretty wise for a lunatic."

Gorgio and two servers approached the table with their pizzas. "And a nice meatball for *Signore* Wylie. No sauce, and no gravy!" Gorgio placed the bowl on the sidewalk for Wylie. *"Buon appetito!"*

Wylie thanked him with a woof and a wag.

Chapter Six

Charlotte, North Carolina
Tuesday, Early Evening

Chris waited patiently in the reception area of Evan Houston's law office. He glanced around the room. There were several people ahead of him, or perhaps a better way of putting it was that they were behind him in the long, agonizing journey of divorce. He flipped through a few of the magazines, but he was too distracted and nervous to focus on anything. He practically jumped out of his seat when he heard a woman screaming from the conference room.

"You're a lying creep! I never slept with Scott, or anyone else for that matter! You're the one who cheated on me!" A door swung open, and a woman in her mid-fifties stormed down the hall with a furious expression. She shouted back over her shoulder, "I'll take you and your teenage girlfriend to the cleaners!"

A man's voice could be heard coming from the room. "She's twenty-two!"

She turned for one last quip. "Yes, one-third your age. How unoriginal."

When she realized she had an audience, she straightened her skirt, tossed her Hermès scarf around her neck, and announced, "Get ready for the fight of your lives, folks. Divorce ain't pretty." Then she marched out of the office.

Chris stifled a smile. It was like watching his own preliminary separation meeting with Lucinda. Except she was the one who cheated, but she also felt the need to make a scene. She blamed Chris. It was his fault she found herself in the arms of another man. But thanks to Evan's calm demeanor, he was able to still the waters and remind them they had a son to think about, and having an acrimonious relationship wasn't going to help anyone. After all, getting a divorce was what they both really wanted.

It was over an hour before the reception area emptied out. Chris had purposely made his appointment for the end of the day so he and Evan could have dinner after and catch up. Even though Evan wasn't going to charge Chris for his time, there were a lot of other people involved preparing documents, follow-up, fees, and a lot of administrative work at the courthouse.

Evan appeared at the end of the hallway. "Come on down!" He waved Chris into his office. "Sorry about the commotion," he said as he motioned Chris to take a seat.

Chris snickered. "It reminded me of the first meeting we had. I guess Lucinda thought drama was necessary during divorce proceedings, but thanks to you, she turned down the noise."

"I do my best, but sometimes I just want to hit all of them over the head with one of my law books." Evan chortled. "That couple? I really can't blame her. He's involved with a woman thirty-eight years younger than he is." He shook his head. "It's so cliché."

"I totally agree with you. Plus, I think men are dense when it comes to women. At one point or another, we manage to get involved with the wrong people. I mean seriously wrong. So many women want a man to rescue them, and men want to feel they've still got the juice."

"I believe it's called a midlife crisis."

"Swell. I hope I can skip that part of adulthood," Chris said wryly.

"You and me both. But we still have a couple of years to mess things up." He laughed.

Evan opened his leather portfolio. "Alright, let's get down to business. I recommended you start keeping track of Dr. Tooth's involvement with Carter."

"Yes, and I asked him if Bruce was helping him with his science project. Carter looked at me and said, 'You're not serious, are you?' It took me aback, but that spoke volumes. He told me Bruce didn't even know he had a science project."

"Good. I mean, that's good for your case. It's a shame Carter does not have any support at home. Do you think Carter has any psychological issues with it?"

"Psychological issues?" Chris frowned and wrinkled his brow. "It never occurred to me. He never complains about Bruce, and he always seems fine when he's with me."

"Do you think there's any chance he may feel neglected?"

"Neglected?" Chris didn't know where this conversation was going.

"I'm trying to build a case for you—and against them. If Carter is experiencing any angst, depression, resentment, or disassociation, it could help. Help you, I mean."

"Geez, I hope he's not." Chris was beginning to feel concern. "He's never expressed it to me."

"Most kids don't," Evan replied.

"Wow. It never occurred to me. He's usually in a good mood when we're together. He rarely discusses his mother or Bruce."

"Maybe the reason he's in a good mood with you is because that's where he feels the most comfortable."

Chris nodded. "I suppose if there was something bothering him, he might not want to bring it up. He's a little self-conscious. You know that puberty thing."

Evan laughed. "I try to forget those days." He started writing on his pad. "When is Lucinda planning on moving?"

"She said six months."

"We need an exact date," Evan noted.

"I'll try to get it out of her."

"Have they found suitable housing?"

"I really have no information except the very loose time frame. The conversation was short. She really threw me for a loop, and then I had a work meeting. All sorts of thoughts were running through my head." Chris looked up at Evan. "If I share them, we have attorney-client privilege, correct?" Chris rubbed the back of his neck. "I could choke her."

Evan let out a snort. "Well, yes, unless you are divulging information of intentionally doing something criminal. But you didn't say you were planning on doing it. It's a fantasy." Evan looked up. "But do try to refrain from such comments. Please."

"Roger that." Chris gave him an assured look.

"We're going to have to meet with her and nail some of this information down."

"I know that is going to set her off, for sure."

"Well, she can't simply do whatever she wants when it comes to your son."

"True."

"I'll have Monica, my paralegal, call Lucinda tomorrow to set up a conference. If they are leaving in six months, we really don't have that much time." He scribbled something else. "I also want Carter to have a psych evaluation."

"Is it necessary?" Chris's concern was growing by the minute.

Evan looked up from his desk. "We need an impartial assessment as to what Carter's homelife is like. Do you think he'd have a problem speaking with a total stranger?"

"Not if I explain the situation."

"Is he aware of the move?"

"He hasn't mentioned it, but I haven't seen him since Lucinda dropped the bomb. I'll talk to him about it after practice, either at Jack's Bar-B-Que or at home, depending on whether or not we're alone."

"Does he seem comfortable living in two separate homes?"

"Honestly, he's never said anything to the contrary."

"Good." Evan wrote a few more notes. "As far as I can tell, Carter is well-adjusted. He has good grades, I assume."

"He certainly does. Otherwise, it's no ball games for him." Chris adjusted himself in his chair. "I try not to spoil him. His mother seems to think I'm too harsh."

"In what way?"

"Just like I said. He has to do his homework, get good grades, and play nice in the sandbox." Chris gave a nervous chuckle, but there was a serious expression on his face.

"Is Lucinda lax as far as discipline?"

"I have no idea. Carter is pretty tight-lipped about the goings-on at Lucinda's. My take is that he looks at it as an obligation to stay with her a few nights and every other weekend. I think he views it as a temporary situation. Honestly, sometimes I think I'm the only one who does any parenting, but Lucinda has never discussed any bad or moody behavior from Carter. Everything is always 'fine' until she needs money for something."

"What does he do for fun when he's there?"

"Fortunately, his friends are nearby. I purposely bought my house so he could visit his friends, regardless of whose house he was staying at. We're less than two miles from each other. He could ride his bike, but I'm still uneasy about traffic. There are too many distracted drivers on the road, and kids don't always pay close enough attention." Chris paused. "He and his buddies often meet up at Wembley Park, a midway point."

"At least the town is starting to put bike lanes on the roads," Evan said.

"Do you really think anyone texting while driving is going to notice? I doubt it," Chris replied. "They're not even observing the signs that say, 'Don't text and drive.'" He let out a huge sigh of annoyance.

Evan nodded in agreement. "So, let me ask you this: If the judge gives him the choice, do you think he'd decide to stay with you full time?"

"It would appear that way. I sure hope so." Chris furrowed his brow. "When we're together, he talks about school and his activities, and his friends. Oh, and apparently, he's discovered that not all girls have cooties, but he's still on the fence about most of them."

"What about Lucinda? What does he have to say about her?"

"The only time he mentions his mother is when it comes to transportation or switching days. As for Bruce, Carter will make a few jokes, like what a doofus he thinks Bruce is. But nothing malicious." Chris paused. "More like Bruce is a part of the furniture. Carter can be pretty funny at times." Chris smiled as thoughts of his son went through his head. "The other day he asked me if it was polite for someone to use dental floss in front of you, but before I could answer, he shrugged and said, 'Must be an occupational hazard.'" Both men laughed.

"Carter is at that age when kids are discovering their sense of humor." Evan continued his questioning. "What about Luna?"

"What about her?" Chris cocked his head. "We've been seeing each other for about three years. Well, the first year really didn't count. We were pretending we were 'just friends.'" He used air quotes.

"I've only met her a couple of times, but she seems right for you. I mean, in a yin and yang kind of way."

"Yin and yang?" Chris sounded confused. "You're starting to sound like her." He smiled.

"On purpose. I like her. She's a free spirit, but also grounded at the same time."

"True. Kind of an enigma," Chris said thoughtfully.

"They get along okay? Luna and Carter?"

"Yes. She's really good with kids. She worked in children's services for a while," Chris continued, as Evan took notes. "Carter's never stayed over when she's at my place, although I'm pretty sure he knows what's going on."

"So when you get together with Luna, and Carter is around, what do you normally do?"

"We'll take hikes. Canoeing. Movies. She's fixed early dinners for us a couple of times before I had to bring him back to his mother's. And he helps her with food prep. For some reason, he enjoys peeling potatoes."

"Maybe he simply enjoys her company."

"Luna has a knack for relating to kids. She says it's part of her sixth sense."

"Oh, don't let Lucinda hear you say anything that sounds woo-woo. She'll have her lawyers twist it into something weird or sinister."

"Good point." Chris pursed his lips.

"I assume Lucinda knows or is aware of Luna?"

"Yes, and thankfully, they've never met, but Lucinda knows about her. If Lucinda's said anything to Carter, he hasn't shared it."

"Anything else that comes to mind?" Evan looked up from his papers. "If the judge allows Carter to make his own decision, and you get full custody, Lucinda will no longer be entitled to child support."

"Boy, is she gonna hate that," Chris chortled. "Well, I think we have our work cut out for both of us. When I speak with Carter, I'll start by discussing Chicago, presuming Lucinda has told him about it." He hesitated for a moment. "Gee, I hope he doesn't say he's *excited* about moving to Chicago."

"Doubtful. Like you said, he's going through enough changes without any help from a moving company."

Chris let out a sigh of relief. "I'm sure you're right. Then I'll let him know I am filing for full custody." Chris had a thoughtful expression on his face. "I'll tell him he'll have to do an interview with a psychologist, because it's required. He's a smart kid. He knows there are lots of rules."

"I'm sure. His father is in law enforcement." Evan smiled as he tried to assuage Chris's trepidation.

"Let's get back to Monica calling Lucinda. She will have a cow if it comes out of the blue," Chris said.

"Most likely. If you want to give her a heads-up, that's fine. Just tell her Monica will be calling to set up a meeting this week. We're going to have to fast-track this if we want a resolution before she moves. Before you go, let me know when you're available so we're not wasting time playing phone tag."

Chris gave him the days and times while Evan continued writing. When he was finished, he stood and asked, "Ready for a beer?"

"Am I ever," Chris answered, and got up from his chair. Evan walked around and put his arm around Chris's shoulders. "You've got a good case. It will be grueling, annoying, and aggravating, but you have a lot going for you."

It dawned on Chris that he hadn't told Evan about his new position and the raise. "I have something else that will work in my favor. I'll catch you up over that beer."

Chapter Seven

Luna's House
Wednesday Night
A Flash from the Past

Luna was stuffed from the pizza and the cannoli. Her first inclination was to flop on the sofa and hit the TV remote, but the box containing pieces of her past was summoning her like the Cape Hatteras Lighthouse. She pushed herself off the couch and stepped over Wylie, who was equally stuffed from the meatball.

Luna moved the colorful hand-blown bowl she'd bought from Patsy Lambert's Hot Sand shop. The mixture of blues and greens reminded Luna of flowing water. Serene. Tranquil. She hoped it would give her a sense of calm as she sifted through the tokens of days long gone.

Junior Year

Luna continued to work on the psychology project with Brendan and was grateful he didn't discuss his girlfriend, Laura, with her. Luna wasn't sure if he was being sensitive to her feelings, but then again, did he even know how she felt? Luna thought perhaps the relationship wasn't going that well, and he was keeping it to himself. But then again, he was spending almost every weekend with Laura. Luna hated how much she cared. But she was stalwart in keeping their friendship spirited, and their banter remained the same as they argued over who had the better voice: Rihanna or Adele, or Adam Levine versus Eminem. Brendan would argue that Levine sounded like a girl, and Luna's retort was that Eminem had a potty mouth and no real voice. One artist they did agree on was Toni Braxton. Luna could sense the pain in Braxton's performance of "Un-Break My Heart," and later, she would experience it for real.

It was shortly after spring break when Luna noticed Brendan was acting a bit sullen. He was much too quiet. After a week went by, she couldn't help but ask, "Brendan, is something the matter?"

"Huh? Yeah. Nah. Well, yeah."

Guys are so not *articulate*, Luna thought to herself. "What's up?"

"Laura and I broke up." He sighed. "It's okay."

Luna sensed it was not okay. "What happened? Unless you don't want to tell me."

"She went back with her ex." He made a face, pretending it wasn't a big deal.

"Well, that stinks," Luna said kindly, but inside, she was doing cartwheels. Maybe she would get a second bite at that apple.

"I'll get over it," he snickered, but Luna knew he was crushed. This was his second relationship in two years that had gone south. The first one was because the girl moved across the country, and they couldn't keep up with each other, three thousand miles apart. This breakup was new. Fresh. Maybe it didn't sting as much.

"You sure you're alright?"

"Me? Yeah. Two for two. At this rate, I'll have an ex-girlfriend every year," he joked.

Luna thought—hoped—she could break that pattern, but a lot had to happen first. She would have to make her feelings known. But not yet. She didn't want to be the rebound girlfriend.

Luna jumped at the sound of her phone. It was Chris. "Hey, dollface. How was your day?"

"Good. We have everything under control for tomorrow's event."

"You are a miracle worker. I hope those kids appreciate what you and Ellie are doing for them." Chris's voice was calm and kind.

"I think they are going to be blown away. Lots of the artists are helping decorate. It's going to be even better than they originally planned." Luna's voice was cheerful.

"Why am I not surprised?" Chris's smile could be felt over the phone.

"We seemed to work some magic, although I don't want to jinx it." Luna crossed her fingers.

Chris continued. "Listen, there is something I need to talk to you about this weekend."

"Everything alright?" Luna's voice sounded genuinely concerned.

"Not exactly. I have a few things I need to figure out."

"Care to share?" Luna was even more concerned at this point.

"*Er*, not over the phone. I'll fill you in when I see you."

"Oh. Okay." Luna was not okay, but she didn't know what else to say to him.

They said their goodnights, and Luna proceeded to recall her past.

Several weeks before the end of the semester, Luna, Brendan, and ten other students were chosen to spend two weeks at a writer's workshop in the Blue Ridge Mountains. Both Brendan and Luna were selected as the "adults-on-duty" and were responsible for overseeing the other students. Nothing serious, but making sure the students attended every meal, workshop, and went to bed no later than eleven. Not that there was much to do. There were no televisions, and cell phones were kept under Luna's supervision. Unless it was an emergency, students were required to be "unplugged."

Every night, the group would gather around the fire pit on the patio and talk about their projects, their thoughts about the day's workshop, and share feedback with one another. One evening, Brendan and Luna were the last two sitting there as the embers began to fade. They were sitting close together. Very close. They were shoulder to shoulder. At one point, Brendan turned Luna toward him and kissed her softly. Then more passionately. The two were intertwined when they heard the sound of a stick breaking several yards away. They disentangled themselves immediately, each apologizing to the other.

"I guess this isn't a good idea." Brendan scooched a few inches away from Luna.

"You're probably right," Luna replied, but her heart disagreed. "We don't want to be accused of setting a bad example, or any other impropriety."

Brendan let out a loud exhale. "Agreed." He stood and held out his hand to give Luna a boost up from where she was sitting. She knew it was the right thing, but she still didn't like it. At least he'd showed some interest. That was a big plus.

She brushed off her pants and turned to him. "Hey, do you think there are any stores open right now?"

"Why? You need something?" Brendan checked his watch. "It's eight thirty."

"You know how everyone was kinda groaning about how long this retreat has been? Yeah, it was fun in the beginning, but I think everyone is ready to go home."

"What did you have in mind?" Brendan had no idea where the conversation was going.

"Yellow ribbons." Luna giggled.

"Yellow ribbons?" Brendan asked; then Luna reminded him of their significance. He rubbed his hands together in a conspiratorial way. "Let's get moving. There's a big box store a few miles from here."

They bought as many yards of yellow ribbon as they could find in the greeting-card section of the store. When they got back to the retreat, they agreed to meet around midnight to be sure everyone was asleep. They then made their way around the ten mini-cabins, adorning the doors with the symbol of solidarity and hostage release. They could barely contain themselves as they snuck from one cabin to the next. Brendan whispered, "We're probably the only ones who know what this means."

"Who cares? This is fun!" Luna squeaked.

The following morning, most of the students got the joke and took the ribbons home as souvenirs. Overall, the retreat was a successful exercise in discipline, fellowship, and collaboration. Romance? Not so much.

Luna and Brendan continued their usual friendly interaction, with Luna hoping it would develop further after the retreat. Once they got back to their regular classes on campus, things seemed normal between the two of them, particularly their close physical proximity when they were together. It was as if they were in a world of their own, allowing others to be spectators as they entertained each other with jokes, both private and public.

The first Saturday in May was a big day for horse racing: the Kentucky Derby at Churchill Downs. It was the start of the battle for the Triple Crown. Luna had always dreamed of going, but getting tickets was impossible, until Brendan told her he had an in with one of the stable hands. It was impossible to find a vacancy at a hotel or motel within thirty miles, so they decided to pack a tent, sleeping bags, and the other items necessary for a night under the stars—and on the ground. Luna was wild with delight. She and Brendan were going camping and to the Derby. What could be better?

The trip from Durham to Louisville was at least an eight-hour drive, so they left Friday afternoon and arrived at dusk at the campground, where hundreds of other racetrack lovers had already settled in. It was like

Woodstock, but with less LSD and music and better constructed bathroom facilities. One step up from Porta-Potties. The overall mood was lively and a little rambunctious, with people sharing stories, food, beer, and an assortment of other alcoholic libations. Luna was careful not to over-imbibe. Waking up in a bag on the ground with a hangover was not an option. Neither was privacy. *So much for romance*, she thought, but Luna was satisfied she and Brendan were together. She hoped there would be a second attempt at kissing, but it didn't happen. Luna figured it was because you could practically touch the people in the adjacent tent. She let it slide. Some other time.

The morning of the race, they were up at the crack of dawn. They had to be at the stables by seven o'clock if they had any chance of gaining entry to the famous racetrack. Brendan phoned his friend, who told him where to park and that he'd give them passes for general admission to the clubhouse. Everything was still closed to the public, and security personnel were all over the grounds. The big race didn't start until after six o'clock that evening, so the two had to busy themselves for the next eleven hours.

Luna was caught up in the high energy surrounding the legendary and distinguished venue that hosted one of the most famous thoroughbred races in history. Brendan's friend gave them a quick tour, pointing out the various sections of the stables and the paddock area. Luna wanted to get up close and personal with the horses, but that was not going to happen. She would only be able to view them from a distance later on.

She read a little about one of the favorites, Big Brown, who'd been purchased by a man who owned a trucking company in New York. He named the horse Big Brown as a nod to UPS's logo and nickname. Luna imagined the horse caught her eye from yards away. "He's going to win," she whispered to Brendan.

"Who are you, Dr. Dolittle?" he teased.

"You'll see." Luna gave him her raised-eyebrow look.

As the day went on, throngs of people began entering the area, the women wearing some of the most absurd-looking hats. *When did it get this crazy?* Luna wondered. In addition to their chapeaus, many were adorned with tens of thousands of dollars' worth of diamonds. *Make that hundreds of thousands.* It was a spectacle of the uber rich and conspicuous consumption.

The day was as long as the lines as they waited to use a flushable toilet. Even though the facilities at the campground weren't completely barbaric, they still needed a few decades of modernization. There were more lines for food and drinks, so Luna and Brendan joined two separate queues and designated an area where they would meet after they spent ridiculous amounts of money on hot dogs and soda. It was the Kentucky Derby, after all.

Brendan made sure he placed their bets early on; otherwise, it would have meant waiting in more lines of hopeful gamblers. There were nine other races before the big one, and they placed bets on all of them, with Luna using her Dr. Dolittle superpowers to pick the winner of each.

They could barely squeeze through the throng to watch the races in person and had to rely on the closed-circuit TVs to see what was really happening. Whenever one of Luna's horses came around the final turn and down the homestretch, she would start screaming as if the horse could hear her. At one point, a woman turned to her and asked, "Do we need to call an ambulance?" But Luna didn't mind the mockery, considering she won a few hundred dollars on a two-dollar bet. Brendan was in shock and awe. Earlier that morning, he'd scanned *The Morning Line* and the professional picks but lost every time. Luna consoled him with, "I'll buy dinner."

Finally, Steve Buttleman, the bugler for the race, began to play the "Call to the Post" for the fastest two minutes in sports. Luna could barely contain her excitement. She grabbed Brendan's shirtsleeves and held them in what felt like a death grip. Brendan couldn't help but laugh at his friend. She was as entertaining as the event itself. As the parade of horses entered the track, over 160,000 spectators sang the state song, "My Old Kentucky Home," a song riddled with controversy, so she didn't join in. She knew no one would notice, and frankly didn't care. At that moment, all she could think about was the race.

The horses were at the gate. Luna was almost hyperventilating as the bell rang, releasing the thoroughbreds. Big Brown could hardly be seen in the thick pack of horses until they came around the clubhouse turn, when he pulled ahead. Luna's lungs were on fire. She thought she might wet her pants. Big Brown kept moving faster, gaining on the other horses. The crowd went wild as the horses approached the finish line, with Big Brown winning by five lengths.

Luna could barely contain herself. You would have thought she held ownership or had placed a chunk of money on the winning horse. But it wasn't really about the money. It was about the excitement she believed she shared with the beautiful animals doing their best to win. Tears were streaming down her cheeks as Brendan swooped her up and gave her a victorious spin, careful not to knock anyone over. Brendan was smiling from ear to ear. Not because he'd won. It was because Luna's excitement was contagious. Brendan put his arm around her shoulders and guided her through the sea of spectators. She turned in her ticket and collected her ten-dollar winnings. You would have thought she'd won a million.

They moved through the swarm slowly until they finally reached an exit. Once they found Brendan's car, they decided to make the trip back to the university instead of camping another night. They wouldn't get back until sometime around two a.m., but it beat sleeping on the ground. Besides, Luna's level of exhilaration was at its peak. It would take hours for her to calm down. They stopped two hours into their journey and found a restaurant that wasn't part of a fast-food chain.

The drive back seemed to go quickly as the two babbled on about the weekend, going over every detail of their adventure. When they arrived at Luna's dorm, Brendan put his arm around her and gave her a big hug and a quick kiss. Too quick for her liking, but it was a kiss, nonetheless.

As the semester was drawing to a close, she hoped Brendan would make plans for them to get together over the summer. They lived several hours away from each other, but the trip was doable. She waited for him to suggest it, but he didn't, and they parted with platonic hugs, promising to keep in touch.

During the summer months, communication between them was sporadic. Brendan's family was going through a crisis. Actually two. His younger sister was diagnosed with MS, and his father was recovering from a stroke. With Brendan being the oldest of the five children, he took on the responsibility of handling all the important issues while his mother tended to his dad. It wasn't until the fall that his father had recovered well enough for physical therapy, and his sister found a good doctor at the Mayo Clinic in Minnesota. But it all took its toll on Brendan. He had one more year of college to go, and the summer had worn him down. He was starting to get depressed. Luna was very concerned and gave him as much support as she could, and as much as he was willing to take. *Men can be so dense.* That seemed to be one of Luna's theme songs.

While the students were signing up for the fall semester classes, a new girl transferred from Minnesota. Her name was Eileen Lovecraft, and she happened to be in one of Luna and Brendan's classes. Luna shuddered when she first spotted her. It was disconcerting. Was it because she resembled Brendan's ex, Laura? She couldn't quite put her finger on it, and the feeling made her uncomfortable. Even Eileen's last name gave Luna the creeps. *Lovecraft?* Jealous, perhaps? Why? Brendan hadn't shown an interest in her. At least not yet. Or at least not to Luna's knowledge. But she couldn't shake the dread. Something was causing a chasm in their relationship.

The first two months of the semester, Luna and Brendan continued to study together and always grabbed a bite to eat afterward, but it wasn't as frequent as it had been in the past. No more concerts. No more movies.

She wondered why he hadn't made another attempt at romance. But she let it go. He'd had a rough summer and probably needed some emotional space.

The week before Thanksgiving, Brendan told her he was going to the Outer Banks to visit family for the holiday. He seemed excited, and Luna was glad he and his family would be sharing happier times. Then, one afternoon as she was walking to class, she overheard Eileen telling someone *she* was going to the Outer Banks. *Not Minnesota? Where her family was from?* It sent a chill up Luna's spine. Several thoughts ran through her head. Brendan's family lived in Greensboro, North Carolina. His father was having physical therapy, and his sister was involved in clinical trials. It didn't sound right to her that they would travel to the Outer Banks, but she didn't question him. She admitted it was none of her business, but still . . .

The day before everyone left, Luna and Brendan gave each other big hugs and wished each other a Happy Thanksgiving. But there was something in that hug. Or was it something that *wasn't* in that hug?

The week after Thanksgiving, Brendan's mood was buoyant, more so than it had been since they'd returned to school. As the two were walking to their class, Luna remarked at the change in his disposition.

He smiled. "I'm seeing someone."

Luna thought he meant a therapist. "Really? For how long?"

"It's pretty new, actually."

The word *new* struck her in an odd way. She wanted him to elaborate, but her gut was telling her she really didn't want to know. He told her anyway.

"It's Eileen," he continued.

Luna thought she might vomit. Vomit from hearing the truth, and vomit from her failure to recognize it. *The worst lies are the ones we tell ourselves.* It was difficult for Luna to refrain from spewing her thoughts and feelings. "Do you think it's because she resembles Laura?"

He stopped short. "You think so?"

Men are so dense. The recurring refrain. "Just sayin'."

He touched Luna's arm. Her tension was palpable. "Are you alright?"

Tears started to well up. "No. I am not alright." She turned so they were face to face. "I'm in love with you."

He blinked several times. "I . . . I had no idea."

"Bull." She turned and walked away as quickly as possible without knocking people over. She took the long way back to her dorm. Her body was shaking uncontrollably, and she gasped, trying to contain her emotions before she got back to her room. But there was no hiding the sheer look of humiliation on her face. She dashed past the reception desk, ran toward the elevator, and pushed the Door Close button several times. Thankfully, her roommate hadn't returned from class, so she had a couple of hours to regroup.

An hour later, Brendan phoned her. "Luna, listen. I'm really sorry I hurt you."

"I'll get over it." She struggled to seem cavalier.

"I want us to still be friends." He sounded awkward.

"Maybe. But not right now. I need time to adjust. I gotta go." She ended the call, folded her arms on her desk, buried her head, and bawled her eyes out again until she fell asleep. She was gutted. Mortified.

A few hours later, a stabbing pain in her neck woke her up. "Ouch!" It took her a few seconds to gather her wits. When she sat up, she noticed the ink on the paper was smudged with drool and tears. "Wow. I should have seen that coming."

Her roommate looked up from the book she was reading. "Seen what coming? You okay? I tried not to wake you."

Luna nodded her head. Her bloodshot eyes and her reddened nose told a different story. A story about someone who'd just learned something dreadful. "Just me being an idiot, that's all."

"Want to talk about it?" her roommate asked.

"Not really." Luna got up, brushed her teeth, put on her pajamas, and crawled into bed.

The next morning, she phoned the professor who taught the class she and Brendan were in and explained she had gotten food poisoning over the weekend and wouldn't be attending his lecture. He gave her the assignment and told her to "feel better." *As if . . .*

Two days later, she knew she had to show her face, but decided to sit in the back row instead of her usual seat next to Brendan. There were almost two hundred students in the large room, and she was comfortable sitting behind all of them. She saw Brendan crane his neck and look in her direction, but she pretended not to notice. The minute the bell rang, she was out the door like lightning. She heard him calling her name and moved as fast as possible to get to her next class. The one he wasn't in. She was grateful they only shared one class this semester. It made it much easier for her to avoid him. He texted her a few times, but she kept replying with, **Please leave me alone**. Finally, he did.

Christmas break was only a few weeks away, and it was a good opportunity for Luna to regroup. The last day, she finally reached out to him. She texted, **Enjoy the holiday.** He replied, **You too.**

Once she was home with her family, she began to feel more like herself. Her brother was in the Air Force and planned on coming home for a few days. Luna knew it would be the elixir she needed before she returned to school in the new year.

After several hilarious conversations with her brother, she realized how uplifted she felt. Then it hit her like a brick. It was the endorphins. Laughter triggers endorphins. Endorphins cause the levels of cortisol to go down, and cortisol is considered a "stress hormone." It made perfect sense. All the laughter she experienced with Brendan gave her surges of endorphins. No wonder she felt so good when she was around him and was so devastated at the thought of losing him. Laughter was the best medicine, and she vowed to include it in her daily routine and never again let one person ruin her mood, her day, or her life. At the very least, she would try.

Luna snapped to attention when Wylie rested his head on her knee. She was in the exact same position she'd fallen into that fateful night, with her head cradled in her arms on her desk. Had she been dreaming? Was she reliving her past, channeling those same emotions? It was a flashback that felt all too real. It was as if she'd stepped into another realm. A fugue state. A different dimension. The dried tears on her face confirmed it. *What was going on?* She *hoped* it was hormones. It was loony, even for her. She leaned over and placed her head on top of Wylie's. "What is wrong with me, pal?" He bumped her chin lightly with his nose. "Nothing? You mean I'm normal?" Wylie cocked his head. "Okay, not normal-normal." She wrapped her arms around his neck. "Thank goodness you understand me."

She looked at the clock. It was past midnight. "Come on, buddy. Time for your last visit to the doggie bathroom." She walked to the kitchen and let him out to run around the fenced-in yard one more time before they both hit the sheets. She made a cup of herbal tea, let him back in, and gave him a treat. "This is literally a midnight snack, pal." He looked up at her with his big brown eyes. He knew. Dogs knew. They were often smarter than people.

Luna tossed and turned all night. She was drawing similarities between the way her relationship had developed with Chris and with Brendan. They were friends first. Pals. Was there something ominous in the phone call earlier? What was on Chris's mind? She hadn't seen him for almost three weeks. Was the impending conversation going to be a repeat of Brendan's rejection of her love and affection? Chris hadn't said "love you" when they hung up after the call. Why not? Did she say it to him? No. Had he said it before? Yes. But how long had it been?

Luna could read people like a book. Except when it came to her own romantic relationships. She presumed the universe wanted her to learn lessons in life, particularly her own. And if you don't learn it the first time, you were likely to repeat it. One lesson she had to constantly remind herself of was that love came in all shapes and sizes and, at its root, it was pure. It should not come with restraints or conditions. She recalled the Richard Bach platitude about setting something free if you love it—but who has that kind of power, anyway? She thought again. It was about releasing and letting go. But one could only do that in one's own mind. One thing was certain: love could be very painful, and right now, she was suffering the pain of losing a friend. She'd lost him once to another love, then ultimately released her pain. But this feeling was something entirely different and much, much sadder.

Her thoughts returned to Chris. Intellectually, she knew her relationship with Chris was solid. It was her emotional insecurity that was speaking much too loudly.

Luna kept punching the pillow, trying to find a comfortable position. It was impossible. Her brain was in overdrive. Wylie was at the foot of the bed, eyeing her every move. "I know, I know. Sorry, pal. My mind is not cooperating."

She flung herself back against the pile of pillows and remembered how she and Brendan had reconciled their friendship. They hadn't been in another class together during the final semester, so she saw very little of him. Several weeks before graduation, Brendan sent her a text congratulating her on her award for her extracurricular work with underprivileged children. When she read the text, she realized her heart no longer felt heavy. She still loved him, but the emotion had morphed into fondness. She replied with her thanks and wished him all the best in his future endeavors.

She wasn't surprised when he told her he was moving to Minnesota. He and Eileen were getting married. Again, she wished him "all the best," and she meant it.

They vowed to keep in touch, but she figured he wouldn't. Much to her surprise, he did. For the next fifteen years, he sent her birthday wishes, and she did the same; occasionally, they checked in with each other about world events.

During the pandemic, he reached out to her to see if she was okay, which began a weekly banter of one-liners from *Young Frankenstein* and *Blazing Saddles*. She could finally share laughter with her old friend again. But then several months passed with no contact. It was also odd that he hadn't responded to any of her emails. She thought perhaps Eileen was jealous and had put a stop to the communication, but Luna decided she was going to make one more attempt to reach out once she got past the event at the center and the weekend ahead.

Chapter Eight

Thursday Morning
Law Offices of Evan Houston, Esq.
And So It Begins . . .

Lucinda sat in the reception area, sending dagger looks at everyone who walked into the office. She was fuming, and she didn't care who knew or what they thought. It wasn't as if people had any right to judge her or her situation. Most people waiting in a lawyer's office were probably there because there was a problem. Evan dealt with family law, so there was a good chance every person in the office had something major going on in their lives. But Lucinda was self-centered. Whatever their problems were didn't matter to her. The only thing that mattered was how this situation was going to affect her plans. She was ready for a battle, especially after she heard Chris's voicemail informing her Monica was going to call to set up an appointment. She kept checking her watch, anticipating Chris would be late due to his job. *His job. Everything had to do with his job.*

Chris walked in exactly on time and was totally prepared for her ire. *What did she expect? That she could take his kid halfway across the country without a fight? Did she not know him after all this time?* Chris was an easygoing guy when it came to many things, but not when it came to his job or his son.

"Lucinda," Chris greeted her. She ignored him and turned her back. "Great," he muttered. He caught the eye of another man sitting across the room. The man gave Chris a sympathetic look. The brotherhood of divorced men, especially those dealing with an angry ex-wife. Chris had paid his dues to this particular club. He leaned forward and rested his forearms on his legs. He was ready for a fight.

Chris spotted Monica walking in his direction. She told them Evan was ready and then escorted Lucinda and Chris into Evan's office. As Chris rose from his chair, the man sitting across the room gave him a thumbs-up. Chris nodded and smiled. Then he chuckled to himself, thinking there should be some kind of secret handshake among this club of exes.

Monica opened the door to Evan's office. "I'll be at my desk if you need me." She turned and left.

Evan stood as the two entered the room. "Lucinda," he said cordially. She nodded but said nothing, sat, placed her purse on her lap, and waited. "Chris." The men shook hands. It wasn't a secret handshake, but it might as well have been. Evan was going to win this case for his friend.

Evan began. "I understand you have plans to move out of state," he said to Lucinda.

"Yes, I do." A curt answer.

"When is this going to take place?"

"In six months." Another curt answer.

Evan pushed ahead. "Do you have an exact date?"

"Not yet."

"When do you think you will know?"

"I'm not sure."

"And is it your intention to take Carter with you?"

"I'm his mother."

"True. But as of now, you have joint custody, and you need to get a court order to take him out of state."

"Not if Chris will agree to it. I don't understand why we have to go through all of this."

"Because you . . ." Chris's voice trailed off. He wanted to say, "Because you can't be trusted," but stopped short. No point in starting an argument on top of a disagreement.

Lucinda shot him a nasty look. "Because I what?" Her voice was shrill.

"Nothing." He leaned back in his chair, letting Evan take the wheel.

"Lucinda, you have to understand that you signed a legal document regarding custody. If you take Carter out of state, you could be charged with kidnapping."

"That is ridiculous!" This time a louder shrill.

"No, it's the law." Evan paused to give her time to digest what the ramifications of such an action would be.

"I would not be kidnapping my son. He's *my* son." Lucinda spat out the words.

Chris couldn't hold back any longer. "He is *our* son. Plural. Yours and mine."

She folded her arms and looked away.

Evan was quite familiar with situations like this one. Everyone thought they were right, and the other person was wrong.

"You are going to need a court order, Lucinda. That's all there is to it."

"We'll just see about that." With that, she got up and stormed out of the office.

Chris looked up at Evan. "Now what?"

"Now we file for full custody. She has been put on notice that she simply cannot do what she wants."

Chris smirked. "That'll be a first. She is not going to take it well."

"Not your problem. She can have all the tantrums she wants, but unless a judge decrees that she can move Carter out of state, she doesn't have a leg to stand on."

"But what if she just packs him up and leaves?"

"Chris. Are you forgetting you are a U.S. Marshal? Kidnapping is your area of jurisdiction."

Chris laughed for the first time. "That woman makes me nuts, although I doubt they would let me take the case. Conflict of interest." He paused. "But did you know that there are over 875,000 abductions every year? And ninety percent are family members, sixty percent of which are women."

"Interesting stats, but I doubt she'll become one of them. Do you think Carter would go willingly without telling you?"

"I would hope not."

"Good. When do you plan on speaking with him?"

"He has practice on Thursday, and I'll be there coaching. Then we usually go to Jack's Bar-B-Que. Sometimes one or two of his friends will join us."

"Good. Glad to hear you have a lot of interaction with Carter and his friends. Does Bruce?"

"Who?" Chris joked.

Evan chuckled. "Keep everything on a routine

schedule, so Carter doesn't feel any disruption." Evan checked his notes. "We don't want him to start to experience anxiety over this. I'm not saying he won't, because he probably will, but maintaining a sense of normalcy will help. If they plan on leaving in six months, that will put the date sometime after the school year begins. Is she aware of how unsettling that can be?"

Chris huffed. "Is she aware of anything other than herself? You know her as well as I do."

Evan nodded. "I'm acting as your lawyer now. She will be her own worst enemy if she continues to be combative. I was relieved you controlled your emotions. The two main things we need to focus on are winning over the psychologist and winning over the judge. As I mentioned the other night, keep a journal of everything pertaining to Carter: how much time you spend with him, homework, baseball, anything and everything. Evidence of your ability to parent him singularly will be key."

"Understood. So, what's next?"

"Monica should have the paperwork ready." He picked up the phone and buzzed her. "Do you have the papers for Mr. Gaines?" There was a pause as he listened and then said, "Great. Thanks."

A few minutes later, Monica appeared with a file. She sat in the chair that had been occupied earlier by Lucinda. The top of the form said MODIFICATION OF CUSTODY AGREEMENT. Chris looked it over. "Do you want me to fill this out now?"

"The sooner, the better. It's going to take some time to get all our ducks in a row. Once the initial paperwork is filed, then we can get a court-appointed psychiatrist or psychologist so there will be no issues with favoritism."

Chris went to work on the forms. "What should I put down for the 'AS OF' date?"

"I suggest September first. That will keep Carter in the same school district."

"Do you think this will be resolved in the next few months?"

"That, I cannot guarantee. But often, when a parent is attempting to violate an agreement, the court gives the case priority treatment. Remember, we're heading into the summer, and people take vacations."

"Speaking of vacations, I wanted to take Carter to the Grand Canyon, but I doubt Lucinda will go for that, especially if I'm filing for full custody."

"Correct. Keep things local and uncomplicated."

Gaines let out a huge sigh. "Plus, with the new job, I may not be able to get much time off."

"Don't let anyone hear you say that. Your stance is that you are available to your son twenty-four-seven."

"Roger that." Chris completed the forms and handed them back to Monica. "Thanks."

Chapter Nine

Stillwell Center
Thursday
The Big Event

Ellie, Luna, and Chi-Chi were accustomed to putting events together, but those were their own events, not someone else's. Still, so far, things were going along as planned. Ellie made sure via social media that people were informed the center would be closed to the public on Thursday beginning at six p.m. for a private function.

Ellie had always considered renting out the space for private occasions, but there was already enough going on all the time. Adding more tasks to the existing workload might put everyone over the top, especially her. But this was an emergency. She remembered when she was in college, many years ago, when a prom or a dance was on the calendar. You spent weeks getting ready. The dress. The shoes. The accessories. Testing various hairstyles. What kind of corsage? *Did they still do that, she wondered? Corsages?* Today, many went to the events solo, or with a friend. Having a date was not the norm anymore, much to the relief of many. No pressure. Just get yourself dolled up and have a good time with your friends.

Ellie was the first one at the center that morning, with Ziggy and Marley in tow. She opened the large patio doors and let them run to the doggie park. Alex would be along shortly to take care of any messes they might create.

Luna was the next to arrive with Wylie, who immediately headed for the patio to see his buddies. She fired up the coffee machine and walked to The Flakey Tart to meet up with Heidi Dugan. Heidi prepared orders of scones and croissants for The Namaste Café, and Luna sold them. Luna had a placard next to the basket stating where the baked goods came from, hoping to prompt people to buy more. It was that type of camaraderie that made the center extra special, in addition to the unique art and specialties it offered.

Luna always added four extra scones to her order, for Chi-Chi, Cullen, Ellie, and herself. It had become part of their morning ritual. The three women would meet at Luna's while Cullen was banished to his workshop. He didn't mind one bit. He'd rather be whittling at something or replacing hinges.

Ellie gave Luna a look of concern. "Are you alright, dear? You look a bit weary."

"Not enough sleep."

Chi-Chi floated in like a colorful sunrise, her hair wrapped in a matching scarf that secured the braids down her back. She pulled out a chair and plopped herself down, a very un-Chi-Chi-like move.

"Whoa. What's up?" Luna asked.

"My brother. He is coming to town this weekend."

Everyone groaned at the same time. Just the mention of his name conjured thoughts of him with Jennine May. "She is going to be all over you," Luna said.

"I know," Chi-Chi moaned. Then she sat up straight. "I have a wonderful idea. I will tell her Abeo is coming, and would she have dinner with him on Saturday."

"Well, that would get him out of your hair."

"And we have dinner plans, do we not?" Chi-Chi reminded Luna.

"True. I thought you would invite him to join us," Luna said evenly.

"Oh, please. I am certain Jennine would be a better option." Chi-Chi sipped her coffee and eyed the other women over her cup.

Luna burst out laughing. "I couldn't agree more!"

Ellie, too, was laughing. "I so much enjoy our morning gatherings."

"I cannot wait to tell her—I mean ask her," Chi-Chi proclaimed with a devilish grin.

"What do you think Abeo is going to say?" Luna asked.

"It does not matter. He will go with her. I will insist."

The three women were on the verge of hysterics when Luna noticed Jennine opening her shop. She motioned in Jennine's direction. "Get to it, girlfriend."

Chi-Chi stood and smoothed her red and gold dashiki, then adjusted her head wrap. "Excuse me," she said politely, then turned and glided across the atrium.

Ellie and Luna were giggling. Jennine was known to be a bit like Blanche from *The Golden Girls*. If there was a man within fifty feet, she would sniff him out. If he was single, she would attach herself to one of his appendages. She had several options depending on how brave or petrified he was.

"I wonder what Chi-Chi is going to do if Abeo and Jennine go back to her place?" Luna rested her chin on her propped fists.

"Maybe they'll go back to Jennine's," Ellie suggested.

"Well, if I know Chi-Chi, she is going to instruct her brother to figure it out." The two friends laughed as they squinted to see if they could make out what the other two women were saying.

Chi-Chi had a slight smile on her face. She placed her hand on Jennine's. Jennine's head began to bounce up and down. Chi-Chi put her hands in a prayer position, bowed, and glided back to the café. She could barely contain her jubilation.

Chi-Chi took a very deep, relaxing, cleansing breath as she entered. "As you would say, 'mission accomplished.'"

Luna and Ellie remained impassive. They didn't want Jennine to see them overly excited. Just another day in the center.

"Bravo," Ellie said with a straight face.

"Ditto," Luna added. She looked over at Jennine's shop. "She must have gone in the back. Spill," Luna instructed Chi-Chi.

"I told her that my brother was coming into town unexpectedly and I had plans, so would she be so kind as to entertain him for the evening?"

"Entertain? I guess that's a euphemism for Jennine and her man-eating tendencies." Ellie continued to keep a straight face. "No pun intended."

Luna couldn't control herself. She got up, walked behind her easel, and howled.

Chi-Chi sat primly in her chair. "Please. I still have terrible visions from their last encounter. I prefer to think of something else now."

Luna peered from behind the large sketch pad. "Okay, but you still haven't figured out how you can get the two of them to stay at Jennine's."

"Do not worry. I will tell him. He must ask if he can see her place. I will tell him to flirt with her."

"Do you think he'll be okay with that?" Luna returned to her chair.

"It doesn't matter. I am okay with that, and *that* is all that matters." Chi-Chi gave a sly grin. "Besides, he is a man."

As the three finished their morning ritual, then cleared their cups, Alex walked through the atrium with the three dogs following him. Ellie went to speak with him. "Good morning, Alex."

"Morning, Ellie. I'm about ready to start hanging the lights. I figured I'd get it done before the center opens. Devon is going to put up a few tinkling chimes, since I'll have the ladder out."

"Good idea. Do you have everything you need?"

"I think so. I'll give you a click when I'm done."

Suki ambled over with a huge box filled with three-inch origami cranes. "I have one hundred. Each guest can take one home."

"How lovely! Thank you, Suki. They will be thrilled. How on earth did you manage to make so many in such a short time?"

"It is my pleasure, but I am not to get all the credit.

My advanced students helped. Please tell me—shall I place all of them in the trees?"

"Put a few dozen in the trees and plants, and we'll get a table and line up the rest near the door. I'll make sure there is a sign telling the students they may have one when they leave. Thank you again, Suki."

Ellie walked back to the café, carrying one of the paper cranes. "Suki made one for each attendee."

"That's so nice. Gee, I wish I had something to give them."

"How about a raffle for a reading?" Ellie suggested.

"Really? I was trying to stay on the down-low."

"Do not make me laugh," Chi-Chi replied. "You have so many clients, you can hardly keep up with them."

"True, but they are all referrals."

"The word is already out," Ellie said. "Unless you don't want to do it."

"Oh, sure! I'd be happy to. But how do we do it? Don't we need a license or something?"

"Probably, but I doubt they'll send the vice squad here." Ellie chuckled. "We can ask the kids to buy a ticket for five dollars. The money will go to the food bank."

"As long as you have bail money when the police arrive, I'm game!" Luna laughed. She knew there were still a very small handful of people who resented Ellie's success, particularly those who'd tried to stop her from building the project. "Do we have tickets?"

"No, but I'll ask Nathan to stop at the office supply store." Ellie picked up her cell phone and hit Nathan's speed-dial number. "Hi, Nathan. Need you to run an errand for me." Ellie explained what she wanted.

"No problem," said Nathan. "Gregory is coming in

at four o'clock so I can go home, change, and grab dinner. I'll be back around six, and he and I will keep an eye on everyone and everything for the party." Nathan was more than happy to accommodate Ellie.

"Wonderful. Thanks. See you later." Ellie turned to Luna and Chi-Chi. "Check that off the list. I'll print out the signs for the registration book, the raffle, and the cranes. Maybe Cullen can make some quick easel frames."

"Let's go ask." Luna motioned for Ellie to follow her into Cullen's showroom.

"I must get to work. I will speak to you later." Chi-Chi floated across the atrium and into her shop.

The bell from Cullen's front door rang in the back of his workshop. "Did he begin working on your dresser?" Ellie asked.

"No, but I have. I started sifting through the contents I took home. The process began a tidal wave of emotions. It was kinda weird. When I started going through the box, it was as if I was reliving the past."

"That's why they call them *mementos*, dear." Ellie had no idea how real Luna's experience was, and Luna wasn't about to elaborate. No one ever had to know how foolish she had been during that particular time in her young, naïve life.

The center was alive with excitement as the hour drew near. The awards were for outstanding service to the community, and Sabrina, one of the pages at the center, was one of the recipients. Ellie was very proud of her apprentice and her interest in the arts. With the main focus on math and science, art, music, and dance were considered less important, but Ellie was determined to encourage and endorse them. The monthly youth string quartet recitals had become more popular with parents. Ellie hoped it was because they were exposing their children to the classics, but she suspected it was because they could let their kids run wild in the gardens. No matter. The audience was growing.

Everyone who was participating in the evening activities brought a change of clothes. Thankfully, Luna had been alert enough in the morning to pack a small bag of cosmetics to cover up her lack of sleep. She ditched the idea of contact lenses and donned her biggest pair of horn-rimmed cat-eye glasses. She swapped her maxi skirt for a light beige summer dress and sandals, and pulled her long hair into a side braid and tied it with an animal-print ribbon. She peered in the mirror, double-checking she hadn't missed any clues of her sleepless and troubling night. Not a knockout, but respectable.

Luna turned around when Chi-Chi entered the tiled bathroom. "Well, hello, gorgeous! You look magnificent!" Chi-Chi was wearing a spectacular black jumpsuit with an embroidered peach and gold cape, and a matching *gele* head wrap.

Chi-Chi gave her a humble bow. "Thank you. I thought it would be nice to represent my heritage in front of these young people."

"You nailed it. Not that I would know one *boubou* or *aso ebi* from another."

Chi-Chi laughed. "Someday I will teach you the fashion of Yoruba. Suki will also be wearing traditional clothing from Japan."

"Very cool. Geez, I hope Brian from The Cheese Cave doesn't show up wearing a foam rubber wedge on his head!" She giggled.

Just as Luna was putting on the last of her undereye coverup, Ellie walked in carrying shop aprons. She also gasped at Chi-Chi's appearance. "Absolutely stunning. Well, I certainly don't want you to wear one of these." She glanced at Luna, who looked like a vanilla ice-cream cone, and handed her a bright blue apron. "Sorry, dear, but that is not traditional attire."

"Ha. It is for me!" Luna chuckled, and then donned the vibrant apron. "Brilliant idea." Luna looked down at her simple dress. "At least it won't clash with what I'm wearing."

Ellie had designed the logo for the center and ordered several dozen shop aprons made in various sizes and colors. All the artists wore them when they were working on their crafts, and many patrons had asked if they were for sale, so she'd ordered more. She hadn't planned on merchandising items for the center, but they became very popular. She then had baseball caps made that also became a favorite. The proceeds went to her favorite charities. Ellie felt lucky she had the resources to provide assistance for animals, women, and the food pantry. George urged her to put herself on the payroll to keep track of her expenses, but Ellie replied, "It's my money, and I am going to spend it on whatever I want. Besides, I want to be around to see the good I've done. Like the center." There was no doubt Ellie was generous and determined.

Ellie looked at Luna. "Are you feeling alright today?"

"Yes. Why?" Luna knew she hadn't been herself lately, and with the lack of sleep, she figured she looked dreadful.

"Oh, my friend. You cannot pretend you haven't had much on your mind."

"True. It's been chaos in my head."

"How so?"

"I mentioned something wasn't sitting right with me. I thought it might be Chris. I know something is happening with him, but I don't know what it is."

"Perhaps he will discuss it with you this weekend." Chi-Chi was trying to comfort her friend.

"I think that's the plan." Luna sighed. "Oh, Chi-Chi, what if he's going to break up with me?"

Chi-Chi balked. "You cannot be serious. He adores you. What makes you say this?"

"I think I'm having PTSD from a previous relationship."

"Ah. Yes, sometimes the past haunts our present. That is not a good thing."

Luna chuckled. "I'm the one usually doling out platitudes."

"Today it is my turn. I am sure it is nothing for you to be concerned about."

"Then there's this other thing."

"What thing?"

"A friend from my past. It was fifteen years ago. I had a huge crush on him, and he fell in love with someone else."

"Do you still have feelings for him after all this time?"

"No. Not in that way."

"So what is the matter?"

"After he moved, we kept in touch on every birthday and holiday. We even had dinner after an alumni reunion. It was good to have my friend back in my life. During COVID, we were emailing each other every day, and then he suddenly stopped."

"Have you tried to get in touch with him?"

"I sent an email a couple of days ago but haven't heard back."

"I am sure he will be happy to hear from you." Chi-Chi's calm voice was soothing.

"I'm sure you are correct." Luna smiled.

"Come. As you say, let's get this party started!"

Cullen was exiting the men's room as Luna and Chi-Chi were leaving the ladies' room. Cullen stopped short and caught his breath. "Chi-Chi. You look stunning."

She smiled. "Thank you. And you look . . . *hmm*, you look like you need a fresh apron."

Cullen looked down at his dusty trousers. "Good idea." He nervously smoothed his hair. "See you in a few."

Luna smiled to herself. She couldn't remember when Cullen had been this awkward.

The guests began to arrive promptly at six. Gasps of delight echoed through the beautifully adorned atrium. More sounds of pleasure drifted from the patio, and moments later, the band began to play.

Everything was perfectly placed, with tables for the registration book, raffle, and the cranes and high-tops lavish with food. The party was in full swing as Ellie and her crew looked on. She looped her arms around Chi-Chi and Luna. "Bravo, ladies. But let's try not to have to do this again." The women cackled, but they knew should anyone have a party emergency, the Stillwell Center would be there to save the day.

Chapter Ten

180 miles away—Charlotte, North Carolina
Thursday Afternoon
Chicago Ain't My Kind of Town

Chris was standing to the left and rear of the catcher. Carter was playing second base. A pop-up fly ball was aimed right at him, and he missed it. *It was such an easy play. What happened?* Chris thought to himself. He always maintained impartiality with the players, never showing favoritism to his son, nor did he reprimand him any more than he would another player. Besides, Chris believed in instructing rather than scolding. His voice was cool and calm. "Eye on the ball, guys."

The batter took another swing at the ball, this time hitting it between second and third base. In an attempt to make up for his last mistake, Carter ran toward the ball, colliding with the third baseman. Chris blew his whistle and flagged the team over to the bench. "Today you're playing against each other, but that is not an excuse for not paying attention. When we get to a real game on Saturday, everyone needs to be sharp. Alert. Mistakes can cost you the game." The boys murmured their agreement. "Okay. Grab some water and pretend you are vying for the World Series." Chris couldn't help but notice that Carter seemed a million miles away. "Hey, pal," Chris called out to him. "You okay?"

Carter gave him an adolescent shrug and walked back to second base. Normally, Carter had no problem telling his father what was on his mind. He hadn't learned about "filtering one's thoughts" yet. Maybe in a couple of years, he'd understand the positive uses of finesse, although many people never did. Chris chalked it up to his age and the awkwardness that went with it.

Another inning went by, and Carter appeared to be concentrating on the game—but still, Chris felt something was gnawing at his son. Tonight would be all about laying the cards on the table, allowing Carter to speak his mind about whatever subject he wanted, although Chris was sure most of the conversation would be about Chicago. Chris still wasn't sure if Lucinda had told their son her plans. It wouldn't surprise Chris if she waited until the movers showed up, but there was going to be a battle before that happened.

After six innings, Chris called the game. "Okay, guys, you looked better these past two innings. Play like that on Saturday."

"You got it, Coach!" several of the boys shouted.

Chris and Carter walked to Chris's Jeep Cherokee and put the gear in the back. As soon as they were strapped in, Carter looked at his father. "Dad? Do I have to move to Chicago?"

So she did tell him. "What did your mother have to say about it?"

"She didn't say anything. I heard her talking to Bruce."

"When was this?"

"About a week ago."

"And you didn't mention it to me?"

"I thought I misunderstood, but then she was making a big stink this morning about going to see a lawyer."

"How much of this conversation did you hear?"

"She was pretty mad. She told Bruce that she didn't care what you did. We were all moving."

"Did she know you overheard her?"

"I'm not sure. As soon as I went into the kitchen, she stopped talking."

"And you didn't ask?"

Carter pressed his lips together and shook his head. "Uh-uh."

Chris drew a deep breath. "Don't worry, son. We'll talk some more after we get a few barbecue ribs in you."

"And fried onion rings?" Carter's face lit up.

"Whatever you want."

"Even though I flubbed at practice?"

"Right now, I'm your dad, not your coach." He reached over and tousled Carter's black hair, the same color as his. Carter also shared his father's slightly exotic look. He could end up being a heartbreaker in a few years, but Chris was resolute on emphasizing integrity, responsibility, loyalty, kindness, and generosity. So far, his plan seemed to be working. Carter was a good kid. He showed empathy toward others. Chris wondered if that was Luna's influence. Not that Chris wasn't empathetic, but that was the core of Luna Bodhi Bodman.

They pulled into Jack's Bar-B-Que's parking lot, and Carter jumped out, brushing the remaining dirt off his pants. "I guess I should have reminded you to bring a change of clothes," Chris said.

"I had them in my backpack, but Mom was in one of her tizzy modes, and we left the house without it."

Chris made a mental note. Lucinda was starting to rack up some failing grades.

They were regulars at Jack's, and the hostess seated them in their favorite booth, where they could watch the big-screen televisions that were hanging over the bar.

The waitress came over to their table. "Howdy there, dudes." Her name was Wanda. She had been working at Jack's since Jack's father opened the place fifty years ago. "What'll you boys be havin' tonight?"

"Hey, Wanda. I'm thinking I'll try something different tonight," Chris said.

"Really? No ribs?"

"I didn't say 'no ribs,' but I'm going to have a side of curly fries this time."

"Oh, you're such a kidder, Marshal." She looked at Carter, who was finally smiling. "And what about you, young man?"

"I'll have my usual and a side of fried onion rings."

"Fried onion rings and cheese fries?" She eyed him over the glasses that sat precariously on the tip of her nose. Wanda never wrote anything down. She could take an order for a table of ten, including appetizers, entrees, sides, beverages, and dessert, and never miss a thing. It was remarkable, a gift very few possessed.

Carter looked at his dad and nodded like a bobble-head, asking for permission.

"Go for it. If you need some help, I'll be happy to oblige." Chris was relieved Carter was behaving more like himself.

"Awesome!" Carter smiled at Wanda.

Chris waited until Wanda was no longer in earshot. "Carter, I want you to try to remember that first conversation you overheard about Chicago." Chris realized he was interrogating his child, but maintained a kind, safe tone.

"Like I said, it was about a week ago. I was in the bathroom, and they were in their bedroom. She asked him when they expected him in Chicago. I thought maybe it was a trip or something, but then she said there was a lot of planning to do, packing, finding an apartment."

"An apartment?" Chris did not like that idea one iota.

"Yeah. I guess until they can find a house or something."

"Is that what she said?"

Carter furrowed his brow. "I really don't remember, but I just figured."

"What about school? Did she say anything about school?"

"I think they heard me, because they started talking real low so I couldn't hear anything else." Carter looked down at the table. "Dad?"

"Yeah?" Chris's intonation matched his son's.

"Was it a bad thing that I put my ear up against the shower to try to hear more?"

Chris burst out laughing. "Son, I am an investigator."

"But it's not polite to eavesdrop, right?" Carter looked embarrassed and confused.

"No, it's not, but there are exceptions. In this case, it was an exception. You want to know what is planned for you and your life, right?"

"Well, yeah." Carter seemed surprised and relieved.

"Okay. Not that I am encouraging rude behavior, but I want you to pay close attention to anything that they say about Chicago. I need you to do some reconnaissance for me. Okay?"

"Sure." Carter was delighted to be in on a secret mission with his father.

"If and when your mother brings it up to you, I want you to act surprised. Can you do that for me?"

"Uh, yeah." Carter rolled his eyes.

Wanda returned with a Sprite for Carter and a mug of beer for Chris. One was his limit, and he was going to savor it. He now had an "inside man." He knew it was time to let his son know his plans for custody. "Carter, I have to tell you something very important, but you must promise me you will not let your mother know we talked about this. You got it?"

"Got it." Carter stared into his father's eyes.

"I filled out papers to file for full custody."

Carter's eyes widened, and his voice got louder. "You mean I don't have to move to Chicago?"

"Shh. This is a secret operation, remember?"

Even though Carter was about to become a teenager, his father's occupation as a U.S. Marshal held him in awe. "Got it." Carter bit his upper lip.

Wanda blasted through the swinging kitchen doors,

balancing a large tray on her shoulder. Chris marveled at how agile she was, considering how many years she had been doing the job.

"I wonder if she ever dropped anything," Chris whispered to his son.

"Want me to ask her?" Carter was definitely acting more like himself now.

"I dare you." Chris sat back while Wanda placed their food on the table.

"Hey, Wanda? Did you ever drop anything?" Carter asked with an innocent face.

"Are you kidding? One time I decorated a couple with two orders of spaghetti, including the meatballs!" She cackled. "They put up such a fuss. The lady was hollerin' about just getting her hair done, her new dress, and all that." She finished placing the cholesterol buffet in front of them. "Boss took the dry-cleanin' money out of my paycheck." She *tsk-tsk*ed. "I've been pretty good since."

"Wanda, with your memory and your balancing act, you are truly one of a kind." Chris grinned and ripped one of the ribs off the rack.

"You're gonna need some extra napkins." Wanda reached in her pocket, pulled out a wad, and plunked it on the table. "I'll get you some of those wipes before you leave."

Chris muttered a "thank you" as he gnawed on the juicy rib.

"So, Dad. If you're going to file for full custody, will I still get to see Mom?"

"We're going to have to work that out. It's going to be a little rough getting used to, but I think keeping you here is in your best interest, wouldn't you say?"

Carter nodded his approval as he stuck his fingers in the onion rings.

"I have to ask you this." Chris thought he knew the answer, but just in case. "If you could choose who to live with, who would you pick?"

"You mean here or Chicago?"

"Yes."

"Here. For real." Carter confirmed his father's hopes.

"Good. I don't know if the judge will let you decide, but there is going to be a lot of stuff he's going to want to hear about."

"Like what?" Carter was licking his fingers.

"Like, does Bruce help you with homework?"

Carter made a face. "You can't be serious, Dad. Bruce barely knows I sorta live there."

"I don't remember the last time he went to one of your games." Chris squinted.

Carter shrugged. "Me either."

"Does it bother you?"

"No biggie. Dad, I don't hate the guy or anything, but he's just one big annoyance."

"What do you mean?"

"I dunno. He'll ask me if I did my homework, but he's never asked me if I need help with it. Heck, he hardly talks to me. Ya know, things like, 'How was your day?'" Carter said it in a deep voice, trying to mimic Bruce.

"Does he ever refer to you as *son*?" Chris had to ask.

"As if. And even if he did, I wouldn't pay attention. He's not my dad. I'm not his son."

Chris was impressed with the strong stance Carter took.

"What about your mom? Does she help with homework?"

"Nope. Only asks if I did it."

"Very engaged parenting," Chris muttered.

"Listen, Dad. I'd rather live with you all the time and just visit her. She's not mean or anything, she's just not there." Carter pointed to his temple.

"Are you saying your mother is a little off?" Chris leaned in.

"Not exactly. She's just got her own stuff she's always busy with. Most of the time, she's out with Bruce, or she's out and Bruce is in his office. Honestly, I feel like a visitor."

"Why haven't you said anything?"

"I guess I'm used to it."

"Does it make you feel bad?" Chris asked.

"No, not really. I mean, I know she loves me and all that, but she is not like most other moms. She doesn't participate in any school activities. Sure, she'll come to a game, but she's not baking any cookies," Carter snorted.

Chris laughed out loud. "I'm really sorry."

"About what?"

"That you feel like you're a visitor at your own mother's."

"Not your fault. I always tell people I live with you. I mean, I do most of the time, so it's not a lie."

"Just a stretch of the truth." Chris eyed him.

"Dad. Look. My room at your house is *my* room. She doesn't even let me put anything up on the walls just in case they have guests." He grabbed another handful of onion rings.

Chris thought about the first time Luna had spent the night and slept in Carter's room.

As if reading his father's mind, Carter said, "I know Luna slept in there once. But you know what I mean." Carter was much more mature than Chris was giving him credit for.

"I'm really sorry you feel that way about staying at your mother's. You should feel it's your home as much as you do when you're with me."

Carter shrugged. "Like I said, it's no biggie. As long as I have my room in your house, I'm good with it."

Chris's shoulders relaxed for the first time in days. He didn't realize how much stress he'd been holding in. "So how are we going to play this?" Chris asked, wondering how much of a sleuth he'd raised.

"I'm going to keep my eyes and ears peeled. I'll text you anything that seems a little goofy."

"No texting. No emails. No electronic fingerprints."

"Right. I guess I'm gonna have to start writing things down," Carter joked.

"Funny, dude. I bet you are the only one in your class who has a signature."

"And I can write cursive, too." Carter opened his eyes wide.

"Has your mom ever mentioned Luna?" Chris tried to sound casual.

"I heard her say something to Bruce about her name. Something about how 'hippy-dippy' it sounded. Then Bruce told her the only difference between her name and Luna's were two consonants and a vowel. They start with the same two letters and end with the same one." Carter snickered. "I thought it was kind of cool of Bruce to come up with that."

"Ha. That never occurred to me," Chris mused. *Some investigator.* "Listen, there's something else. You are going to have to sit down with a psychiatrist."

"A shrink? Why?" Carter held up a rib midair.

"So they can evaluate you. Make sure you are having happy thoughts," Chris said. "Seriously, they want to make sure you're well-adjusted, and if you are capable of making a decision on your own as to who you'd rather live with."

Carter nodded. "What if I just tell them?"

"Not that easy, son. Just answer the questions honestly. Don't try to fake anything. It's their job to see through the bunk. But I have complete faith in you." Chris squeezed a lemon wedge into his palms and wiped them with a napkin. He noticed Carter watching him. "Gets the sticky stuff off. And the smell."

"How come I never saw you do that before?"

"Maybe you just weren't paying attention while you were stuffing your face." Chris grinned.

Wanda sauntered over with a basket of wipes and the check. Chris pulled out a couple of twenties and placed them on the plastic tray. "Ready, partner?"

"Ready."

Chris walked behind Carter and placed both hands on his son's shoulders. "We've gotta make a stop on the way home."

"Ice cream?" Carter crossed both fingers.

"I have some in the freezer." He leaned in and whispered in Carter's ear. "But first we gotta get you something for that zit that's about to explode."

Carter instinctively touched the part of his face his father was referring to. "And don't keep touching it," Chris instructed him.

They pulled into the lot of a national pharmacy chain. "I hope you're not eating too much junk," Chris said, as they walked past a very long aisle filled with chemically treated snacks. Chris jerked his thumb at the rows of chip-filled bags. "There isn't one thing on those shelves that's good for you." Chris had had this conversation with his son many times, but the boy was a burgeoning teenager, so it didn't hurt to drop some reminders.

"Yeah, I know." Carter frowned. He didn't want to tell his father that his mother sent him to school with a packet of MSG-and-sodium-enriched snacks all the time. But Carter wasn't a dummy and rarely broke open a package. Normally, he'd toss the bag over to someone sitting at the same cafeteria table. Then Carter wondered, by not telling his father, was he technically lying? He decided to broach the subject. "Dad? If someone leaves out information, does that mean they're not telling the truth?"

"It depends. In court, they want you to tell the whole truth, but again, it depends on what information they're seeking." Chris thought he might be talking over his son's head. "What's on your mind? Can you give me an example?"

"If Mom does something that I know you don't like, and I don't tell you, is that a lie?"

Chris was growing suspicious. "For example?"

"She packs one of those snack bags in my lunch all the time."

Chris chuckled. "As long as you don't eat it."

"Not usually."

"Well, if you want to keep that complexion of yours

clear, you'll steer away from junk, including soda. Sugar, too much salt, and preservatives aren't good for you. I mean, you probably won't die from it, but an apple or a handful of nuts are a better option."

"Got it."

They approached the section that carried dozens upon dozens of different brands of facial cleansers, treatments, serums, and lotions. Chris grabbed a jar of charcoal facewash and Axe aqua and bergamot body wash, the same as he used at home. "You like this stuff, right?"

"Yeah. Mom always says I smell like you when I come back after spending a weekend with you."

Chris laughed and realized he had been using the same personal hygiene items for years. "Does she get bent out of shape about it?"

"Nah. I think it's kinda funny. I think I smell better than Bruce." Carter snickered. "Maybe she's trying to give him a hint."

"Well, now you can smell like me all the time. You're taking this stuff to your mother's." Chris slapped the bag against Carter's chest.

"Cool."

As they were nearing Chris's house, Carter turned to his father. "Dad? Are you and Luna ever going to get married?"

Chris was stunned by the question. "I . . . I don't know. Why?"

Carter shrugged. "You've been seeing each other for a couple of years."

"I know, but she lives two hours away. One of us would have to move, and I'm not in a position to do that now. Besides, you don't want to move, right?"

"Correct. But if she wanted to move, would you ask her?" Carter was digging for info.

"I wouldn't expect her to give up her life in Asheville."

"Why don't you ask her?"

Chris was solemn for a moment. "How would you feel if I did?"

"It's okay with me. I like her. She's fun and funny."

"Let's see. If I get full custody, and I marry Luna, all three of us would be living together."

"Yep." Carter was nonchalant.

"And you wouldn't mind?"

"I wouldn't. But maybe *she* would!" Carter howled.

Chris broke into a chuckle. "Very true." Then his thoughts went to what life might be like for the three of them. Together. A family. It was definitely something he should seriously consider.

Chapter Eleven

Buncombe County
Cards on the Table

Cullen was unusually nervous. Was it because he'd planned a ruse to get his sister and her boyfriend together? Or was it because he was planning on having "the talk" with Chi-Chi? In either case, he couldn't stop pacing the back of his workshop. Luna brought him his usual breakfast treat of scones and a latte. Normally, Cullen would grab the scone from the plate and take a huge bite, but not that morning.

"You okay?" Luna eyed him closely.

"Yes. Why do you ask?"

She was still holding the plate with the untouched scone. "Because you usually dive into this." She held it up in front of his face and then set the coffee on the workbench.

"Stomach is a little off." Cullen wasn't lying. He'd had butterflies all morning.

"Oh, I know—you're excited about your date with Chris," she teased.

"Aren't you the funny one?" He grabbed the scone from the plate. "It's about tomorrow night."

"What about it?"

"You know. Dinner. Me. Cooking. Chi-Chi. And all the rest."

"Ah. Right. Cullen, it's going to be fine."

"Are you sure about that?" He knitted his brow.

"I know I've been a terrible judge when it comes to my own romances, Chris notwithstanding. I just happened to luck out with him."

"It took you an entire year to 'luck out.'" He made a finger quote with the hand that wasn't wrapped around the pastry.

"True. But look how long it took for you to ask Chi-Chi out to dinner. Several months. And now you're a couple."

He brushed the crumbs from his mouth. "I suppose."

"Don't be daft." Luna rolled her eyes and shook her head.

"Okay, so sue me. I'm nervous." Cullen slowly ate the rest of the scone to avoid further conversation.

"Well, don't be. If anyone should be nervous, it's me."

"How so?" he mumbled.

"Chris wants to talk to me about something."

"And that's bad, why?"

"Same reason you're nervous. We're insecure."

"Yes, you mentioned that the other day. Must be in our DNA." He finally smiled.

Luna took the empty plate, turned, and walked toward the showroom. "Don't forget the boutonniere. Turquoise." She chuckled. True, she was nervous, and that strange feeling hadn't left her. Was it the old memories? No, because she'd had that sense of discomfort before she saw the dresser. Maybe the tablet would help. She sat behind her easel, shut her eyes, and began to draw. When she felt she was finished, she opened her eyes and saw a stick figure of a boy holding hands with a stick figure of a man. *Chris and Carter, perhaps?* Well, that wouldn't be unusual. She heaved a big sigh. Granted, she felt less of a sense of foreboding than she had earlier that week, but there was something in the air. Something wasn't quite right. She looked at Wylie, who was sitting at her feet. "Do you have any clues you could share?"

He put his head down and covered his eyes with his paws. "You're not helping." She leaned over and gave him an affectionate rub. She spotted Chi-Chi opening her shop. She was wearing a beautiful yellow kaftan with matching yellow ribbons woven in her braids. "Yellow ribbons!" Luna jumped up and grabbed her laptop. She sent an email to Brendan's last known address, quoting one of the lines from *Blazing Saddles* in the hope it would trigger a response. She waited patiently as Chi-Chi walked across the atrium, followed by Ellie. When the two women entered the café, Luna closed her laptop and began to make their coffee. "Good morning, my beautiful friends."

"E káàrò!" Chi-Chi smiled. She looked like a big helping of sunshine. "Good morning."

"And a fine good morning to you! You look lovely." Luna smiled back. "Ellie, you too are looking lovely. I especially like your shoes." Luna pointed to Ellie's saddle shoes. Ellie's wardrobe was simple but stylish. Even when she was sitting on the floor of her office, she looked put-together. Maybe it was her white, blunt, chin-length haircut that gave her a sophisticated air. Not a lot of women could pull it off. Luna pulled her braid around to the front. "I've been thinking of cutting this off."

Both Chi-Chi and Ellie asked, "Why?" at the same time.

"It's a little dated." Then Luna looked at Chi-Chi's long hair. "Not yours. You do so many different things with yours. Mine is either pulled back with a headband, in a ponytail, or a braid. I feel like I'm boring."

"Are you saying you're thinking of a makeover?" Ellie tilted her head.

"I'm not sure, but I think my odd mood might be because I'm in a rut."

"You? Rut? Hardly," Ellie protested.

"Seriously. I've had this same Boho look for fifteen years. Maybe more."

"Was there something in that dresser that is making you feel passé?" Ellie asked as she pulled out a chair.

"You have such beautiful hair." Chi-Chi took hold of Luna's braid. "It would be a shame to cut it."

"I'm finding a few gray hairs. I dunno. Maybe something to freshen it up." She pulled her hair from Chi-Chi's hand and scrutinized it.

"I would suggest you wait a few days before you do anything drastic," Ellie urged.

"Huh." Luna wasn't known for waiting and wanted to take a pair of scissors to her hair immediately. "Maybe I'll make an appointment at the salon next week. I don't want to shock Chris."

"Good idea. Why don't you ask him what he thinks?" Ellie said.

"Ask Chris what he thinks about my hair?" Luna balked. "What do men know about hair, except when they are losing their own?"

Chi-Chi and Ellie laughed. "That doesn't seem to be Chris's problem. At least not yet," Ellie added.

Luna's eyes brightened. "What if I go to a wig store and try a few on? This way, I'll have an idea of what I like and what looks good on me."

"Now that sounds like an excellent idea," Chi-Chi said.

"Sometimes I'm smarter than I look." Luna chuckled. "But right now, I'm not thrilled with how I look."

"Perhaps I should help you with your makeup today. And we can do something interesting with your hair," Chi-Chi offered.

"For instance?" Luna was intrigued.

"What if I do gypsy braids instead of this?" Chi-Chi picked up the end of Luna's hair again.

"Gypsy braids?" Luna asked.

"It's a mixture of box braids and loose tendrils. A slightly undone look," Chi-Chi suggested. She pulled her phone from the hidden pocket in her kaftan and searched for photos until she found a style she thought would look good on Luna. "Like this."

"I like it. And I like that ombre coloring too," Luna said, referring to the gradient change from medium brown to brownish blond.

"Do not get ahead of yourself or me. Let us start with the braids. But I do agree. The colors would look nice with your complexion."

Luna checked the time. "How long will it take?"

"About an hour."

"Do you have time now?"

"I do not. But I can do it before we go to dinner."

"Perfect. I'll surprise Chris when we meet up with the guys later."

Ellie brought her cup and plate to the sink. "That sounds like a very good plan. I must get to work, but I want to see your masterpiece before you leave."

"Leave it, Ellie. I'll take care of it," Luna called over to her.

"Thank you, dear. Have a good morning." Ellie gave Wylie a pat on the head before she went out the door, followed by Chi-Chi.

Luna checked her email. No response from Brendan. Nothing. Strange. She scrolled through the contact list on her phone. Brendan Nelson was still there. She sent a text. Sometimes people responded to text messages faster than email, and sometimes people would only send text messages. They didn't even call anymore. Social media. The Internet. All an illusion of communication. People spewed out messages, hoping someone would care. Someone would listen. Luna flicked herself on the cheek and repeated Ellie's words: "'Let's not be cynical, dear. As long as the people you care about communicate with you, that's all that matters.' Right, Wylie?" He let out a low yowl. "At least you pay attention."

The minute the center opened, people began pouring in. It was slightly overcast, which brought folks inside, but they were still able to have lunch outside on the patio, walk through the gardens, or take their pooches to the dog park.

Luna glanced across the inner lavish courtyard and noticed a sign on Jennine's door. She couldn't read it from where she sat, so she picked up the walkie-talkie and buzzed Chi-Chi.

"What's up with your neighbor Jennine?"

"I do not know. Why do you ask?

"There's a sign on the door. Go see what it says," Luna urged.

Chi-Chi huffed. "If that is your wish."

"Well, it is. And it should be yours, too. Remember, she's out with your brother. What if something happened?"

"You make a good point. Hold on." Chi-Chi walked over to Jennine's door. "It says, 'Be back in a jiffy.' What does this *jiffy* mean? I hear it all the time, but it makes no sense to me."

"It's a unit of time. Some argue it's one-one-hundredth of a second, while others claim it's one-sixtieth of a second. Because it's such a quick period of time, it's become slang for *very fast*."

"I do not know if I will ever understand your slang."

"Well, we've got plenty of it." Luna laughed, then went back to the original question. "I wonder where Jennine went?"

She had barely finished her sentence when Jennine appeared from the back of her shop, wearing what looked like lingerie. "Oh, Chi-Chi," Jennine said. "I'm so glad you're here. What do you think of my outfit? Do you think your brother will like it?"

Chi-Chi was aghast. Her first reaction was to say, "Only if you're going to a bordello." *That* was a word she knew. Instead, she took the polite route. "I am not sure where you are going, so it is difficult for me to have an opinion."

Jennie flashed her capped teeth. "Well, I know where I *want* to go." She winked at Chi-Chi.

"I am certain you do." Chi-Chi's stomach was turning somersaults. "I thought you were going to go out to dinner."

"Oh, yeah, that too. So whaddya think?"

"I think it's very . . . diaphanous."

Jennine furrowed her brow. "Dia-what?"

Chi-Chi thought quickly. "Gossamer. Delicate." She was not accustomed to stretching the truth, and those two words were the only ones that were appropriate, other than calling the outfit cheesy or flimsy.

"Yes. Delicate. Exactly what I was going for," Jennine cooed.

In addition to my brother, Chi-Chi thought to herself. "I made a reservation for you at Blue Ridge."

"Fancy." Jennine was impressed at Chi-Chi's choice of restaurants. "Glad I went home to change."

"I must get back to work." Chi-Chi turned and moved quickly to her shop. She clicked on her walkie-talkie. "We will not be going to Blue Ridge," she said to Luna.

"Whatever you say. So, what is Jennine up to?"

"What do you think she is up to?"

"From here, it looked like she was getting ready for a role in an old Hollywood movie."

"I do not like horror pictures." Chi-Chi smiled at her own joke.

Luna chuckled. "You're funny. It doesn't matter where we go, but we should call ahead."

"Yes. Let's go to the steakhouse. I need a piece of red meat."

"Wow. Jennine really gets under your skin, doesn't she?" Luna asked, knowing the answer.

"I do not want to discuss it. We shall eat meat, creamed spinach, and baked potatoes."

"You got it, girlfriend. Let's leave at six. Sabrina and Lucy already agreed to cover for us."

"Excellent."

"What time is Abeo arriving?" Luna asked.

"Around five. That will give me one hour with him, and then he will be on his own." Chi-Chi snickered.

It was just after three when Chris arrived at the center. First stop was Luna's. She was with a client at her easel while Sabrina covered the front. If Luna had a reading, she would pay Sabrina or Lucy extra money to mind the café. Chi-Chi was right. Luna had more clients than she could handle and was feeling a little guilty about pulling the pages away from their regular routine. But no one seemed to mind. Stillwell Art Center was an oasis of cooperation.

Chris tipped his fingers in a salute and motioned he was going to Cullen's. Before the guys headed out, they stopped at the café to discuss their plans for later. Chris immediately walked over to Luna and gave her a hug and a kiss. On the lips. Very important. They all figured they would be finished with their dinner around the same time and decided to meet at Luna's for a nightcap. Afterward, Chi-Chi would go back to her—hopefully—empty house. She and Cullen still hadn't slept with each other, and Chi-Chi was adamant about keeping it that way. At least for the time being. Not that Cullen ever made a move. They kissed plenty, but only in private, and that's where it ended.

* * *

The guys drove to the exhibit center, chatting about the latest baseball stats. Chris wanted to tell Cullen about his promotion, but also wanted to tell Luna first. Maybe he'd make an announcement after dinner. Then he had second thoughts. It should be something they shared together. In private. He also didn't want to discuss the impending custody battle. That was a lot of important information he had to keep to himself for a few more hours. Once they arrived at the car show, it was easy to be distracted. The smell of polish and leather filled the exhibit hall. Everything from a 1912 Ford Model T to a 1969 Chevy Camaro and a Volkswagen bus were on display, fetching tens of thousands of dollars. The bus had a sticker price of 63,500 dollars, more than a current luxury SUV. Cullen was amazed. A green 1955 Chevy Bel Air caught his eye. Then the price tag made him do a double take. That, too, was over 63,000 dollars.

Chris made his way over to a 1959 red Ford Thunderbird with a V8 engine. "Only twenty-five-thousand dollars. Not bad, really."

"I always figured you for a T-bird or a Mustang," Cullen remarked. Then he turned to Chris. "Maybe this isn't such a bad idea after all. I'm going to chat with the owner of that Bel Air and see if I can get a fix on what investment in time and money is required in order to make a profit."

"I'm going to continue to drool over this baby." Chris leaned into the window of the driver's seat. It was in excellent condition. But did he really need a new car? He strolled among the other pristine cars. It could be a good hobby, if he ever had the time.

About an hour later, Cullen caught up with Chris. "Sorry. I really got a boatload of information. Most of these guys love to talk. And talk. And talk."

"I get it. The T-bird dude was trying to talk me into buying that car. I had to walk away, because he almost had me pulling out my credit card," Chris said.

"It is a beauty," Cullen added.

"Don't encourage me. I have a lot on my plate, and buying a new-old car isn't on the table right now." He thought for a moment. "Did that come out right?"

Cullen laughed. "Spending too much time with my sister, *eh*?"

"Actually, no. Don't tell her, but I really do miss her."

"Wow. Don't tell *me* that, either!" Cullen joked.

Chris couldn't keep it in any longer. In fact, it might be a good idea to run his thoughts past Cullen. "Listen, I'm about to embark on a very serious mission."

Cullen looked stunned. "Seriously?"

"It's not work-related." He was saving that tidbit for later. "Lucinda and Bruce are moving to Chicago. He has an opportunity to join a practice there. So I'm filing for full custody."

"That *is* a serious mission. I suppose you have no other choice, right? It would be terrible for all of you if Carter had to move."

"Correct-o-mundo. I can't let her take Carter to a city where major crime is up and he's eight hundred miles away."

"She can't just up and leave, right?"

"Not if I have anything to say about it. Besides, we have a binding agreement, and neither of us can take Carter out of the state without notifying the other person. She wanted to do this just between us. Didn't want to go the legal route. Doesn't she realize I work in law enforcement? I knew she was an airhead, but I didn't think it was filled with helium."

Cullen let out a guffaw. "Wow." This time, it was a different kind of *wow*. A heavy load kind of *wow*.

"We were in my lawyer's office the other day to discuss this, and she left in a huff."

"Shouldn't she have her own lawyer?" Cullen asked.

"Yes, but I wanted someone to start the conversation. See how she'd react. I could have bet on her having a hissy fit."

"She can't possibly think she can just up and leave with your son."

"She thinks being a mother is some kind of free pass for anything. 'A boy needs his mother.' That routine. And from what Carter said, she has very little interaction with him. You know what he told me? He said he felt like a visitor when he was at his mother's house. It nearly broke my heart. A kid shouldn't have to feel that way with his own mother."

"Wow." Cullen's vocabulary was reduced to monosyllabic words. "And he never said anything to you?"

"Not a word. But Carter is like that. He doesn't want to disappoint me. Her. His teachers. He's a borderline overachiever. But I'm not going to discourage that, unless it becomes a problem."

"Parenting is no picnic," Cullen pondered.

"Carter and I have a great relationship. He'll talk to me about anything. Anything except how he feels being at Lucinda's. I guess the problems there have become more evident to him the older he gets. When he was younger, he had a lot of distractions. Lucinda's parents would visit on a regular basis, so he was usually surrounded by people who paid attention to him. They moved to Scottsdale, so he rarely sees them now. Plus, he's going through puberty."

"Wow." Cullen blinked several times. "I don't know how you do it. I can barely figure out my sister, let alone be responsible for a kid. And I've known her for almost forty years."

Chris laughed. "I don't know if anyone will ever figure out your sister, but it's fun trying."

The two walked to their car and drove to one of Chris's favorite bistros. Good food, casual atmosphere. They continued their conversation, with Chris saying, "I'm worried about how Luna is going to take this change. It's going to be a pain in the butt until the legal work is wrapped up. Lucinda is not going to go quietly, but if the judge gives Carter the option of staying with me, she will have the biggest conniption in the history of North Carolina."

"She wouldn't dare just take him, would she?"

"She may be a helium-head, but she's not completely daft. She knows she would be committing a federal crime by taking a child illegally out of state, and as it happens, I am a federal marshal who works in child abductions."

"Excellent point."

"Besides, I think Carter would put up a fight. He knows the rules. And he doesn't want to go. We discussed this the other night. We're lining up our ducks, and I'm preparing for a lot of screaming and yelling. On her part, not mine."

"What does Luna think about all this?" Cullen asked.

"I haven't told her yet, so please don't mention this to her until I have the opportunity. What I want is your opinion. What do you think she'll say? Her reaction? If I get full custody, it's going to change things. When she comes to Charlotte, Carter will be at home with me. And it will be a challenge to come here every other weekend, unless I can find somewhere for Carter to go. Maybe he can stay at a friend's, but we're not there yet. It's going to be an adjustment, for sure."

Cullen sat quietly for a moment. "Luna loves you. And she loves Carter. Sure, it will be an adjustment, but Luna is a free spirit. She'll go where the universe takes her." Cullen smirked.

Chris laughed. Cullen wasn't wrong. If it felt right, Luna would go with the flow. He hoped it would feel right to her.

They finished their dinner, got the check, and drove to Luna's house. Chris had left his car at the center; Luna was going to drive him back there the next day. The lights were on, and soft bossa nova music glided from the windows. They could hear Chi-Chi singing along with the sultry music. *Had she any idea how seductive she was?* The men looked at each other as if reading each other's minds. "I give you a lot of credit, my man," Chris said. "I'd be taking a cold shower every night."

"Don't think I don't." Cullen snickered.

Luna greeted them at the door and gave Chris a peck on the cheek. Chi-Chi continued to sing and sway to "The Girl from Ipanema" by Antônio Carlos Jobim. Cullen thought the words—about a man who does not know how to tell a woman he loves her—could not be more appropriate at that particular moment.

Luna put down her glass of wine, took Chris's hands, and started to move back and forth with the music. That prompted Cullen to do the same with Chi-Chi. Wylie wisely moved out of the way. A dreamy dance party was taking place in the living room. The next song on the album was "Manhã De Carnaval," a slow, repentant song known in English as "A Day in the Life of a Fool." But Astrud Gilberto sang it in Portuguese, which was so much more romantic. The two couples were in sync with the music and each other. Luna's eyes began to tear. Chris lifted her chin and said, "You okay?"

She rested her head against his chest. "Never been better."

Chris hoped his news wouldn't taint her mood later, but he had to tell her. She was part of his life, and if he intended to keep it that way, he had to lay the cards on the table. Things were about to change.

The couples danced to the alluring music for almost an hour. It wasn't until the music stopped that they realized no one had spoken the entire time.

Chi-Chi was the first to say something. "I am sorry to break this beautiful mood, but I must see what trouble my brother has gotten into."

"I don't know if you really want to do that," Luna said. "Maybe you should call to be sure he's not at your house with you-know-who."

Chi-Chi nodded and pulled her phone from her purse. "Should I text him?"

"Probably a good idea," Cullen encouraged her.

Chi-Chi typed: **Abeo, are you with Jennine? And not at my house?**

"Now we wait." She sighed. Several minutes went by with no word.

"Maybe he's busy." Luna raised her eyebrows.

Chi-Chi sighed again. "I do need to get to sleep."

"Here's an idea. Why don't you drive past Jennine's house and see if her car is there?" Luna offered. "I have her address."

"I'll follow you if you want." Cullen looked at Chi-Chi.

"If Abeo is there, I do not want him to see my car," she answered.

"We'll leave your car at the Stop N' Go. He doesn't know my car." Cullen was happy to oblige in the reconnaissance mission.

Chi-Chi's eyes grew wide. "That is a marvelous idea." She hesitated. "But what if they are at my house? Then what do I do?"

Luna and Chris looked up at the ceiling.

"You can stay with me," Cullen offered. He quickly added, "In the guest room." He wanted Chi-Chi to feel comfortable, should the situation arise.

"Thank you." Chi-Chi gave him a weak smile. She was anxious to find out if her house was her own that night.

Everyone said their goodnights. "It was a lovely evening. Thank you," Chi-Chi said, with a bit more confidence.

Cullen followed Chi-Chi to the store, where she parked her car by the side of the building. She then joined Cullen in his car. As they approached Jennine's house, Cullen slowed down. "Is that her car?"

"Yes! Yes, it is." Chi-Chi was feeling less anxious.

She slumped down in the passenger seat. "Can you see anything?"

Cullen peered over the steering wheel. "The lights are on, but, oh dear. Oh my." He stepped on the accelerator and moved quickly past the house.

Chi-Chi had her hand over her mouth to stifle her laughter. "I suppose they were there? Together?"

"Oh, yes. Very together." Cullen was blushing over the sight of Jennine doing some kind of fan dance in front of her guest. "Wow." It was the word of the day.

Chi-Chi couldn't stop giggling. "Now you know how I felt when I found them in my living room."

"And you can't un-see something like that." He shuddered. Yes, Jennine was Blanche from *The Golden Girls*, for sure. Cullen drove back to the mini-mart. "Let me follow you home. It's late."

"Thank you. That is very thoughtful of you." She got in her car, and Cullen proceeded to tail her.

When they arrived at Chi-Chi's, Cullen got out and walked her to her front door. He stopped her as she was about to turn the key. "Chi-Chi, there's something I have to tell you."

"Is everything alright, Cullen?" A look of concern crossed her face.

He held her at arm's length and took a deep breath. "Chi-Chi. I love you. I've known it for a long time. I just never had the nerve to come out and say it. So there you have it."

Chi-Chi threw her arms around him and gave him the sweetest kiss. "Thank you."

Thank you? What does that mean? Thoughts were racing through his head. He choked out, "Excuse me?"

"Thank you for telling me. Please come in. I think we should discuss this."

Cullen gulped. He had no idea what was coming.

Chi-Chi gestured to the sofa. "Please, sit." He sat with his forearms on his thighs, his hands gripping his knees, readying himself for bad news.

"There is something I must tell you."

Uh-oh, here it comes. Massive humiliation.

Chi-Chi sat next to him and took his hand. "You know I am very fond of you. There is something you should know."

He was holding his breath.

"I was once married." She paused, letting the information sink in. "My parents arranged it."

Cullen's mouth dropped open.

"And it was a terrible arrangement. His name is Debare, a very mean and cheap man. After almost a year, I could no longer stand to be with him. It was very difficult for me to tell my parents. I was afraid they might disown me." She stopped for a moment. "But much to my surprise, they were not at all angry. They were relieved." Cullen listened with a blank look on his face.

"Evidently, his parents gave my parents very bad information about him. Actually, it was what they did *not* tell my mother and father." She got up and poured each of them a glass of water, then continued. "After we were married for three months, my husband applied for a loan and wanted my father to cosign. Before he put his name on the paper, my father did a background check on Debare. He had a gambling problem and owed tens of thousands of dollars to credit card companies."

"And his parents failed to mention this?" Cullen was appalled.

"Yes. You see, my family had more money than his, and we were all citizens of the United States. His parents believed if he married into a good family, he would turn his life around."

Cullen nodded. "Obviously, that didn't happen."

"No, it did not. But it explained a lot of his behavior. I was only twenty-one at the time, but I was not willing to forgive all of his sins if he was going to continue committing them."

"Very good point," Cullen replied.

"So, we got divorced. I have not spoken to him since."

Cullen was quickly doing the math. "You haven't spoken to him in over sixteen years?"

"This is true. The day the divorce was final was the last time I ever saw his face." Chi-Chi looked at Cullen. "I am sorry I have not told you this before."

"Oh, no. It's okay. I'm glad you did." He was still wondering where that put him on her list of priorities. "Does Luna know about this?"

"No. Only my family."

"I shall never mention it."

"Thank you. Now that you know, I hope it has not changed your opinion of me."

"Not at all!" he exclaimed.

Chi-Chi let out a big whoosh of air. "I am glad. I did not like the idea that I was keeping a secret from you."

"It's private. I mean, it's part of your past, and I don't blame you for not telling me. It's not important. At least not to me. That didn't come out right. Your being divorced is not important. *You* are important to me."

Chi-Chi looped her arm through his and rested her head on his shoulder. "I am so relieved." She sighed. "Oh—and I love you, too."

Luna was resting her head on the back of the sofa, basking in the romantic atmosphere of candles and music. "This is really nice."

"Yes, it is." Chris moved to sit next to her. He turned her face toward him. "I have two very important things I need to discuss."

Luna shot up like a geyser. "What? What is it?" She *knew* something was amiss.

"Please don't get yourself worked into a tizzy. Do you want the good news or the challenging news?"

Her head was spinning. "All of it!"

"The good news is I am getting a promotion. And a raise."

Luna sat on her heels. "That's great! What's the challenging stuff?"

"Lucinda plans on moving to Chicago. Bruce is going to be a partner in a dental practice there."

"What about Carter?" Luna immediately realized that was going to be the challenging part.

"I'm filing for full custody," Chris replied.

"Well, good! You should have it anyway," Luna huffed.

Chris looked surprised. "You realize that will make us a threesome on most weekends." Then he laughed. "Sorry, wrong wording." He was beginning to feel less anxious about Luna's reaction. "What I mean is, I'll have him every weekend except when he's staying with a friend."

"That's okay with me. I love Carter. We're besties.'"

"So he's told me." Chris brushed one of Luna's wisps from her face. "Like the hair, by the way."

"Thanks. Chi-Chi did it for me."

"Anyway, things are going to get dicey until this is settled."

"When are they planning on moving?"

"She said six months."

"What does Carter think about all of this?" Luna asked.

Chris looked forlorn. "He told me he's always felt like a visitor at Lucinda's. Ever since his grandparents moved, he's been feeling disconnected. But he's happy when he's with me. He said if he was given the choice, he'd rather stay with me."

"That's great!" Luna exclaimed. She wrapped her arms around his neck and nuzzled him. "I am very happy for you."

Chris was stunned but not surprised. Luna had a big, open heart when it came to other people. Chris also knew she was vigilant at keeping her own heart safe. Sometimes he could feel her pulling back, but he knew it was a defense mechanism. If nothing else, Chris had learned how to read people. Not necessarily the same way Luna could, but it was something that helped create their bond. He appreciated her intuitiveness. She appreciated his strength, integrity, and methodical thinking. They were an odd but good match. *Yep. Who'd a thunk it?*

"There's going to be a lot of adjustments and disruptions until this is settled. But it has to happen within the next five months. She hasn't even told him yet. Carter overheard Lucinda talking to Bruce."

"This is kinda sudden, isn't it?"

"Very, but Bruce's uncle is retiring in a couple of years. He has a good practice and wants Bruce to come on board and eventually take it over."

"Well, that's good for Bruce and Lucinda."

"Exactly. What I don't understand is why she hasn't told Carter yet."

"Maybe she's afraid he'll do something rash?"

"Carter? Nah."

"You know that, and even *I* know that, but Lucinda doesn't. She doesn't know what makes Carter tick." Once again, Chris was briefly taken aback by Luna's insight, but then again, it should come as no surprise. "One day when we were hiking, Carter made some comment about his mom. You were off on a phone call, and he and I got to chat a bit. He's pretty funny, too."

"He gets his sense of humor from me." Chris grinned.

"Obviously, because from what he's told me, Lucinda has none."

"Helium-head." Chris chuckled. "Listen, she's not a bad person. She's just selfish and self-centered. She doesn't mean any harm unless you get in her way." He snickered.

"I suppose we have different definitions of a bad person, but you know you have my support," Luna murmured. "So tell me about your new job!" She became animated. "Tell me! Tell me!"

"I'm going to be working in WITSEC. The witness security program."

"As in witness protection?"

"Correct."

"So you'll be working with criminals, eh?" She gave him a little nudge.

"It depends. Often, it's people who witnessed a crime and need protection until they testify. But, yes, there will be criminals from time to time."

"And you'll be babysitting them?"

"Not exactly. I'll be managing agents who facilitate their relocation. I won't necessarily be a handler. Every situation is a little different."

"That is so cool." Luna was enthralled.

"It is." He pulled her close and held her tight. "I'm happy you're okay with all of this."

"Absolutely."

She was relieved the cards were on the table. She'd been right about the stick figures, and it appeared the question marks she'd first drawn had been answered. *Or had they?* There was still that little thing nagging at her, and she couldn't quite put her finger on it.

The following morning, Chris noticed the box of keepsakes. On the top of the pile was the program from the Kentucky Derby.

"I discover something new about you every day, Luna lunatic."

"And what might that be?"

"You like horse racing?" It was half a question.

"Not as big a fan as I used to be. It's become a new toy for the oil-rich. It's a transaction now. These magnificent animals mean nothing to them. They're just numbers on a balance sheet." Luna got into a tear when it came to animals. "These people have no appreciation for the horses. It's only their bottom line that counts and how much they can brag to their friends." She was huffing at this point.

Chris looked alarmed. "Okay, dollface. Take it easy."

"It's just so disgusting." Luna's eyes welled up. "People are savages. It's all about money and power. Humanity is dissolving."

"Hey." Chris put his hands on her shoulders and looked her in the eye. "It's not like you to be cynical."

"Ellie said the same thing," Luna scoffed. "Probably hormones." She didn't want to mention the friend who seemed to be MIA, which was more and more vexing to her as each day passed without a response.

Chris snickered. He was relieved it was she who'd suggested the monthly roller-coaster ride. Granted, they were intimate, but hormones are a touchy subject. Definitely off-limits. "Well, did you actually enjoy it?"

"What? The Derby? For sure. It was quite an experience. None of which I care to repeat. It's a once-in-a-lifetime event. I did it. Done."

"Who did you go with?" Chris sensed there was something she wasn't telling him.

"A friend. College buddy." Luna wanted to end the conversation as quickly as possible.

Chris knew when to stop the interrogation and changed the subject. He began to tell her about the cool Thunderbird that had caught his eye.

"Midlife crisis?" she joked.

"Huh. That hadn't occurred to me. I just thought it would be cool to tool around in a vintage piece." He cleared his throat. "But your brother might be onto something. You can buy a decent car for less than five thousand dollars. If you have the time and inclination, you can turn it for a hefty profit."

"That could be a good project for you and Carter. Is he into cars yet?"

"No. He's barely discovered girls. But I think he might enjoy something to add to his repertoire." He snapped his fingers. "Let's see. He's twelve now. In five years, he'll get his license. That would be plenty of time for him to refurbish a car."

"Him? Are you going to participate?" Luna chuckled.

"Of course, but the car would be a good incentive for him. He can have it when it's finished."

"That actually sounds like a good plan. And you can do it at his and your leisure. It's not as if that work would be on a schedule like his ball games."

Chris kissed her on the forehead. "You're brilliant, you know that?"

"Kinda." Luna smiled.

Chapter Twelve

Monday
Where in the World Is Brendan Nelson?

The center was closed for the day, and Luna took the opportunity to do some sleuthing. Brendan had never returned her text, so she decided to call. She got a recording saying the mailbox was full. It was perplexing. Brendan wasn't the type to let something go unattended, especially his voicemail. Ever since that summer, when he'd managed his sister's healthcare, he'd felt responsible for his family and was always on call for any skirmishes, misunderstandings, or emergencies. He was the eldest, so it was incumbent on him to keep the peace among his five siblings.

She checked her junk mail. Nothing there. Something wasn't right. She reached out to a mutual friend.

"Anthony! It's Luna. How are you?"

"I am rather excellent. And you?"

"Couldn't be excellenter," Luna joked. She was always coming up with new words or portmanteaus, joining two words to form one, like *mockumentary* for mock and documentary, or *brunch* for breakfast and lunch. She had come up with one recently: *shneakers*, shoes that have rubber soles like sneakers. It was a mystery why the fashion industry hadn't adopted it yet.

"What's going on?" Anthony was always upbeat.

"Have you heard from Brendan?"

"Now that you mention it, I haven't. Been too busy with the kids. Yeah, he usually reaches out during the holidays, but I didn't hear from him last year."

"Me either. We were emailing daily during the pandemic, but then all communication stopped."

"I suppose you tried to email him? Text?"

"Yep. I even tried to call, but the recording said his mailbox is full."

"Now that's strange. And a bit unsettling. He'd never allow that."

"My thoughts exactly. Is there anyone you can contact to see if he's okay?"

"I'll reach out to his nephew. I have his info somewhere."

"Great. Thanks." Luna let out some air. "Be well and behave."

"What fun is that?" Anthony hooted. "I'll be in touch. One love."

One love. It had been his sign-off ever since she first knew him. And he was right.

Not being a particularly patient person, Luna decided to do some searching on her own. She Googled Brendan. Nothing. She Googled his wife. Nothing. She went to LinkedIn and sent a message through their site. That could take a few days. She drummed her fingers on the table. She had to do something to busy herself. There was still a lot of stuff to sift through, but she'd left the box of mementos at home. More drumming. Maybe she'd ask Cullen if he needed some help. Besides, she wanted to interrogate him about his dinner with Chi-Chi. She fixed a cup of cappuccino for him and signaled to Wylie. "Come on, pal. Want to go to the dog park?"

He let out an enthusiastic *Woof!*

Luna walked to the sliding doors, and Wylie made a beeline to the designated doggie area. Ziggy and Marley were already sitting in the shade of a white oak. During the construction, Ellie had made it a point to keep as much of the vegetation as possible, especially the trees. The landscaper built the gardens around the foliage.

Cullen was at his workbench when Luna entered. "So? How did it go?" she asked.

"How did what go?"

"The dinner you were planning for Chi-Chi." Luna folded her arms and tapped her foot. "Spill."

"I'll have you know, little sister, I told her Saturday night after we left your place."

She gave him a shove. "Get out!"

Cullen was beaming.

"I gather she took it well?"

"Yes, as a matter of fact, she did."

"So? Details, please."

"I don't kiss and tell." Cullen made a gesture of locking his lips and tossing the imaginary key over his shoulders.

"Oh, man. Don't do that to me," Luna whined.

"I am a gentleman. If Chi-Chi wants to share anything with you, that is her prerogative. I, on the other hand, choose to remain silent."

"Ugh," Luna snorted.

Cullen was quite amused at his sister. And after his conversation with Chi-Chi, he was in a very fine mood. Almost light on his feet.

"I am going to assume you have taken the relationship to a new level." She raised her eyebrows.

"Get your mind out of the gutter," he chided.

"Oh, stop. That's not what I meant. And that is not something I want to know about, either."

"Let's just say we have come to a mutual understanding about our feelings for each other."

"Thank you! That's all I wanted to hear." She gave him a big hug.

"So what brings you to my humble workshop, besides harassing me?"

"I thought maybe you could use some help with my dresser."

"Actually, that's not a bad idea. Do you want to do a complete update reno, or a restore?"

"I'm thinking an update. The past is the past."

"Good. I'll strip it down. Meanwhile, look through the paint chips and the hardware samples. It's a simple shaker style, so you could do a lot with it."

Luna flipped through the paint chips. "How about a red lacquer with Asian design pulls? I can put it in my dining room and use it as a sideboard."

"Excellent idea."

"I know," Luna mugged.

"Always the modest one," Cullen tossed back.

Luna turned pensive. "So." She took a deep breath. "I tried to get in touch with my friend Brendan in Minnesota," she admitted.

"And?"

"And nothing. He hasn't returned emails or texts. And yes, I tried to call him, but his mailbox was full."

"So? What's the big deal?"

"It's as if he's vanished into thin air. I even called our mutual friend Anthony, and he hasn't heard from him, either."

"It's hard to keep track of people when they live almost a thousand miles away."

"Yeah. But that's just it. We had been emailing regularly during COVID. You know, to keep ourselves occupied while we waited to be unmasked. And then we kept in touch once a week or so, once we were sprung from lockdown."

"When was the last time you heard from him?"

"Before his birthday. Last November. I sent him a funny e-card, but never got any notice he received it. Then I didn't hear from him for my birthday. First time in fifteen years."

"And you're just starting to wonder what happened?"

"*Life* happens. Time manages to slip past you. I know it's no excuse. But finding all the mementos made me realize how long it had been since I heard from him."

"What are you going to do? You can't exactly fly to Minnesota and hunt him down. Maybe he doesn't want to be connected with his past."

"But why?"

"Beats me, but people do things that others can't understand."

"Aren't you the wise one today?"

"Yes. Yes, I am." He walked over and checked the paint chip Luna was holding. "That'll be striking."

"And that, dear brother, was my plan."

"Okay, now go find someone else to play with. I have work to do."

Luna stuck out her tongue and gave him a raspberry.

"Always the mature one." Cullen chuckled and shook his head. "Now scram."

Instead of going back to the café, Luna decided to go for a walk in the gardens. Maybe it would help her feel more grounded.

Luna sat under a maple tree that still had one of Devon Scott's wind chimes hanging from a branch. It was peaceful. Lovely. She thought she would suggest to Ellie that they keep it there. It added a bit more Zen to the Zen Garden. She stood and faced the sun. It felt good on her face. She did a few Qigong movements, embracing a new day with a bright future ahead. Luna knew it would be an adjustment for her, Chris, and Carter, but there was a lot of caring among them, and she was confident they could work it out. After a few quiet moments, she sensed someone approaching. It was Chi-Chi, with a big smile on her face.

"E káàrò!" Chi-Chi called out to Luna. "I thought you might be here. It is a beautiful day, is it not?"

"Yes, it is. You are here late today," Luna noted.

"I had to pry my brother from the clutches of Jennine," Chi-Chi huffed. "Imagine. He had been with her for two days!"

"That must have been an ugly scene." Luna snickered.

"He was supposed to meet me at the shop and inspect the stones he brought the other night. I am glad I put them in my safe. He is drunk on whatever that woman has done to him."

Luna cackled. "Please, stop. I don't want my imagination to get anywhere close to that." She patted the bench she was sitting on. "Join me."

"Have you spoken to your brother today?" Chi-Chi asked slyly.

"Yes. I was in the shop picking out a color and hardware for my dresser. I'm going to turn it into a sideboard for my dining room." She waited for Chi-Chi to carry on the conversation.

"Did your brother mention anything to you?"

"About what?" Luna was trying to contain her glee.

"About the chat we had the other night?"

"I don't follow you." Luna was lying, but she didn't want to betray her brother's trust.

"Please. I am not a fool."

"Okay. He said you had a talk, and it went well."

"And you didn't ask?" Chi-Chi gave her a suspicious look.

"Of course, I asked, but he was tight-lipped."

Chi-Chi settled her back against the bench. "He told me he loved me."

"Oh, that's wonderful, Chi-Chi." Luna put her arm around her friend. "I am so glad he finally was able to tell you."

"You knew about this?" Chi-Chi was taken aback.

"I knew how he felt about you. I also knew he wasn't sure how to convey it. He's not the overly expressive type. Just in case you hadn't noticed."

Chi-Chi chuckled. "Yes, he did seem a little uncomfortable."

"Remember, I am his sister. I know what goes on inside that skull of his. I've never seen him this gaga over anyone before. Sure, he's had girlfriends, but he was never head over heels about any of them. I was beginning to worry that he'd never meet anyone."

"Probably as much as he worried about you before you met Chris."

"True. But he'd never say it to me, either." Luna laughed. "Ready for coffee?"

"Yes. And a scone, please."

The two women walked arm in arm back to the café, where Luna prepared their morning coffees. "Why don't you ring Ellie?"

A few minutes later, the three were gabbing about the news, music, and pondering why there weren't any more good movies.

"Too much superhero, action, adventure. It's dizzying," Ellie stated.

They moved on to a new subject, and Luna proceeded to tell them about Chris's promotion. "He'll be doing some training, but most of his responsibilities will be paperwork. He called it being a glorified clerk."

"Hardly," Ellie scoffed.

"The good part is that he will be doing nine-to-five office work most of the time, so he'll be able to have a better schedule for Carter. Chris has been juggling it for a long time. And, if things go the way he wants, he'll have full custody of Carter."

"Carter? Full custody? What happened?" Ellie asked.

"Lucinda and Bruce are moving to Chicago. He's joining his uncle's practice."

"This seems sudden. Or did Chris know about it?" Ellie asked.

"He just found out last week. Apparently, they plan on moving in the fall. Chris said she hasn't told Carter yet, so they've made a pact. Carter is going to spy on Lucinda and Bruce." Luna cackled. "He told Carter he was filing for full custody, and Carter was more than happy to hear it."

"Well, it appears you had a full weekend." Ellie smiled.

"Indeed."

Ellie turned to Chi-Chi. "And what about you, my dear?"

Chi-Chi began to blush and fan her face. "Let us say that I am very content with my relationship with this woman's brother."

"This is what I like to hear. My girls being loved by two wonderful men. And trust me, there aren't many of them out there."

"Don't we know it." Luna chuckled.

Within the hour, they finished their *tête-à-tête*. Chi-Chi had returned to her shop when Abeo slinked in like a criminal. Full of shame. Chi-Chi uttered a *tsk-tsk*.

"Oh, but you were the one who set up the dinner, were you not?" He tried to throw the blame in her direction.

"It was dinner that I arranged. Whatever transpired afterward was of your own doing."

Abeo jerked his head. "Have you met that woman?" He shivered. "She is someone you do not contradict."

Chi-Chi laughed. "Why are men so stupid?"

"It is not stupid. It was an ambush."

"Stand up," Chi-Chi ordered.

"What?"

"I said stand up!" she repeated. He obeyed.

"You see? You are taller than I am. You are bigger than I am. You are not a victim."

"You don't know that woman." Abeo shook his head. "It is very difficult to say 'no' to her."

"Repeat after me: 'No.'"

"No," he obliged.

"See. It is that easy." Chi-Chi was laughing to herself. It had gone exactly as she intended. Though she hadn't anticipated it would go on for two days.

Back in her café, Luna opened her laptop again. She was on a mission. She typed in both Brendan's and his wife's names again. Still nothing. Once again, she found herself drumming her fingers on the table. She jumped when her phone buzzed with a new text. It was from Anthony. It had a crying emoji and a postage stamp–sized photo of Brendan with a very brief obituary. She started to shake. She kept reading the short notice over and over:

Brendan Nelson, age 37, born November 28, 1986, in Greensboro, NC. Died January 27, 2024. A summer memorial is being planned.

Tears were streaming down her face. "This can't be. It just can't be," she said out loud. She read it again. "But why? How? And there's no mention of any of his family members, including his wife." She immediately phoned Anthony.

He answered with, "I can't believe it. Did you get my second text?"

Luna was sniffling. "No. I've been frozen on this one."

"Well, you need to read the next text. It's bizarre."

"Hang on." Luna swiped her phone to read the second notice:

> Eileen Lovecraft age 37, born July 5, 1986, in Minnetonka, MN. Died January 30, 2024. A summer memorial is being planned.

"I don't understand," Luna whimpered. "What happened?"

"Nobody seems to know, or if they do, they're not talking." Anthony sighed. "When I reached out to his nephew, all he did was forward the obits. Very bizarre."

"Indeed. There is no mention of any family members, and neither is mentioned in the other's notice. That is *very* bizarre." She reached for a napkin and wiped her face. "Any news about the memorial?"

"Nope. This was all he sent."

"But summer is coming, and nothing about a memorial? For either one?"

"Nope," Anthony said again. His voice was somber. "I'm devastated. I don't even know what to say."

"Me either," Luna sobbed. "Is there anyone we can call? His brothers? Sister? Parents?"

"I sent an email to his brother at his job as soon as I saw the text, but he hasn't gotten back to me yet."

"Okay, Anthony. Thanks. I think. Keep me posted, and if I find out anything, I shall do the same."

"One love." Anthony ended the call.

Luna continued to stare at the minuscule notification. No cause of death. No family. No nothing. She immediately logged into her laptop and searched the Hennepin Coroner's Office, checking for death certificates. Nothing. Not for either of them. Luna was mystified, shocked, and very, very sad. "This isn't right. It can't be." She kept repeating the words over and over. Wylie came running into the café as if he sensed his "mommy" was in distress. Luna wrapped her arms around him. "Oh, Wylie. This is just so terrible." She buried her face in the nape of his neck and began to sob uncontrollably.

Ellie happened to be passing the café when she saw Luna slumped over Wylie. She rushed in. "Luna! Are you alright?"

Luna looked up. Tears were streaming from her bloodshot eyes. She could barely speak. "It's . . . it's my friend Brendan."

"The one you've been trying to reach?" Ellie said.

Luna tried to control her hiccupping. "He's dead, Ellie. I can't believe it."

Ellie pulled out a chair and sat next to her hysterical friend. She placed her arms around Luna and let her sob against her chest. She was like a ragdoll. Ellie rocked her back and forth until Luna gained some composure. "What happened, dear?"

Luna blotted the snot and tears from her face. "No one knows."

"I don't understand." Ellie truly didn't.

Luna turned her phone so Ellie could see the diminutive notice under Brendan's photo. Then Luna showed her the one for Eileen.

Ellie read the notices out loud. "This is very odd, isn't it?"

"I just got off the phone with a mutual friend. That was all he could come up with. No one in Brendan's family seems to be forthcoming with any information."

"Oh, dear, dear, Luna. I am sure there is an explanation."

"But according to this, it happened months ago. And no one has any information? Still? Nothing?" She was heaving deep breaths.

Ellie didn't know what to say to soothe her friend's distress.

"What's even more bizarre is that I checked the Hennepin County Coroner's office, and there is no death certificate for either of them."

Ellie sat helpless. She shook her head. "I am sure something will turn up eventually." She knew it was a bit of an empty comfort, but it was something to say.

"Something isn't right about this." Luna held two wads of napkins against her eyes.

Ellie decided to remain silent so Luna could let off some steam.

"I mean, he was so well-liked. He had so many people in his circle of friends, not to mention his very large family. Why aren't any of them mentioned? And why aren't either Brendan or Eileen in the other's obit?" She sniffled. "I just don't get it."

Ellie got up. "Let me fix you a cup of tea." She had no idea where the idea came from that a cup of tea would soothe anything, but it sure seemed to keep the Brits stoic. Perhaps placid would be a better word? In either case, Ellie pondered whether or not the Brits put scotch in it. Now *that* would make sense. She rummaged through the basket that held an assortment of herbal teas. Chamomile was known for its relaxing properties, so she opted for two bags.

Luna was ruminating on the days when she and Brendan were best buddies. Ellie let her talk. More like *babble*. But it seemed to have a calming effect on her.

Ellie finally broke in. "Have you told Cullen?"

"No. I literally just found out a few minutes before you walked in."

"Hmm. I see." Ellie sat down again and placed the brewing tonic in front of Luna. She was about to suggest a diversion. "I've been thinking more about my idea of showcasing indigenous art for the holidays. But I need an ambassador."

Luna looked up. "What do you mean?"

"I was wondering if you would like to take a trip to Sedona. On me, of course. You've visited Tlaquepaque, haven't you?"

Luna's mood began to change. "Oh yes. It's spectacular."

"Truth be told, I was inspired by it, and the Torpedo Factory, which is how Stillwell was created."

The two began discussing how the artisan village came into being. In the early 1970s, Abe Miller, a Nevada businessman, visited Sedona often. At that time, the city had only one traffic light, and Abe spent many vacations there. He particularly loved the many acres of a sycamore grove located at the south of 89A next to the bridge to Oak Creek. The property was owned by Harry and Ruby Girard, and after two years of coaxing, he persuaded them to sell it to him.

Miller was a real estate developer and a lover of Mexican art. He was a visionary, and his vision was to create a living artist community. He hired Bob McIntyre, a well-known architect who was keen on helping Miller bring his vision to life. They spent months traveling through rural villages in Mexico, taking photos and drawing sketches. The plans were fluid, changing from day to day as the Spanish Colonial complex came to life. It was a combination of tradition and innovation with a natural, organic feel. The patios, courtyard, plazas, and tiled walls were built by amateur artisans, which contributed to the authenticity of the design.

Miller also insisted the trees remain, and everything be built around them. Today, the sycamores still grew within the structures, including one in the Rowe Fine Art Gallery that twisted through the roof.

"The atrium is a nod to Miller's intentions of incorporating landscaping with art." Ellie smiled. "You see, I am not the brilliant visionary everyone thinks I am."

"Oh, but you are," Luna protested. "You truly combined the inspirations of both art centers here."

"True. I was inspired by their inspirations."

"Isn't that what inspiration is supposed to do? Inspire others?" Luna's face finally brightened.

"Indeed." Ellie patted Luna's hand. "So what do you think about my idea? I'd like you to go to Sedona and speak to some of the artists who create ornaments there. I'm thinking perhaps five or six artists, if there are that many who can contribute. I haven't been there since we broke ground here, so I'm not entirely sure what's available. That's why I'd like you to be my scout. Take a week?"

Luna blinked several times. "Oh, that would be wonderful. I have a very good friend from college who lives there now. We keep talking about getting together, so this would be perfect." She hugged Ellie. "Thank you. Thank you for your confidence in me."

"Of course. You are a very creative woman. You also have very good instincts."

"Yeah. Sometimes." Luna gathered all the wadded-up napkins and tossed them in the trash. "When do you want me to go?"

"Whatever fits your schedule. Sometime within the next month?"

"I'll check with Chris, Cullen, and Chi-Chi and see what they have going on." She sat back down and whispered in Ellie's ear, "I have to ask Cullen to . . ." She bobbed her head toward Wylie. The dog looked up at her. "Yes, I'm talking about you."

"Excellent. I'm sure either Sabrina or Lucy can cover for you."

"Good." Luna looked down at her phone. It was as if Brendan was looking right at her. She turned the phone over. "I'll also have to check with Gail to see what her schedule is like."

"Well, then, we have the beginning of a plan." Ellie got up. "I need to get back to work. Try to take it easy for the rest of the day. You've had quite a shock." Ellie gave Luna a hug and Wylie a pat on the head.

"Thanks, Ellie." Luna gave her a weary smile, but at least her lips were turning in the right direction. Luna walked out with Ellie and headed for the ladies' room. Fortunately, the center was closed to the public, so she didn't have to be concerned about how she looked. She knew she was a mess.

She splashed cold water on her face. It felt good but

did nothing to mask her red, swollen eyes and nose. She gripped the edge of the long slate vanity and shoved her face close to the mirror. "Geez. This is the second time in a week you look like you went through the spin cycle of a washing machine." She dabbed her face with a few paper towels. Maybe she should go home. Take the rest of the day off. Leave the coffee machine on, so anyone who was working could help themselves. Cullen could check on it before the end of his workday.

"Get a grip." She stood up straight and scrutinized her face again. "Maybe a makeover can shift this heavy energy." She thought about the question mark on her easel. Was Brendan's death the question? That made sense, because there was no answer. She took a few deep cleansing breaths and returned to her shop.

Luna sat in front of her large drawing pad, shut her eyes, and began to sketch. When she opened them, she found a rudimentary drawing of a boat. It was like something a child would draw. "Now what does *this* mean?" She didn't know anyone with a boat.

It had been about an hour since her meltdown. Luna thought she looked respectable enough to interact with other humans and walked to Cullen's workshop.

"You again?" he teased, until he noticed how blotchy her face was. "You okay?"

"No. I am not okay." Luna started to sniffle again. She pulled out her phone and showed Cullen the infinitesimal acknowledgement of her friend's death.

"Oh, Lu. I am so sorry." He put his arms around her. "What happened?"

"That's it. Right there. That's all she wrote. Or he wrote. But nobody wrote anything else." Then she scrolled to the next text. "Check this out."

Cullen squinted and stared. "His wife?"

"Yes." Luna sucked in her lips. "There are no other names in either obit."

"Wow." Back to the monosyllabic words.

"Yep." Luna sighed. "Well, there's nothing I can do about any of this."

"True. And I suppose you've tried to ferret out additional information yourself."

"Yep. I even checked the coroner's office. It's baffling."

"Oh, and I know how you get when something baffles you."

"Cullen, he was my friend. A good friend. It's not going to be easy to let this go."

"Listen to me. You're going to have to. You can't track down his family and demand information. They are probably still grieving."

"But what about the memorial?" Luna whined.

"Let it go, dear sister. If anything comes up, I am sure you will hear about it."

She sighed. "I suppose you're right, but . . ."

"Nuh-uh. Don't get yourself all twisted up."

"Too late. I already am," Luna huffed.

"Well, untwist yourself, girlie. Find something to occupy your mind."

"It's the timing of all this, too, Cul. You brought my dresser here, I found souvenirs of Brendan, and now he turns up dead."

"Well, that wasn't exactly the course of events. You discovered those items months after he died. You just didn't know he was dead. You tried to make contact, and you got the news." Cullen looked at her. "This is not a coincidence, Luna. Like I said, he was already dead."

"Okay, okay. I get that he has left the planet."

"Sorry, kiddo, but not everything has to be connected."

"Have you met me?" Luna snickered.

Cullen took her by the shoulders and gave her a kiss on the forehead.

"What's with my forehead lately? People keep kissing it."

"Because you're so cute." Cullen chuckled.

Luna perked up. "But I do have some exciting news."

"Good. Care to share?"

"Ellie wants me to go to Sedona and scout out a few Native American artists for a holiday decoration display she's planning in the atrium."

"That's great! You'll have a chance to see Gail?"

"I hope I can stay with her. Ellie just told me about it an hour ago. I have to get my equilibrium back. It hasn't quite sunk in yet. She wants me to go to Tlaquepaque, the art center there. She also confessed she got the inspiration for the atrium landscaping from the developer. He built it around a grove of sycamore trees. There are live trees growing inside buildings." She pointed to the atrium. *"Et voilà!"*

"When are you going?"

"Like I said, I haven't wrapped my head around it yet. I need to speak to Chris, you, Chi-Chi, and of course, Gail."

"Okay, you're speaking to me now. What do you need?"

"Wylie-sitting?"

"Of course. You don't even have to ask me. You might have to ask *him*, but I'm good with it."

"Thanks. I think this trip will do me a lot of good. Sit on a few Red Rock vortexes and open up to the universe." She hesitated before she went on, but being Luna, she couldn't help herself. "Maybe it will tell me what happened to Brendan."

"Two things. One, it sounds like the perfect place for you." Cullen smiled. "And two, you need to let this Brendan thing go. You're the one who always says, 'The universe is unfolding as it should, so let it do its job and unfold.' Don't obsess about this. You need to focus on your mission for Ellie. And have some fun with Gail." He was relieved to see his sister's mood lighten up.

"Right. I had better call her now to see when she's available. Then I'll give Chris a buzz." She got on her tippy-toes and planted a sisterly kiss on his forehead.

"What was that for?"

"It's forehead-kissing day. Didn't anyone tell you?" Luna twirled around and headed back to her café. There was lots to do.

Chapter Thirteen

Asheville, North Carolina
That Same Day
The Makeover

The minute she returned to the café, Luna phoned her long-time college buddy. "Honey pie!" Luna always referred to Gail that way.

"Sweetcakes!" was always Gail's response. "What is going on?"

"Got a minute?" Luna asked.

"Absolutely. Speak to me."

"Ellie wants me to go to Sedona to check out some of the artists at Tlaquepaque. She's doing an ornament exhibit featuring native and indigenous artists. She wants to display them with a placard explaining the origin of the pieces. I have to find five or six artists who would want to participate."

"Oh, that is fantastic! I don't think anyone would say no," Gail said.

"Well, you know how some artists can be."

"True. True. But I know several that would jump at

the opportunity to have their work shown in a prestigious art center in Asheville."

"Oh, good. That will save me a little time. Give us more time to play!" Luna began to immerse herself in the planning of her trip. "So . . . can I stay with you?"

"Do you have to ask?" Gail laughed. "Of course, you can."

"I don't want to impose on you and Robert."

"Our B&B is available the entire month. You and I can stay there together. We'll be out of Robert's hair!" Gail hooted. "I sent you the pics, right?"

"You did. And it's beautiful. I can't believe you laid all that tile yourself."

"Remember? My father made my siblings and me help him lay the paving stones for the rear garden."

"That was a rather impressive undertaking."

"I could probably become a mason, but now that I'm getting regular manicures, that's out of the question." She laughed. "Once I laid that last piece of tile, I decided that tile work, masonry work, or any other kind of construction work was going to be done by professionals. I'll supervise," she declared.

"Isn't it funny how when we get older, there are things we wouldn't dream of doing now?"

"Ooh, baby. You can say that again!" Gail roared.

Luna laughed. "Ha! Yes, there are things we would undo if given the opportunity."

"Ah. Historical revisionism. If only."

"Politicians do it all the time!" Luna pointed out.

"Well, that is true."

"How about historical eraserism?" Another new word for Luna's dictionary.

"I like that. Can I use it?" Gail chuckled.

"Be my guest."

"And *you* be *my* guest."

"That's fair." Luna took a breath. "I have to make a few phone calls to clear the decks. How about I get back to you tomorrow or the day after?"

"Perfect. This is going to be . . . So. Much. Fun. How about we plan it around the solstice? We'll get up and watch the sunrise from Bell Rock. Like we did when I first moved here."

"Fantastic! And your other mission will be to book us a spot at that fabulous spa on Oak Creek."

"Where we went in the hot tub? And it was forty degrees outside?"

"That's the place! My treat!" Luna offered.

"You don't have to do that."

"I know I don't *have* to. But I *want* to. It'll be an early birthday present."

"Fab! Okay, sweetcakes. I gotta run. Check in when you have a date, and we'll nail everything down. Love you!"

"Love you too!" Luna ended the call. She felt a sudden burst of energy and a total mood shift. She sent Chris a text, asking if he had a minute to talk. She didn't like to interrupt him when he was at work. She included *No rush* so he wouldn't think it was an emergency. He responded he'd call within the hour.

In the meantime, Luna began to check online for hair salons. Chi-Chi did her own hair and cut Luna's when she needed an inch or two removed to freshen the ends, so there wasn't anyone around who could recommend a salon. Maybe Ellie. She buzzed her via the walkie-talkie. "Hey, Ellie, can you recommend a good salon?"

"Of course, dear—Les Cheveux. Ask for Felipé. And please be sure to pronounce it with an accent over the last E," Ellie instructed, with a bit of a giggle.

"Thanks, Ellie. I shall call them and ask for Felipé." Luna had been sporting the same hairstyle since college. And her granny dresses needed an update, as well. She went to the Les Cheveux website and checked out their extensive gallery of styles and color. She gravitated to the ombre style again. The one she particularly liked started as a warm brown at the roots and continued for about three inches, then gradually turned to a lighter brown, and then a brownish blond at the end. She would have to cut her hair in order for it to look right. She pulled her long braid around and measured about a foot, maybe more. It was going to be drastic, for sure.

Instead of being nervous about cutting her hair, Luna was excited. For some reason, she felt as if she were getting a fresh start. Not that she needed one, but all the change in Chris's life would invariably impact hers. She noted the photo and phoned the salon. She crossed her fingers in the hope they would have an opening before she chickened out. Fortunately, they had a cancellation for later that day, and Luna scooped it up. She began to browse through a few retail websites to see how she could change up her wardrobe. The hippy-dippy bohemian look was so last decade. Several, in fact.

Luna jumped when her phone rang. "Hey!" she greeted Chris.

"Hey, dollface. What's up?"

"Ellie asked me to go to Sedona to scout out Native American art at Tlaquepaque."

"That sounds like fun. Sedona is right up your alley," Chris replied.

"Yes, it is. I'm going to stay with Gail."

"Someone better notify the authorities," Chris chided.

"Very funny," Luna remarked. "I wanted to see what your schedule was like so I can plan accordingly."

"I just got out of a meeting with the director. I have to go to a special training lab for two weeks and am waiting for Evan to get back to me to see if he has any idea how soon we'll get a hearing."

"Right."

"Lucinda is moving very soon, so that may push the needle, but you know how bureaucracy goes. The upside is that *she* can move, but without Carter. Not until the judge decides who has custody. And then there's school. He'll start here, which will also help my case. The courts don't like disruption."

"True. I remember when I was in social services, the child's best interest was always the most important thing. Not what mommy or daddy wanted."

"Carter needs to have an evaluation, too, but that won't happen until the paperwork is filed."

"Lots of balls in the air," Luna noted.

"Exactly. That being said, I can't plan my orientation lab until I get a handle on what's happening with Carter. I don't want to be out of town when he's with the shrink."

"But when you are out of town, where will he stay? With Lucinda, I presume?"

"That's another thing. There is a baseball camp he wants to go to. That's also a two-week stint, and I'm hoping I can arrange for both things to happen at the same time."

"You certainly have a lot of things going on. I don't want to add to your list of things to juggle."

"I don't mind juggling you at all," Chris teased.

"Gail suggested I go out there for the solstice, June twentieth. We'll climb Bell Rock to watch the sunrise."

"That sounds rather spectacular."

"It is. We did it several years ago when she first moved there. We got up before dawn and put on our hiking boots. The morning light was just bright enough so we could climb. We thought we would be the only people there, but as we ascended, we came across about a dozen people who had the same idea in mind. You're right. It was spectacular."

"I don't want to hold up your travel plans, but I'm in a bit of limbo-land right now. You should probably put your trip together, and we'll wing it until I get a better grasp on things."

"Sounds like a plan."

"Luna? Thanks for checking with me."

"About what?"

"Scheduling." He chuckled.

"Oh. That. You mean the thing couples normally do?" Luna egged him on.

"Yes, dollface. Couples. You. Me." He paused. "And I thought you were the smart one."

"Well, I am. I was simply being considerate." She threw the conversational ball back.

"You always are."

"Please don't tell me I'm too nice. I hate it when people say that to me. It makes me want to be *not* nice."

Chris laughed. "That will never happen."

"You're probably right, although I do have my limits. Just sayin'."

"You? Limits? Hardly."

"Okay, okay. You got me." Luna chuckled. "I've gotta run. We'll talk later."

"You got it. Enjoy the rest of the day."

Enjoying the rest of her day was exactly what Luna had in mind. She didn't tell Chris about the news of her friend Brendan's death. There was nothing he could do about that. She also didn't mention the planned makeover. She wanted to surprise him. But she was going to tell Chi-Chi and ask if she would go with her. She picked up the walkie-talkie and buzzed her friend.

"Want to go on a mission with me?"

"Oh, my. I am not sure what that means. What kind of mission?" Chi-Chi scrunched up her face, waiting for a Luna-lunatic type of reply.

"Remember I said I was considering a makeover?"

"Yes?" It was more of a question than a statement.

"And that ombre hairstyle I liked?"

"Yes?"

"I made an appointment for two o'clock."

"Today?"

"Yes. Today. I don't want to chicken out."

"I see. What time do you want to leave?"

"Well, I was also thinking about buying a few new items for my wardrobe."

"You are going for many changes, I see."

"Well, an update, if nothing else."

"So you want to do some shopping." *That* was more of a statement than a question.

"I was looking online, and there's a shop in Asheville called Natural Elements. I'd like to check it out before I go to the salon."

"You mean before *we* go to the salon." Another statement.

"So you'll go with me?"

"I cannot let Luna Bodman experiment without adult supervision. What time shall we leave?"

"You are the best! How about in an hour? We can grab some lunch."

After saying goodbye to Chi-Chi, Luna dashed into Cullen's workshop. "Can you take Wylie for me?"

"Sure. What's up?" He wiped his hands on a shop towel.

"I have a few errands to run." She wasn't telling him what she had in mind. He'd either try to talk some sense into her or be indifferent. And she wasn't in the mood for anyone to throw another bucket of water on her.

Soon, the two women got into Luna's car and drove twenty minutes to Asheville. During the drive, Luna relayed her unnerving information about Brendan.

"I am so sorry to hear this," Chi-Chi said with deep affection. "I know it must be hard for you to absorb such disturbing news, especially when there is no explanation."

Luna let out a huge sigh. "You got that right. It's all a little spooky, even for me. I tried to talk to Cullen about it. You know, the dresser, the mementos, then this news. He said not everything is connected, that it's just a strange coincidence."

"Perhaps he is right on this particular occasion." After Chi-Chi's attempts at squelching Luna's concern, she changed the subject. "Tell me. What kind of wardrobe are you thinking about?" she asked.

"I saw some cute capri leggings. There's a blue tie-dyed pair and a floral pair, and one chambray."

"The tie-dye suits your existing wardrobe."

"True. I don't want my legs to go into shock with too abrupt a change in clothing." Luna laughed. "My plan is to pair them with tank tops, a short-sleeved cropped jacket, and a kimono. This way, I can have multiple outfits without going completely crazy."

"Oh, girl, you went completely crazy many years ago." Chi-Chi kept a straight face.

"Why does everyone always pick on me?" Luna put on a fake frown.

"Because it is easy." Chi-Chi laughed.

Natural Elements proved to be a boon for Luna. The boutique was having a sale! A perky salesperson greeted them. Luna described the clothing she'd seen online, and the woman was happy to point her in the right direction. "Look!" Luna whispered to Chi-Chi. "It's a BOGO sale."

"I see that. Buy one and get fifty percent off the second pair."

"Exactly. That means I shall buy two pairs, which means I'll actually be getting one for free!"

"And you said you were not good at math." Chi-Chi smiled.

Luna dug through the pile of leggings on the display table and found the blue tie-dyed pair and the floral in her size. Chi-Chi combed the adjacent table and pulled out the chambray. "Oh, they have them in black, too." She handed the leggings to Luna.

"Go try these on."

Luna made her way to the dressing room. The salesperson walked over and asked if they needed help. Chi-Chi rolled her eyes. "My friend is on a mission to update her wardrobe."

The salesperson eyed Luna up and down. "I think we can bring you into the new millennium." She grinned.

It was Luna's turn to roll her eyes. "I thought Boho was in fashion again."

"It is. But . . ."

"Don't you start picking on me, too." Luna made a face.

"My friend is very sensitive." Chi-Chi smirked.

"How about I pull a few things together to go with those leggings." The salesperson raised her eyebrows at Chi-Chi, thinking Luna might not have any fashion sense whatsoever.

"I want a few tank tops, crop jacket, a kimono, and a tunic," Luna called over her shoulder before she shut the louvered door to the dressing room.

The woman worked her way across the shop and quickly pulled items from the rack. "Try these." She hung them on the hook on the outside of the dressing room. A few minutes later, Luna exited wearing the blue tie-dyed leggings with a navy tank top and a cropped denim jacket.

"You look adorable!" the salesperson gushed.

"That's not exactly what I was going for, but I kinda like the way this comes together." Luna went back inside and tried on another outfit. This time, it was the rust-and-yellow paisley tunic over the black leggings and black tank.

"Very smart-looking. Sophisticated," the salesclerk cooed.

"I'll take smart and sophisticated," Luna said. She twirled in front of the mirror. "Next! Should I do the chambray or black leggings with the kimono?" she called through the louvers.

"You can do either. Chambray if it's casual, black if it's a little more formal. Like dinner. You can create several outfits with the pieces you have," the salesperson advised.

Luna swung open the door. "Ta-da! That's exactly what I had in mind. It'll be much easier for me to pack."

"You traveling soon?"

"Yes, I'm going to Sedona."

"Wonderful. I've never been, but I've heard great things."

"It's magical." Luna sighed. She handed over the leggings, tanks, jacket, kimono, and tunic. "It's still pretty Boho-ish." Luna smiled. "I'll take all of it."

The salesperson's head snapped up. She couldn't remember the last time when a customer came in, knew what she wanted, and purchased almost a dozen pieces in less than a half hour. "Perfect," she gushed, while calculating her commission in her head.

Luna squeezed Chi-Chi's arm. "This is so exciting."

"I am very happy to see you are more like yourself today. Last week, you were in a state. You seem more relaxed now," Chi-Chi replied.

"I am. I have a mission to complete." Luna chuckled.

"Yes. We know that you are not happy unless you are on a mission," Chi-Chi needled her.

They walked to the counter while the salesperson

carefully wrapped each item in tissue and placed everything into two rigid burlap shopping totes. Luna handed over her credit card.

"But you do not know how much it is going to cost." Chi-Chi looked at her with concern.

"It doesn't matter. I checked the prices when I was online and knew what I could afford. The sale was a bonus!" Luna's eyes grew wide.

"Do you need new shoes?" Chi-Chi didn't want to encourage her friend to spend more money, but it was a valid question. If you're going to do something, go all the way.

"Probably a pair of booties."

The salesperson added her two cents. "They'll look great with the outfits you chose."

"Can you recommend a store?" Luna asked as she returned the plastic to her wallet.

"There's a boutique around the corner. Cute, trendy, but the prices are reasonable."

"Great! Thanks!" Luna grabbed her bounty of fashion goodies. "And thanks for your help."

"My pleasure. Have a nice trip!"

"Thank you!"

"Goodbye." Chi-Chi nodded and smiled.

They meandered over to the shoe store, and Luna checked the time. "We have about an hour for the next phase of my transformation. Coffee?"

"I am not sure if caffeine is what I need to watch your transformation. Perhaps decaf."

Luna chuckled. "Let's check out the shoes first."

"You are the leader in this adventure."

Luna spotted a pair of Doc Martens in the window.

Chi-Chi guided Luna's attention to the Sofft slouch boots. "Those are much more feminine. You do not want to look like a lumberjack, do you?"

"You're right. Besides, I have a similar pair, and they're just a little beat-up."

"Then I suggest you try those." Chi-Chi pointed to the Sofft boots again. "You can take your mechanic boots to a shoemaker and have them refurbished."

"Good thinkin'. See, that's why I needed you here."

"I have come to realize that you truly do need adult supervision most of the time."

Luna poked Chi-Chi with her elbow. "Hey. You're starting to sound like my brother."

"I have learned a lot of things from your brother."

Luna gave her a sideways glance. "Am I going to have to kill him now?"

"You had better not." Chi-Chi wagged a finger at Luna in jest.

Luna approached a young man behind the counter. "Hi. Do you have the Sofft slouch waterproof in a seven?"

He looked over his wire-rimmed glasses. "Let me check." He then disappeared into the back of the store.

Luna mumbled to Chi-Chi, "And let's not forget new glasses, too. He reminded me how dated they look," she chortled.

"We should wait until after your salon appointment."

"Again! Good thinkin'."

The man returned with a seven and a seven and a half. "Just in case."

Luna slipped off her everyday walking shoes and stepped into the soft leather bootie. "Mmmm . . . comfy."

"Yes, they are known for their comfort." He sounded a bit snide.

Luna nodded a few times. "Yes, I am aware. Thank you." She rolled her eyes at Chi-Chi, who bit her lip to keep from laughing.

Luna stomped around in the boots and decided they were exactly what she needed. "I'll take them. Thank you," she said, and handed him her credit card.

Chi-Chi took the shopping bag from the clerk, and they ventured back to the car.

"Not bad for an hour's work!" Luna exclaimed, as she tucked her shopping treasures into the back of her SUV. They hopped into the vehicle, and Luna punched the salon's address into her GPS. "I'm a little nervous," she squealed.

"Yes. I understand. I do not know what I would do without all of my hair."

Luna jerked her head. "I'll be getting rid of my hair!"

"This just occurred to you?" Chi-Chi looked at her suspiciously.

"Well, yes, and no. I mean, I was more focused on the look, rather than the process."

"Yes. It means you will have to cut your hair if you want it to look good. Your hair is much too long for that coloring."

"True. But I'm ready for it. Honest. I feel like I'm letting go of my past. Consciously and subconsciously. Physically, emotionally, and spiritually."

"I did not realize your past had such a hold on you," Chi-Chi mused.

"Neither did I. Not until I opened the drawers of my

old dresser. Strange, isn't it? We hold on to things, not just in physical form, but in our head." She took a breath. "I mean, I know all of this intellectually, but I think it's the symbolism we cling to without being fully aware of what we are doing."

Chi-Chi thought for a moment. "I believe I understand what you are saying. It's like the women who still wear the same hairstyle they had in high school." Then she burst out laughing. It suddenly dawned on her she was referring to her friend.

"Thanks, pal."

"I did not mean you. The ones with the big bangs."

"And the massive amounts of blue eyeshadow!" Luna barked.

"That is exactly what I am talking about."

"And you are correct, my friend. I've had the same hairstyle since high school. The only exception is that I never had bangs. Or blue eyeshadow!" Luna smirked. "I had no idea I was one of those people."

"You are not."

"Well, if I am, that's about to change."

"As long as *you* do not change." Chi-Chi patted Luna's hand.

"I'm shedding my past. I think it's a very symbolic gesture."

"I could not agree more."

"Do me a favor, please? Look up Locks of Love?"

"Yes, the donation site. I used them several years ago. Ah, here. There is a form you can fill out. I will send you the link."

"Thank you. I'll be happy to know my hair went to a kid who lost their hair because of cancer treatments. Boy, that must be horrible. Your body is subjected to intense treatments that kick you in the tush, and you lose your hair as a thank-you. It's terrible."

"But they are making progress every day."

"True. And so is cancer. When I was a kid, you rarely heard of anyone getting cancer. Now, they say one out of every three people will be diagnosed with one form or another. It's scary."

"It is. And that is why we count our blessings every day."

"So true, girlfriend. So true." Luna pulled into the parking area for the salon. "Here goes!"

They walked into Les Cheveux and were greeted by a bald man. Luna attempted to stifle a chuckle. Not a good endorsement. Chi-Chi was thinking the same thing and could not suppress her big smile.

The man in the black shirt, black pants, diamond stud earring, and the shiny chrome dome brushed his cue ball with his hand. "Is this what you have in mind, dearie?" Everyone burst out laughing. "Puh-lease. I get that reaction with every new client." He became animated. "*Do I really want a Baldilocks working on my hair!*" He spun on his heel. "Of course, you do, darling."

"Of course I do?" Luna sounded dubious.

"You must be Luna. I'm Felipé." He accentuated the *É*. "Not Phil or Fel-eep. It's Fel-eep-é. Now that we have that straight, follow me, darling." He looked at Chi-Chi. "My, you are one delicious thing. You can come, too."

They followed him past a row of minimalistic white chairs that ran along the black walls of the sleek reception area. A large white vase with palm fronds sat on an oblong glass table.

Next was another room in reverse color with a row of eight black salon chairs that faced individual mirrored stations hung on white walls. Three of the stations were occupied with customers, and the stylists were wearing black smocks with the salon's logo. One stylist had an ear-hugging asymmetrical cut with the short side colored in bright fuchsia. The second stylist had a chin-length cut with black bangs and blond hair. Luna was getting nervous. Felipé could tell by the look of horror on her face. "Don't panic, lovie. They are victims of a hair show." He called out to them, "I told you not to go. You both need to do something. You're scaring the customers."

He showed Luna to a chair and gestured for Chi-Chi to take the next seat. He leaned against the station and folded his arms. "Let me guess. You want to lop off those locks."

"I need a change. Oh, and now that you mentioned locks, I want to donate my hair to the charity."

"That's wonderful, darling. And because you are being so kind, we will not charge you for the haircut. You can fill out the paperwork here, and we'll ship it to them."

"Terrific," Luna replied. "I was looking through your gallery." She pulled up the style she liked on her phone and showed it to him.

"Darling, you are in luck. That particular 'do is one of my creations." He tilted his head this way and that, looking at Luna from various angles. "I think that would do well for you."

He looked at Chi-Chi.

She shrugged.

"Today I am her chaperone, but she makes the decisions."

Felipé chuckled. "Okay. Patrice is going to get you set up."

A young woman showed Luna to a dressing room and gave her a smock. "You can take off your top if you'd like and hang it on the hooks. We're going to put a cape over this, so you might be more comfortable. You'll be sitting under a heat lamp." Patrice closed the door and waited outside.

Luna followed the instructions, removed her peasant shirt, and pulled the smock on. She wrapped the belt around her waist. She took another look at her long braid. "It's been swell." Then she flung it back over her shoulder.

Chi-Chi was waiting in the chair, reading a cooking magazine. "Are you ready, my friend?"

"As ready as I will ever be," Luna said nervously.

Felipé returned. "Okay, darling, I am going to turn you around so you are facing away from the mirror. Cutting hair this long can be traumatic, and I don't want you to freak out. Okay?"

"Okay!" Luna breathed out the word. "Chi-Chi? Are you going to stay and watch this?"

"I do not know if I should." She was being sincere. "I may have an expression on my face that you will misinterpret."

"Oh great." Luna looked at Felipé. "How long is this going to take?"

"As long as it takes, dear. We do not rush this sort of thing."

"Ballpark?"

"Two hours, at least."

"Ah. Then I think I shall go for a walk in the neighborhood," said Chi-Chi. "There is a brewery Cullen has been talking about. They do some sort of tour he seemed interested in. I shall get some information for him."

"That's very thoughtful," Luna said. "Even if you're leaving me alone here. With this man!" She laughed nervously.

"It is better if we see the final results together," Chi-Chi said calmly. "Good luck."

"Thank you," Luna said.

"I meant to Felipé." Chi-Chi grinned and left.

Felipé pumped the chair up so he could be face to face with Luna. "I'm thinking to here." He touched her collarbone.

She winced.

"It will be alright. Trust me."

"I have no choice, do I?"

"No. You are in my power now," he said in jest.

He loosened her braid and took a wide-tooth comb and pulled it through her soon-to-be-gone, waist-length hair. "You have nice hair, and I have to tell you it is really a good idea to cut it. As we get older, our hair thins." He rolled his eyes and leaned in. "I ought to know," he continued. "Brushing and combing these locks will pull more hair out."

Luna agreed. "Yes, I've noticed more in my brush and comb."

"And let me tell you something, those celebrities who have all that long hair? Fake. Fake. Fake. Nobody has real hair like that, unless you're eighteen years old."

"That's about when I let it grow."

"See?" He pulled his scissors from a leather case, grabbed her hair, and pulled it into a ponytail just below her shoulder blades. From there, he unceremoniously lobbed off over a foot of hair. "For the children," he said. "You are doing a good thing. You truly are."

Luna could feel the difference already. The warmth and weight of her mane was no longer there. She was surprised that it actually felt good. He continued to clip and snip until he was satisfied with the length. "Alright, my pretty. On to the next phase."

Luna reached around her back. It was truly gone. She took a few breaths and muttered, "It's okay, it's okay, it's okay."

"You're gonna be gorgeous."

He next rolled out a cart with several tubs of various shades of hair color. Felipé and his assistant proceeded to part Luna's hair in quarter-inch sections. Starting at the bottom, he began to paint, then foil, another section, paint, then foil, until her head was covered in foil strips. "Now we wait for the magic to happen!" Felipé said with great enthusiasm. "Can we get you anything? Coffee? Water? Tea? Crumpets?"

"You have crumpets?" Luna said with surprise.

"It is teatime, dearie."

"How about smoked salmon and cream cheese sandwiches? Or cucumber and cream cheese? Perhaps some cheese and chutney?" Luna was teasing, but there was a surprise in store.

"Oh, darling. You have come to the right place." He snapped his fingers, and Patrice rolled in another cart loaded with three tiers of sandwiches, scones, and cakes.

"Whoa! That looks incredible! No wonder Ellie likes to come here. And now I know where she got her penchant for scones. We have them every morning." Luna was delighted at the yummy feast set in front of her.

"Shall I fix you a plate?" Patrice offered.

Luna pointed to a few items. "I'll have one of those and two of these."

Patrice added a few other things. "Just in case."

Several minutes later, Chi-Chi returned. "Are you having a party without me?"

"Please. Join in." Felipé gestured to the cart.

"Do you do this every day?" Chi-Chi asked.

"It depends on which clients are coming in. I must confess, Ellie phoned and told us all about you. Both of you, as a matter of fact. You will tell her we took good care of you, won't you?"

"Of course!" Luna exclaimed with cream-cheesed lips.

"This is quite lovely," Chi-Chi said. "Perhaps I should cut my hair, too?"

"Don't you dare," Luna said.

Felipé looked at Chi-Chi. "Ditto. You have gorgeous hair, and you do it beautifully." He was referring to her box braids tied in a scarf.

"Thank you. I occasionally take a flat iron to it, but that takes me a very long time."

"We have a special straightening system. It takes about two hours, but it will last for up to six months."

"That is very interesting. I may consider it. But not today." She popped a piece of cake in her mouth.

Several more minutes passed until the timer buzzed, indicating it was time to wash Luna's hair. Within the hour, she would be leaving with a new hairstyle. When she returned to the chair, she was still facing away from the mirror. Felipé and Patrice began spraying her wet hair with several treatments. One was to protect her hair from the heat, the other was to give her volume, and the third was for gloss and shine. Like two pistol-packing cowboys, the stylists whipped out the blow-dryers and went to work, tousling, finger-waving, and primping. Luna could tell it was looking good by the expression on everyone's faces. She was itching to see for herself. Within a few minutes, Felipé asked, "Are you ready for the big reveal?"

"Am I ever!" Luna exclaimed, and Felipé spun her around.

"Oh. My. Gosh. I look like a totally different person." She tossed her head back and forth, her hair brushing against her collarbones. "Is that really me?"

"In the flesh, dearie." Felipé stood back. "You're loving it, I can tell."

"Absolutely!" Luna kept turning her head from side to side. "Why didn't I think about doing this sooner?"

"Better late than never," Felipé responded.

"You look beautiful," Chi-Chi said admiringly. "No one is going to recognize you."

"I think that might be a good thing." Luna took the handheld mirror from Patrice, who spun her around to check the back. "It's fabulous! Thank you so much!"

"A pleasure." Felipé gave a short bow.

Patrice removed the cape and sent Luna back to the dressing room, where she found one of her shopping bags. She smiled. Chi-Chi wanted Luna to get the full effect of her new look. Luna decided on the chambray capri leggings, a white tank top, and the denim jacket.

She stared at herself in the mirror. "Hello. My name is Luna. Nice to meet you." She was elated. Wired for sound, as some say. She exited the dressing room and was met with applause.

"You look wonderful, my friend." Chi-Chi embraced her. "Chris and your brother will be dumbfounded."

"I wonder if either of them will even be able to figure me out." Luna laughed. It was true. She looked completely different with her new hairstyle and her new clothes. "But first I need new glasses. These whoppers are too big, and my wire-rims are too outdated."

Felipé crossed his arms and placed his finger against his lips. "I think maybe a cat-eye frame. Something with one of the colors in your hair."

"So far, you haven't steered me wrong. I will consider your suggestion."

The entourage moved back to the reception area, where Luna paid the hefty tab of 500 dollars for her color. It was worth every penny, as far as she was concerned.

Felipé gave her a peck on each cheek. "You look marvelous, darling. Good luck!" He turned to Chi-Chi. "Shall I make an appointment for you?"

Chi-Chi hesitated. Luna jumped in. "Come on, my friend. If I can do it, you can do it."

"And you say it can last up to six months?" Chi-Chi asked Felipé.

"Yes."

"And I can still braid it?"

"Absolutely. You will have all the options."

Chi took a deep breath. "Alright. I shall do it."

Luna was giddy. "I'll come with you for moral support. As long as they serve high tea."

"Of course," Felipé replied.

Chi-Chi looked through her phone calendar.

"Make sure it's not when I'm away," Luna added, and provided the dates of her travel plans.

"June thirtieth it is," Felipé confirmed. "You girls go have some fun now, but stay out of trouble."

Chi-Chi laughed. "That is why I am here."

Luna was walking on air. "I can't believe how good all of this feels. My transformation. My metamorphosis."

"It is true. You have gone from a caterpillar to a butterfly."

Luna frowned. "I was a caterpillar?"

"Do not be ridiculous. I was simply using a metaphor. Do not be so touchy." Chi-Chi gave her a tap on the elbow.

"Ha. Let's call Cullen and tell him to meet us for dinner."

"You still need to get new glasses."

"Right. There's a one-hour place on the way back. We'll stop there and then call him."

"One more thing," Chi-Chi added. "You should stop at Blue Mercury and have them recommend some makeup."

Luna looked surprised. "Why? Do I look awful?"

"No, you do not look awful, but with your new hairstyle and color, perhaps they can recommend something that would go better than what you have been wearing. Maybe you will not need anything, but if you are going all this way, it could not hurt. We shall pick out your glasses and go to Blue Mercury while we wait."

"Good idea. See? This is why I need you with me." Luna grinned.

When they arrived at Spectacular Spectacles, Luna gravitated to the rack of cat-eye–shaped glasses.

"Love your hair," one of the clerks commented.

"Thank you!"

"Can I help you with anything?" the clerk asked. She was a woman in her forties and was wearing a name tag in the shape of eyeglasses that said MAUREEN.

"I need a new pair and am thinking about this shape." Luna pulled on a pair of cat-eyes with a tortoise frame.

"I think that's too busy for your hair. The frame is good, but maybe in a solid?" Maureen handed Luna a pair of amber frames.

"They're perfect!" Luna exclaimed. "Can you have them ready in an hour?"

"That's what we do here," Maureen assured her.

"Terrific!" Luna replied. She turned to Chi-Chi. "Can you call Cullen and tell him to meet us at Three Brothers at, say, seven?"

"Of course, I can." Chi-Chi punched in Cullen's number on her speed-dial and relayed the instructions.

"What are the two of you up to?" Cullen asked with mocking suspicion.

"You will see. Bye." That was Chi-Chi, alright— blunt and to the point.

Luna and Chi-Chi walked two blocks to Blue Mercury, where a young man greeted them with, "Love your hair!"

"Me too!" Luna said in response. She was delighted about receiving two compliments in the past fifteen minutes.

"What can we help you with today?" the man asked.

"I want to be sure I'm wearing the right makeup for my hair. I just had it done."

He brought her near a lighted mirror and checked her face, this way and that. "Your foundation is fine, but I think you might want to ditch the pink blush and go with a more peach and russet tone. Same thing with eyeshadow. Do you normally wear it?"

Luna was grateful her puffy, bloodshot eyes had calmed down since that morning. She removed her big glasses. "Most of the time I just do a quick swipe of light brown. If I'm doing something special, I use a deeper shade in the crease."

"Let's try this." He took a palette off a hook and began to apply a light gold pearl shadow under her brow, and then swiped a chestnut brown to the rest of her lids, followed by a few strokes of black eyebrow pencil and a smudge of brown eyeliner pencil. "Now your eyes have similar tones as your hair, but they stand out because of the eyeliner." He stepped back. "Most people think they have to draw one steady line, but you can dot the rims and then blend it." Then he tried a peach shade of lipstick with a little gloss. "Perfection!"

"I think I'm going to try to wear my contacts more often," Luna said. "Now that I've figured out how to wear makeup without looking like a clown!" She turned to Chi-Chi. "What do you think?"

"I think you look beautiful." Chi-Chi smiled warmly.

"I'm waiting for a pair of cats-eye glasses in a solid amber frame." She winced, hoping she hadn't ruined her new glow.

"That will be perfect," the clerk replied. "Either way, you are stunning."

Luna did a double take. She could not recall anyone ever calling her *stunning*. "Cute." "Pretty." "Lovely." Never *stunning*. Chi-Chi was stunning. Luna began to blush. "Thank you."

Chi-Chi was grinning. "My friend has gone through a great transformation today," she explained to the make-up artist. "She used to have hair down to her waist, wore baggy granny dresses, and wire-rimmed glasses most of the time."

"You could have fooled me," the man said earnestly.

Luna laughed. "Well, it took me long enough to get here. I'd been sporting that look almost half my life."

"Now you can start a new one." He began to pack a few samples in a bag. "Try these on your own. If you like them, you can call me, and I'll send them to you, or you can pick them up. Or if you live close by, we can deliver it."

"We're at the Stillwell Center," Luna said. "I run The Namaste Café, and Chi-Chi is the creative genius at Silver and Stone."

"Wait. Are you the one who has the coffee shop there?" He ducked his head slightly and whispered, "You do readings?"

"Uh, yes," Luna whispered back.

"I was going to stop in, but the café was busy." He looked her over from head to toe. "You were the one with the long braid and maxi dress?"

"That would be me. Correction. That *was* me. This is the *new* me."

"I approve," he said.

Luna reached into her purse and handed him her

business card. "Please call and make an appointment. Gratis."

"That's very kind of you," he replied.

"You have been very kind to me. Thank you." She took her small bag of samples, shook his hand, and said, "Please don't hesitate."

Chi-Chi and Luna walked back to the eyeglass shop and picked up Luna's new frames. Maureen was right—they went well with her hair, and now her makeup, too. On the way to Three Brothers, Luna could not wipe the smile off her face. Chi-Chi looked over at her. "It is nice to see you smiling again. And again. Now I understand what they mean by 'retail therapy.'" She laughed.

"And hair, and makeup, and glasses therapy." Luna chuckled.

They were the first to arrive at the pizzeria. Gorgio greeted them. "Nice to see you, Chi-Chi. And who is your new friend?"

Chi-Chi didn't answer, and Luna stared at him without saying a word. Then her face broke out in a big smile. It gave her away immediately.

"Luna! *Que bella*! I didn't recognize you!" Gorgio was truly surprised.

"I needed a change," Luna explained.

"*Molto bene*! Change is good." He inspected her new threads. "Everything. *Bellissima*! You want to sit inside or outside?"

Luna looked at Chi-Chi. "Outside?"

"It's your day, my new friend."

Gorgio walked them to a table on the sidewalk and handed them menus. "Something to drink?"

"I think I'll have a pinot gris. Really chilled," Luna said.

"I shall have the same," Chi-Chi answered.

Gorgio walked briskly inside and returned with a bottle in a stainless-steel cooler, along with two glasses. "Make that three glasses, please. Cullen is joining us," Luna explained.

"What are you in the mood for?" Luna asked Chi-Chi.

"Nothing too heavy. I put too many little cakes in my stomach."

"Cappellini? It's light. Maybe pomodoro or with lemon and garlic?"

"Now I am hungry," Chi-Chi said while perusing the rest of the menu.

"I think I'll have shrimp scampi over capellini," Luna said. "And a side of broccoli rabe. I'll stink of garlic!"

"That sounds delicious. I do not mind you smelling like garlic." Chi-Chi laughed. "But I will have my capellini with lemon."

Luna and Chi-Chi toasted to Luna's "refurbishment" and waited for Cullen to arrive before they placed their order. Several minutes passed, and then Wylie trotted toward the table, with Cullen lagging behind. Wylie immediately nudged Luna's arm. Cullen stopped. *Who is that?* he wondered. Then he heard his sister's voice. "Holy Toledo!" He pulled out a chair and stared. "Wow. Look at you." His mouth was agape. "Is this a permanent thing?" He eyed her hair, then her clothes. She pulled off her glasses so he could see her makeup before she plunked them back on.

"What do you think of your sister's new look?" Chi-Chi asked.

"She will always be the same character, but now it is in a different costume," Cullen roared. "I have to admit, you look pretty darn good."

"Why, thank you. I feel pretty good, too," Luna said.

"What brought all of this on?" he asked.

"Believe it or not, the dresser. Going through all my old stuff made me realize part of me was stuck in the past. Trapped by things that I hadn't really resolved on a subconscious level."

Cullen hesitated, then said, "Do you think the news about Brendan had something to do with it?"

Luna let out a sigh. "It was the final push I needed. Going through the box was illuminating, but getting the news about him was the catalyst."

"Well, it might have been bad news, but some good came from it. You really look terrific." He could not stop staring at her.

"I agree," Chi-Chi chimed in.

"Does Chris know about this?" Cullen poured a glass of wine from the bottle that was sitting on the table.

"No. I want to surprise him," Luna replied.

"I can tell you this— he will be blown away." Cullen raised his glass. "To the new you!"

Chapter Fourteen

Ten Days Later
Off to Sedona

Luna was a whirling dervish prior to her trip. She had several readings to do, a few wardrobe tweaks, organizing the café schedule and deliveries, and making sure all of Wylie's needs were taken care of. Chewies? Check. Toys? Check. Food? Check. Doggie bed? Check. If she missed anything, Cullen could manage.

She was disappointed she hadn't been able to see Chris before she left. Between her travel plans and his schedule, it was too much of a crunch, and neither wanted to put the other one or themselves under additional pressure. She had been so distracted with her to-do list that she almost forgot he hadn't seen her renewed look. A lot of people did FaceTime on their phones, but Chris wasn't into it, and Luna couldn't care less. As long as they had frequent conversations, there wasn't any need, and even if he'd asked to do a video call—which he didn't—she would have made an excuse. She wanted to see his reaction in person.

It worked out that Chris would take his training courses while Carter went to baseball camp, and Luna was off to climb a vortex. Chris left before she did, but they made a plan for all three to get together for the Fourth of July weekend in Asheville. It might get a little dicey with sleeping accommodations, but Chris was going to explain it all to his son. He didn't want Lucinda to get goofy over it, but Carter was almost a teenager, and he had a pretty good idea what adults did when they were alone. He lived with two of them, although he hardly ever heard the bed springs squeak. Chris vowed that discretion would be the order of the day when Carter was at Luna's. Chris was sure Carter's imagination might run wild, but he wasn't going to give his son any additional ammunition.

If the weather was good, Chris planned to set up a tent in Luna's yard. He'd also bring his telescope. There was much less light pollution at Luna's.

To celebrate the Fourth of July, Ellie hosted a barbecue on the patio of the center for all the artists and their families. To finish off the evening, a small but dazzling fireworks display would light up the sky and the gardens. It should prove to be an enjoyable evening, and for Carter, a new experience. Another reason to choose living with his father. His dad had fun friends.

The day before Luna left, she asked Chi-Chi to stop over to help her select her wardrobe. She didn't want to overpack, especially with her new clothes. Chi-Chi picked up some Mexican food on the way, "To get your tastebuds accustomed to the cuisine."

Luna poured them beers. It seemed to be a better beverage when the heat hit the palate. After dinner, Luna fidgeted with her clothing, packing and unpacking, until Chi-Chi took the wheel. "I shall decide for you. You will never make your flight tomorrow if you do not finish packing tonight."

"Always the adult on duty." Luna gave her a hug.

"It is a shame you were not able to see Chris before your departure."

"I know, but we have a wonderful weekend planned for the Fourth. He's bringing his son here for the barbecue and fireworks."

"Ah. That will be the first time, correct?"

"Carter has been here a few times just as a day trip, but it will be the first sleepover." She rolled her eyes.

"I am sure it will be fine. He seems like a very nice young man."

"That he is. Takes after his dad."

"I would hope so." Chi-Chi laughed as she folded the recently purchased items. "There. You have several options. I am sure you will not be going dancing."

"Only on the rocks, and it will be my woo-woo dance." Luna grinned. "I'm really excited about this trip. I haven't seen Gail in two years. Maybe three? Time just flies."

"Indeed it does, and I must fly home now." Chi-Chi wrapped her arms around her friend. "You be a good girl. Do not get into any trouble."

"Promise!" Luna hugged her back, then walked her friend to the door. "I'll be in touch. Will send photos!" She waved as Chi-Chi got in her car and drove away.

Luna inspected her tote. Ticket? Check. Wallet? Check. Credit cards? Check and double-check. She was ready. Cullen planned to take her to the airport. There was only one airline that had non-stop flights to Phoenix, but it also had the worst cancellations. When she made her reservation, she decided it would be better to fly to Atlanta, then on to Phoenix. At least if she got tied up, she would have a few options. She made a reservation for a car rental in Phoenix. The shuttle was an option, but it would take longer than if she drove herself.

Luna was up at the crack of dawn, pacing the kitchen. Her flight left in three hours, and Cullen was due in thirty minutes. Why she had to arrive at the airport two and a half hours ahead of her flight time was a mystery. The Asheville airport was nowhere near the size of other airports. The security line could not possibly be very long. But then again, people moved slower in this part of the country. Cullen arrived on time, and Luna gave Wylie big hugs and told him to "be a good boy for Uncle Cullen." He woofed back that he would behave.

Things went smoothly at the airport, taking less than fifteen minutes to check in and clear security. Now all she had to do was wait—something she was never comfortable with.

The flight was half full, and Luna had a row of seats to herself. She began to read a book, and before she knew it, they were landing in Atlanta for a thirty-minute stopover. She took the opportunity to step off the jet and stretch her legs in the waiting area. She was relieved she didn't have to run through the massive Atlanta airport to change planes. The place was bustling, and it would be easy for anyone to become confused and disoriented if you weren't familiar with the biggest transportation hub in the country. It serviced more passengers than any other airport and had held the title of busiest airport for over twenty years. While being the busiest, it was not the biggest, dwarfed by Denver, Dallas, Orlando, and Dulles.

They called her flight, and Luna returned to her seat, but for the second leg of the trip, she had a seatmate. One of those who couldn't shut up. She thought the next four hours were going to be torture. She snickered when she recalled the *Seinfeld* episode when Elaine pretended she was deaf so she didn't have to speak to the limo driver. But that wasn't going to work; Luna already had said, "Hello." She asked the flight attendant for a pillow, hoping her seatmate would get the hint. No such luck. Luna sighed and pretended to be a good listener.

The flight arrived on time in Phoenix. Luna made a beeline to the baggage claim and then hustled to the car rental agency. She punched in Gail's address. The clock said it would take two hours and twenty minutes to get there. *Ha. That's what you think.* She couldn't wait to get on the open highway, roll down the windows, and sing her lungs out to whatever was playing on the radio.

She drove north on Interstate 17 and exited at Route 179, where the Red Rocks loomed in the distance. It was truly awe-inspiring. Spectacular. As she drove, Luna recalled some of the local history she'd read up on.

One hundred sixteen miles north of Phoenix and 110 miles south of the Grand Canyon sat Sedona, Arizona, known as the southern gateway to Red Rock Country. The legends of the area's mystical powers had been widely known for decades. It was also a haven for artists and nature lovers alike.

The waters of Oak Creek had carved the deep canyon of scarlet, amber, pink, and rose into rock formations with names like Cathedral Rock, Bell Rock, and Devil's Bridge. There were many interesting formations, but only a few were deemed "vortexes," places that radiated a specific and particular energy. The four best known Sedona vortexes were Airport Mesa, Cathedral Rock, Boynton Canyon, and Bell Rock. Luna had spent one of her birthdays at Airport Mesa, and a summer solstice at Bell Rock. She could attest to their unique vibrations—but then again, this was Luna, a woman with extraordinary and inexplicable perception.

Years before, circa 700 A.D., prehistoric Hohokam and Sinagua Indians built sheltered communities in the canyon walls. The vista from these cliff dwellings gave the inhabitants a vast overlook of the plains and desert that stretched for miles and miles, below and beyond. During one of Luna's past visits, she and Gail had climbed through a network of cliff dwellings where age-worn paintings were faded on the stone. The ghostly ruins marked the settlers' disappearance, but there was no clue as to their sudden departure. The mystery remained unsolved. Luna had received a very disturbing feeling as they wandered through the maze of stone dwellings, imagining living on the edge of the cliff.

Then they came to a spot where Luna felt violence and terror had occurred, and she urged Gail that they should leave as quickly as possible. Later, Gail admitted she'd had a similar experience once before, but she chalked it up to acrophobia, her fear of heights. The place wasn't outfitted with ropes and railings like a normal tourist attraction, so it was totally possible for one to literally fall from a cliff. The visit had been an interesting experience, but one Luna wouldn't want to repeat.

In the late 1800s, settlers arrived, and in 1902, Theodore and Sedona Schnebly opened the first post office. A steep, unpaved route from the north was named after the family. Schnebly Hill Road was breathtakingly scenic, with drops of more than 2,000 feet from a wooded mesa into the fairyland of Sedona. Gail had informed Luna that the road was used for many Jeep commercials. "And we are in a Jeep! No worries; I'll get you home safe!" As they had bounced their way down the rough terrain, Luna noticed a sign indicating that the road was closed between the months of November and March. It was terrifying in the summer. She could only imagine how treacherous it could be in the winter. She had to admit it was a glorious view, but she wouldn't sign up to do it again.

Gail promised no heart-stopping adventures this time around. In addition to delving into Sedona's art world, they would spend time restoring their spiritual, mental, and physical well-being. All good things. This was where Luna knew she needed to be at this moment in her life.

She pulled into Gail's driveway, where she was greeted by a Bernese mountain dog named Max. "Hey, Max! Remember me?" He bowed down on his front paws. "You do!" She gave him a hug and a cuddle.

From the distance, Luna heard a voice say, "What about me?" Gail came running from the front door. "Sweetcakes!" She threw her arms around Luna and rocked her back and forth. "Look at you! All grown up!" Gail stood back and eyed Luna's new appearance.

"What do you think?" Luna asked.

"I. Love. It!" Gail was animated. "I can't believe you're here. In the flesh!"

"Me either. Ellie couldn't have picked a better time for me to make this trip."

"Oh? Do tell." Gail put her arm around her pal and walked her into the house. "Robert wants to say hello. He's got a session tomorrow, and the driveway will be jammed with vehicles, so you can follow me. It's just a few minutes away."

"No problem," Luna responded.

Robert was a music producer who worked mostly on commercials. He and Gail had met in Los Angeles several years ago when she was a studio musician. Gail was one of the few people who could play a ukulele, guitar, piano, *and* sing backup. She was talented and reliable and had steady work, with Robert calling on her frequently. After several months of working together, they went out to celebrate Gail's birthday. It turned romantic, and they got married. During a trip to Durango, they stopped in Sedona and fell in love with it. Robert was able to set up a studio in their house, where he and Gail continued to work together on jingles. Luna admired their relationship and the gamble they'd taken to uproot themselves from Tinseltown. Los Angeles had lost its charm for them. The influx of celebrity wannabes with little or no talent, the regurgitated television shows, and the superficiality had been wearing thin. It was a leap of faith, and it paid off. Gail continued to give all the credit to Sedona. "This place just called to us. We responded."

Luna knew exactly what Gail meant. "Most people get messages but ignore them, and consequently, they live frustrating lives wondering when it's going to be their turn to flourish."

"I hear ya," Gail remarked.

"It's fear. Fear of change. Even if change could possibly improve their lives, it's still change, and change is scary."

The two went on to discuss the workshop they'd once attended conducted by Shakti Gawain. She had everyone write down what their dream job or situation would be. After a few minutes, she had them write down what was the worst thing that could happen if they pursued those dreams. She asked them to read their responses over a few times. Then she asked them to write down, *What is worse than that?* It was a real eye-opener. Really, what was worse than losing your savings? You could always get more money. But your health? Your life? Unless it was a threat to your physical and mental well-being, why not take the risk? If people didn't take risks, they would still believe the world was flat.

"I really enjoyed that workshop," Luna mused. "I feel as if it set me on the right course. I have to admit, it's still dicey trying to discuss metaphysics with people. A *lot* of people. I used to be defensive about it. Now I toss some science at them. You know, stuff like, 'we only use a small portion of our brain.' Then I throw in a dash of quantum physics." Luna chuckled. "That usually stops them in their tracks. Their eyes glaze over, and they change the subject."

Gail laughed out loud. "Love it!" They came around the circular driveway in front of the house.

"Wow. So much has grown since I was here." Luna marveled at the succulents and trees.

"My hobby. Keeps me off the police band radio," Gail chortled.

Luna and Gail left their purses and tote bags in the

entry and walked down a hallway that led to a patio. On the other side was a small building slightly larger than the size of a two-car garage. The exterior matched the main house and was beautifully landscaped courtesy of Gail, a woman of many talents. "The place looks beautiful," Luna exclaimed, noticing the different varieties of succulents.

"Thanks. I think I'm almost done." Gail led the way.

"What do you mean, 'almost done'? It looks pretty done to me." Luna could not see anything that looked unkept, undone, or out of place.

"I want to add a few more things, but that can be next year's project."

"It's spectacular. I'm not used to seeing this kind of plant life except at a greenhouse."

"I'm thinking about making tabletop succulent gardens and selling them."

"That's a brilliant idea."

"Yeah, I need to keep myself busy when we're not recording, or I can get myself into too much retail trouble." Gail laughed.

"I totally get it."

Gail opened the door that led to a small lounge area with soundproof glass that separated the engineer booth and the recording area.

"This is amazing," Luna said with admiration. "You were just beginning to build this the last time I was here."

"Yeah, it was getting a little crowded in the spare room, so I put on my shop apron, grabbed a hammer, and went to work," Gail replied.

"You are amazing," Luna gushed.

"It was either me working on this or having to rent a

space. This was the best option. Now if we get musicians from out of town, they can stay at the B&B."

"You are brilliant." Luna was truly in awe of her friend.

"More than anything, Robert and I wanted to stay here, so we did whatever it took to make it happen."

"I'm so happy for you." Luna smiled.

"Thanks, sweetcakes."

A minute later, Robert came out of the engineering booth. "Luna, you lunatic! Wow! You look terrific! I would never have recognized you. How are you doing?" He gave her a big bear hug.

"I'm just dandy, especially now that I'm here. The place is amazing."

"I have to thank my general contractor." He jerked his thumb at Gail. "My only concern was that she might jam her fingers, and then I'd be out a ukulele player."

"You get a lot of calls for that?" Luna grinned.

"Believe it or not, we do. Lots of island-themed stuff these days, especially for tourist destinations."

"Huh. I never would have thought of that."

"Come, I'll give you the sixty-second tour." He walked her through the engineering booth. "Luckily, times have changed, and we don't need such massive equipment."

"I can see that. I remember those big two-inch reels."

"You weren't born yet!" Robert laughed.

"Yeah, but I know what they looked like!" Luna chuckled. "This is great, Robert. It's very inspiring."

"Building your own recording studio?"

"No, taking your talent with you and being able to thrive."

Gail put her arm around Luna. "This is why I love her." She turned to Robert. "We're going to head over to the B&B and then grab something to eat. Do you want to join us?"

"I'd love to, but I have to finish some edits and transmit them tonight. But you girls have fun."

Gail gave him a kiss, and the two women walked back to the house, where Gail retrieved a small overnight bag. The B&B was less than a ten-minute drive from their house, which made it very convenient for guests, traveling musicians, and paying tourists. It had been a "tear-down" cottage when Gail had the bright idea to buy it and renovate it. At first, Robert didn't think it was a very sound investment, but Gail took control and pulled it together. Luna knew that was one of the reasons she and Gail were besties. When it mattered, both of them took command.

Luna followed Gail's Jeep around the circle, made a few turns, and then soon pulled in front of the renovated two-bedroom cottage. The front yard was filled with indigenous plants and rocks.

"Low maintenance," Gail pointed out. "Grab your stuff and follow me."

The front door opened to a main room with a regular-sized kitchen on one side, separated from the living space by a long cabinet. The opposite side of the living area had built-in cabinets that hid a large-screen television. A sliding glass door led to a small patio surrounded by more indigenous plants. The two bedrooms were opposite the kitchen with an adjoining bath.

"This is great, Gail!" Luna took in all of her friend's handiwork. "I can see why you don't want to lay another piece of tile or brick again."

"I'm using the ukulele as my excuse to avoid all future renovations."

Luna laughed. "I don't blame you. It's a lot of work, don't you think?"

"Do I ever!" Gail laughed. "Let's put our stuff away, and then we can go to Enchantment and watch the sunset over the Kachina Woman." Gail was referring to a rock formation overlooking Boynton Canyon that resembled the mythical Hopi spirit. "Oh, and it's a full moon tonight!" Gail whooped.

"Perfect!" Luna was ecstatic. In some odd way, she always felt as if she had come home when she visited Sedona. Perhaps in a previous life.

Luna freshened up from her long journey and changed her clothes. Tonight, it was going to be her regular jeans, a tank top, and her denim jacket. Even though it was June, it still got chilly at night in the desert.

They hopped into Gail's Jeep Grand Cherokee. "Huh. I just realized Chris has an SUV just like this, but his is silver," Luna commented.

"Well, you know I have to have a red car. For the Red Rocks!" Gail laughed.

On their way to Enchantment, Luna began telling Gail about Chris's promotion and filing for full custody.

"Are you ready to be a mommy?" Gail raised her eyebrows.

"As if." Luna laughed. "Carter is a good kid. We get along well. Besides, they live over two hours away, so it's not like I'm going to be packing his lunch."

"You never know," Gail taunted her. "I don't think you've been interested in anyone this much since Brendan."

Luna sucked in her breath. "Oh my gosh. With everything going on, I didn't tell you the horrible news."

"What horrible news?" Gail turned to look at her.

"He's dead." Luna's eyes filled up with tears.

"What happened?" Gail's eyes were wide as saucers.

"Nobody seems to know. There was a postage stamp-sized obit in the paper, and then a few days later, there was an obit for his wife."

"Holy cow!"

"Holy cow is right! Get this—when I looked up his name in the Hennepin coroner's office, there was no record of his death."

"That is bizarre. Could it have happened somewhere else?"

"Maybe. I know they were hoping to buy a place in St. Kitts."

"Did you check the newspapers there?"

"No. It hadn't occurred to me."

"Well, we'll do some digging on our own later. For now, let's enjoy the moon, stars, and the good energy."

"Sounds like a plan."

After they arrived at the Che Ah Chi restaurant, a hostess showed them to an outdoor table on the brick deck. The panoramic view was stunning, displaying the colorful striations on the canyon walls. "I understand why you moved here," Luna said, as she took in the magnificent view and the crisp air.

"We've talked about moving again a few times, but where would we go?"

"Good question. I often wonder where I will end up twenty years from now." Luna looked around at the other guests. Most were in their mid-fifties.

"Maybe an island paradise?" Gail grinned.

"I love where I am. Stillwell Center has given me a home. A place. You know, where I can be me."

"And I know how hard that is!" Gail was only half teasing.

The waitress came to the table and asked what they wanted to drink.

"Margaritas?" Gail raised her eyebrows.

"Only one. You know what that stuff does to me," Luna replied.

Drinks were served, and they ordered dinner, then watched the sun set behind the canyon walls. Several minutes later, a large full moon began to climb over the eastern buttes. The two friends chatted as they enjoyed the local cuisine and discussed a plan for the next day.

Gail had a list of places and artists to see. "I don't know what you want to do for breakfast, but I picked up some muffins and croissants to get us started. Coffee, of course, for the owner of Madame Namaste Café."

"Perfect."

"We'll head out to Tlaquepaque and visit Celebrations Navidad, Adorna, Cucina Sedona, and El Picaflor. Celebrations Navidad has a lot of ornaments, hence the name." Gail chuckled. "I checked their website, and there are lots of Sedona-centric items. Snowy cactus, Kokopelli, hand-carved gourds."

"Thanks for doing this." Luna reached over and grabbed Gail's hand.

"Of course! Such a good excuse for us to play! Depending on how the morning goes, we can grab some lunch there. It's a bit too hot to hike in the afternoon, but we can take a stroll as the sun goes down."

"Sounds divine."

"Oh, we should also probably stop at the grocery store after lunch. There isn't much at the B&B."

"Only if you let me buy!"

"Deal!"

They sat until the moon was fully overhead. "This is paradise. Not a tropical one, but paradise nonetheless." Luna looked toward the heavens. Even with the full moon, there were thousands of stars. She shouted when she spotted one shooting across the night sky. "Look!" The rest of the diners turned to stare at her. "Sorry. They don't let me out very often." Some of the other people smiled; some frowned. "I guess you have cranky people here, too," Luna whispered.

Gail laughed. "And they're not from around here, either!"

Luna made sure the waitress gave her the check. There was a little back-and-forth between her and Gail, but Luna won the tug-of-war.

When they returned to the B&B, Gail opened her laptop. "Let's do some investigating, Miss Marple. What was Brendan's last name again? Nelson?"

"Yes. His wife's name was Eileen."

Gail typed "St. Kitts newspapers" into the search engine. The *St. Kitts-Nevis Observer* came up. She clicked on the link. "When did this happen?"

Luna pulled out her phone and checked the notice. "January twenty-seventh."

Gail scrutinized the online site and checked for obituaries. "Whoa!"

"What is it?"

Gail turned her laptop around to face Luna so she could read:

American couple feared dead in St. Kitts due to boating accident.
No other details are available at this time.

"But it doesn't have their names." Luna stared at the two sentences. "How can we find out more?"

"That I cannot tell you. Not because I don't want to, but because it's a Caribbean island. Lots goes on down there, and unless you're going to hire a private detective, I don't think you'll get very far."

"Maybe Anthony will know more." Luna checked the time. It was past midnight on the East Coast. "This will have to wait until tomorrow."

"There's nothing you can do about it now, sweetcakes. Want to watch a movie?" Gail had decided to stay with Luna at the B&B so they could get an early start.

"Have you seen *Bad Sisters*? It's a series, but we can probably binge-watch it while I'm here. It's British and darkly funny. I'm up to the third episode but will start from the beginning with you."

"Sounds like it's right up my darkly funny alley."

Chapter Fifteen

Sedona
The Next Day

Luna was up early. Her body was still on East Coast time. She checked her watch. It was five a.m. She couldn't get back to sleep, so she powered up her laptop and did a little more digging for information about the two Americans who'd been killed in a boating accident. She swiped through website pages. Finally, three weeks after the accident was first reported, and in very small print, a headline read:

> Boating accident victims identified as Brendan Nelson and Eileen Lovecraft.

There was nothing else. No cause of the accident, and this time, it didn't mention they were Americans. Maybe the tourism board didn't want bad publicity and kept it on the down-low. She didn't remember any news coverage in the States, but then again, she hadn't been looking. She went back to the Minnetonka local news website to see if there were any updates. Zip. Zilch. Zero. It was so peculiar. She sent a text to Anthony with what she'd discovered. He replied with a frowning emoji and a question mark. The question mark reminded her of her earlier drawing. Were they related? She knew there was still nothing she could do, so she closed her laptop and shuffled into the kitchen to make coffee. The sun was beginning to show its face, and she took her mug of java and retreated to the back patio, where she could watch the colors of the day emerge.

A sense of peace flowed through her. So much had transpired over the past few weeks. This was her opportunity to hit the reset button. She closed her eyes and felt the sun wash over her face. It felt good. Warm. Safe. It was as if the canyon whispered, "Welcome home, daughter." She wondered—could she live here? Not without Chris. Not without her family. For now, she was tied to North Carolina, but she promised herself she would make more frequent journeys to this magical land.

She turned when she heard footsteps approaching. Gail had a mug of coffee in her hand. "This is delicious. I guess having a café is a plus when it comes to making the perfect cup of joe."

"I put a dash of allspice in the grounds." Luna winked.

Gail took a big whiff. "Ah, that's what it is. It's subtle."

"Yeah. Just like me." Luna laughed. "I hope I didn't wake you."

"Not at all. I'm usually up around six, but the aroma of the coffee beckoned me."

They clinked mugs. "Here's to a fabulous day!"

Gail went back into the kitchen, put the morning pastries on a tray, and brought them back outside. "I made an appointment at the spa for tomorrow afternoon. I figured we'd do Bell Rock, then more art shopping, and then have a leisurely remainder of the day."

"Sounds divine!" Luna sipped her coffee and tore off half of a muffin.

They sat in silence for a few minutes before Gail spoke. "Thanks for turning me on to *Bad Sisters*. Brilliant! I can't wait to binge the rest of it."

"I find I'm watching more international shows lately. They're more authentic. Ellie, Chi-Chi, and I were discussing this the other day. I just wish I could figure out how to cut the cable cord and just go to streaming, but the idea makes me a little nervous."

"What do you mean?" Gail asked.

"FOMO."

"Fear of missing out? But why?"

"Old habits. I turn on the TV for local news and weather. I haven't figured out how or if I can do that if I cut the cord."

"Hmm. I get it. Robert rigged something up for us so we can get the local news and major networks, but we don't have the other nine hundred stations nobody watches. Well, I guess some people do, but I don't have kids, and I don't care about every sport known to man or woman. And my Spanish isn't good enough to sit through a telenovela."

"Exactly! Maybe Robert can explain how I can do that at home."

"I am sure he can help. It's good to have a techno wizard in the house." Gail chuckled. "Although there are times when he's in the studio twenty-four-seven, and I don't see him for days." She raised her eyebrows. "Sometimes that's not such a bad thing, either." She chuckled. "Don't get me wrong. I love Robert to pieces, but too much togetherness can get on your nerves."

Luna smiled. "I don't have that problem with Chris." She sighed. "I love my freedom, but it would be nice to see him more than every other week. And now, with the new job, and the custody battle, who knows how often I am going to see him? I work most weekends."

"Honeybunch, I am sure the two of you will figure it out."

Luna nodded. "I have a feeling we will." Then her mind went back to what she had discovered earlier. She got up. "Be right back." She returned with her laptop and showed Gail the small notice identifying the victims of the boating accident.

"Oh, honey. I'm so sorry." Gail wrapped her arms around Luna. "At least you know now."

"Yeah. It still doesn't make me feel any better." She sighed.

"I know, sweetcakes. I know." Gail stood. "Come on, let's shower and get ready for our artsy adventure."

Luna smiled. "Good idea."

Later that morning, they began their mission in search of authentic holiday ornaments, starting with Celebrations Navidad. Gail introduced Luna to the shopkeeper, and Luna explained where she was from and handed him a brochure for the Stillwell Art Center.

"Yes. I am familiar with it." He spoke in a soft voice. It was hard to tell the man's age. His skin told of many long hours spent in the sun. His hair was a mix of black, gray, and white and pulled back in a braid that went down his back, past his shoulder blades. Luna tilted her head toward his back. "I used to have one of those until a couple of weeks ago. How long have you had it?"

"Many years." His eyes also told of many years of experience. Some good. Some bad. The man was not much for conversation. He was a listener. Luna could tell from her years of social work. There were talkers, and there were listeners. Although being a listener wasn't always equivalent to being understanding or comprehending.

Luna carried on. "Would you be interested in having some of your ornaments on display at Stillwell? Ellie is showcasing authentic indigenous art. Her intention is to bring more awareness and discoverability to this vast array of talent." She swept her arm, indicating the items hanging in his shop. He said nothing. Yet. "Each artist's work will be hung in the atrium. You can see the photo in the middle spread." She waited for him to open the brochure and say something. Still, nothing.

The man looked at her as if to say, "Continue," so she did. "There will be a placard in front of the displays, and people can have the opportunity to buy them."

He stared down at the brochure. "Yes. Thank you. How many items do you wish to exhibit?"

"Five or six different pieces, but also some inventory to sell."

He looked up. "I do not mass produce these items. Each is one of a kind."

"Oh, I understand. What I meant was if someone wants to purchase one, we can fill the spot with another."

"I see." He studied the photograph again.

The suspense was driving Luna nuts. She held her breath. She didn't want to be too pushy. Then she wondered if he wanted to be paid in advance, so mentioned it before it became a question. "We will gladly pay you upfront."

"What if you do not sell all of them?" Again, he spoke softly and slowly.

Luna responded with a lively reply. "Well then, all of my friends will be getting Celebrations Navidad Christmas presents."

He smiled. Finally. "How soon do you want them?"

"Not until November. Will that work for you?" Luna held her breath again.

He squinted, as if he were calculating something in his head. "I shall sell you twenty-four pieces. That is all I could manage. We get very busy over the holidays, and I am already working on items." That was the most he had said thus far. "Come back later, and I will give you an invoice." He nodded and retreated to a room in the back.

Luna and Gail gave each other a bug-eyed look. They shrugged in unison and quietly left the store.

"Isn't it curious that someone who makes such joyful things seems so somber?" Luna observed.

"There are many people like that around here. I think they carry a lot of old wounds. Wounds from the past, maybe in this life or one before," Gail said solemnly. "Remember the cliff dwellings and that chilling vibe you got?"

"Boy, do I." Luna shivered.

"It's an interesting dichotomy. The locals are very peaceful and spiritual people, and yet they often seem to be carrying a burden, something that they don't share or discuss."

"Ellie and I were talking about the Lumbee tribe when she got the idea to showcase indigenous art. They were only recognized as a tribe in the late fifties, yet they still are not recognized by the federal government, so they can't get a casino license."

"Bureaucracy," Gail huffed.

"I think it's politics for sure. But other casinos also don't want competition," Luna explained.

"As if there isn't enough money squandered on gambling. That is one of the things that will always bring in cash. Look at the billions the lottery brings in!" Gail paused. "For a very short time, Robert and I lived in Henderson, outside of Las Vegas. We thought being near an airport and entertainment was the way to go, but the energy in the atmosphere was way too much. You could *feel* it. I know *you* know what I'm talking about. Maybe it doesn't affect people who grew up there. They're used to the frenzy. But for people like us, well, we needed less delirium. We were leaving LA, which has its own unique delirium, and when we stumbled onto Sedona, we knew this was exactly where we should be."

A gentle, warm breeze drifted around them, setting off the tinkling of wind chimes, to confirm Gail's words.

They moved from one shop to another, searching for items. Luna noted all the skeleton-inscribed pieces. "It's kind of creepy for a holiday decoration, don't ya think?" She handled one of an owl, with a skeleton painted over it.

"It's the Mexican influence," Gail replied. "*Día de Los Muertos*. Day of the Dead."

"Yes. November first and second. I always light candles to honor my relatives who have passed on, but I never used skeletons." Luna cringed. "I suppose I should know all about this, but a girl has her limits. Especially when it comes to creepy stuff. I don't mean to be disrespectful or anything, considering I believe the spirit lives on. I guess I prefer to remember loved ones with skin on their bodies and recognizable features."

Gail laughed. "Good point. Shall we?" She gestured for them to move on to another shop.

Luna stopped abruptly.

"What is it?"

"That laugh. I know that laugh." She immediately turned in the direction the sound was coming from. She turned and raced toward the figure, who disappeared behind some foliage.

Gail was several steps behind. "Luna! Where are you going?"

Luna tried to keep up with the man, but he got into his car and drove off before she could see his face.

"Luna! What is going on?" Gail was huffing to catch her breath.

Luna was also breathing deeply. "I . . . I could have sworn that was Brendan's laugh."

"Oh, sweetcakes." Gail put her arm around Luna. "I know it's been a big shock, but he's gone." She turned Luna to face her and looked straight in her eyes. "I know you want to believe he's still alive, but you saw it with your own eyes this morning."

Luna heaved. "Maybe I'm losing my mind."

"Doubtful. He's been on *your* mind, so it's only natural you'd draw similarities. Come on. Let's get some lunch. How about Oak Creek Brewery?"

They took their time heading to the restaurant. Once they were seated, Luna said, "I could use a beer right now." She checked the menu. "I think I'll have the Steamboat Rock BLT."

"Ah. Bacon! Never met a slab I didn't like." Gail chuckled. But she could tell Luna was still rattled by that haunting laugh.

"Don't you think it's kind of strange that we were just talking about the Day of the Dead, and then I hear Brendan's laugh?" Luna asked.

"That's what I was talking about. Maybe he was sending you a message. He was laughing, right?"

"Right."

"Come on. You of all people. How many times have you said to 'pay attention to the signs'?"

"A zillion." Luna stared into her empty mug. "Even his gait was like Brendan's."

"I'm going out on a limb here, but I didn't see anyone or hear anyone."

Luna gave her an odd look. "Do you think I imagined it?"

"No. But I think maybe it was a message, and you should take it at that." Gail reached across the table and grabbed Luna's hand. "It's okay. Wherever he is, he knows you cared about him and you miss him."

"And there is nothing I can do about it," Luna replied.

"Exactly. So try to shake it off and think of hearing that voice as a good thing. It was a message, just for you."

Luna's eyes filled with tears. "Sometimes I think I'm losing it."

Gail's brow furrowed. "What do you mean, 'losing it'?"

"A few weeks ago, I felt haunted by something I couldn't put my finger on. I tried meditating and drawing and came up with a question mark. Then my brother had my old dresser delivered. It was almost like a wave of . . . well, that's just it. A wave of I don't know what. Not necessarily a bad wave. Fog. Fog is probably the best description. Like I've been in and out of a fog."

"Hormones?" Gail asked.

"Could be." Luna shrugged. "I don't remember ever having fog PMS."

Gail chuckled. "F.O.G.P.M.S. Fear of getting PMS!"

Luna had to laugh. "I think it's everyone's fear. Especially men. They certainly don't want to be around when it's happening."

Gail signaled for the check and asked, "Ready, Freddy?"

"Did you know that expression came from a mid-twentieth-century comic strip called *Li'l Abner*? Al Capp, the cartoonist, used it throughout the series, until it was revealed that Freddy was the local undertaker." Luna paused. "Hmm. More death stuff."

"And you know this because . . ."

"My brother. He finds all sorts of old stuff restoring old pieces of furniture. He bought a dilapidated highboy that was filled with newspaper cartoons. Filled, as in hundreds of them."

"That's kinda cool. What did he do with them?"

"Sold them to a collector, but not before he read through a bunch of them." Luna remained pensive.

"What now?"

"The death thing."

"You are going to have to stop this." Gail was trying not to lose her patience.

"Sorry. You're right. Why am I so obsessed with this Brendan thing?"

"Because it was a shock. Our minds do strange things when we are shocked. You oughta know."

"Yep." She linked her arm through Gail's. "Let's check back with, with—what was that artist's name?"

Gail gave her a blank look. "Ha. Neither of us bothered to ask. Some team we make!"

"Well, we know where he is," Luna said brightly, as they made their way back to Celebrations Navidad.

The older man was still behind the counter at the store. He looked up and nodded. No smile. No facial expression. Luna couldn't help but wonder again why a man who made such fun pieces of art would be so sullen. No one at Stillwell was like that. Sure, there were some with idiosyncrasies, like Johnny Can-Do, who didn't want to be seen in public. But he had a good reason. His face was scarred. And then there was Jennine, who, well, idiosyncratic was not necessarily an apt description. *Man-crazy* was more to the point. Luna supposed *man-crazy* could be considered a unique characteristic. But then, it was really a matter of perspective. *To each his own*.

The women silently and gingerly approached the counter as if they were entering a church chancel. Perhaps they were. It was this particular man's sanctuary.

According to science, everything has its own unique energy. An electromagnetic field of neurons, protons, electrons, and quarks interacting at various levels and vibrating in a manner that cannot be discerned by the naked eye. In Sedona, those vibrations were amplified. You could *feel* so much of the energy. It was almost palpable.

Luna was the first to speak. "Hi again."

He nodded and handed her a sheet of paper. She looked it over. It listed all the items he would provide, the prices, and delivery date. "May I put it on a credit card?" she asked.

He slid the electronic box toward her. She swiped the card and paid the 600 dollars for the ornaments, plus 42 dollars for shipping and handling. "Do you have something in particular you'd like included on the placard?" she asked.

He handed her a postcard with the name of the shop, address, and a brief description.

"Thank you." She searched the bottom of her tote and found a paperclip that she used to attach the card to the invoice. She didn't know what else to say and so held out her hand. "It was nice meeting you." She wanted to say his name, but she still didn't know it.

He shook her hand. "Elan."

Gail stifled a laugh. "Elan" meant *friendly*.

"Nice to meet you, Elan," said Luna.

"Thank you, Luna Bodman. Peace." He turned and retreated to the other room.

This time they scurried out. Luna could tell Gail was holding something in. "What?"

"His name means friendly."

"Oh stop," Luna said. "Wait here a minute." She turned and went back into the store.

"Elan?"

He came out. "Hello, Luna. What can I do for you?" This time, he was smiling.

"You can tell me why you were so dour earlier. I mean, not that it's any of my business, but you make so many pretty things."

"Many people come here to steal my ideas. I know a cactus is not original, but my cactuses are mine, and you came from another art center."

"I totally understand. I am so sorry you got that impression from me. Us."

"No. I was tired. My grandson kept us up all night. While you were gone, I looked further into Stillwell Center. It is an honor you are considering my work to be on display."

"Whew. Well, it will be an honor to have your pieces on exhibit. I promise to send you photos."

"I would like that. Thank you." At this point, his facial expression had turned to pleasure, and he smiled.

Luna extended her hand once again. "Thank you, Elan."

She was practically skipping out the door when she bumped into Gail.

"I thought I was going to have to come in and rescue you."

"I got him to smile," Luna said in a singsong way, and curtsied.

"Luna, you lunatic. You crack me up. You were not going to leave until you got that man to smile."

"Well, yeah. Especially when you told me his name meant *friendly*."

They linked arms again and made a few more stops before they returned to the car. "I think Ellie will be happy with what we found today. The artists seemed to be very enthusiastic." Luna stopped. "I just got an idea."

"Uh-oh." Gail sighed.

"No. It's good. I think Ellie might be able to swing it—what if she invited the artists to come to Stillwell? She always does events, and this would be another way of showcasing their art. They could speak about it if they wanted. The event would get so much publicity."

"Girlfriend, you are a genius. Do you think Ellie will go for it?"

"I believe she will. It will cost a little for transportation and hotels, but Stillwell will get a ton of exposure. It would be a win-win for everyone." Luna checked the time. It was almost six in Asheville. She decided to phone Ellie.

Ellie's voice was always soothing. "Hello, dear. How are things in the Southwest?"

"Great! We spoke with five artists today. All showed interest. In fact, I've already purchased two dozen pieces. I hope you don't mind."

"Not at all, Luna. I trust your judgement. That's why I sent you."

"They're handmade holiday ornaments and retail for around twenty-five dollars. They'll arrive end of October."

"That's wonderful, Luna."

"So, Ellie, I got this crazy idea. I know, I know, most of them are crazy."

"I never said that, dear," Ellie responded. "But go ahead. Tell me."

"What if we, I mean you, invite the artists to come to Stillwell. We could hold an event where people can meet the artists. Unless you think our resident artisans would be jealous. You know, that someone else is getting attention."

"That would be foolish on their part. It's an opportunity for everyone. I think it's a splendid idea, Luna. We can work out the details once we decide what other pieces we'll feature."

"Fab! Thanks for this, Ellie. I am having a wonderful time here."

"Well, make sure you come back." Ellie chuckled.

"Absolutely! We'll talk soon. Tell Cullen and Chi-Chi 'hi' for me."

"I will. Have fun. Bye."

Luna was beaming. "Yay! She went for it. This is going to be so cool." She stopped. "Maybe we can get Ellie to buy you a ticket, too? After all, you have been helping me curate. And you can stay with me and Wylie."

"I don't want to impose," Gail said flatly.

"Impose? Puh-lease."

On their way back to the B&B, they stopped at the Safeway supermarket. Gail had a list of items from Robert and needed a few things for them to nosh on at the B&B.

"I'll grab some fruit," Luna said, and headed to the produce department. She was looking through the melons when she heard that haunting laugh again. "Get a grip," she whispered to herself. When she looked up, she saw the back of a familiar head moving toward the rear of the store. Those tight black curls. The height matched, too. And he was wearing the same dark green shirt as earlier. Luna shook her head. "You have got to stop this." She took a deep breath and fidgeted with a few casabas. When Gail caught up to her, she noticed Luna's face was pale.

"You okay?" Gail touched Luna's forehead with the back of her hand. "You look like you might faint."

"Must be the heat. I know, it's a dry heat. Yeah, yeah." She wasn't about to tell Gail she'd had another Brendan sighting. It was getting out of hand. "I'll be fine. Just need some water."

"Okay. You wait here." Gail went to the refrigerator section where they kept cold beverages and grabbed a Gatorade G2. She figured Luna could use the electrolytes, even though the sugar wasn't necessarily the best thing, but this new version of the thirst quencher had less than the original formula. One of the many things Gail had learned since she'd moved was to be aware of what she was putting into her body. Her life was so rushed in LA, she rarely ate healthy meals. Now she was more conscious about maintaining a healthier lifestyle. She shrugged. "One of these won't kill her." She dashed back to where Luna was waiting and handed her the bottle. "Drink up."

"Thanks." Luna gladly took the bottle and gulped the drink down.

"You okay now?"

"Fit as a fiddle," Luna lied. She was still rattled, but she was intent on talking herself into a sense of calm.

Their conversation quickly turned to what to do for dinner. "How about steaks on the grill, salad, and some hash browns?" Gail suggested.

"Oh, yummy! Is there wine?"

"Is there wine?" Gail scoffed. "Baby, I got all kinds and colors."

"And this is why we're best friends." Luna had finally shaken off her sense of dread. Maybe there really was something to replenishing your body with electrolytes. She always went for the caffeine.

She paid for the groceries, and they got back into the car. First, they stopped at Gail's house and dropped off the supplies for Robert. Gail went out to the patio and noticed the small red light was on, indicating there was an active session in the studio. She went back into the kitchen, wrote a note, and put the perishables away.

Luna waited out front with Max. He was going on a sleepaway with them tonight. Robert was busy, so Max was lonely.

All three piled into the Jeep and headed to the B&B. Max was so happy, his tail was beating like a drum against the back seat. Luna turned. "Happy, boy?" He opened his mouth and yowled. His voice was as big as he was. Luna kept petting his head, as she and Gail sang along to "Ain't No Stoppin' Us Now" by McFadden and Whitehead.

When the song was over, Gail sighed. "I loved the music of the late seventies and early eighties. Stuff you could sing and hum. Feel-good music."

"I couldn't agree with you more. But don't get me started." Luna was about to tell her how she and Brendan would debate who were the best artists, but she stopped herself. She had to make a real effort to get him out of her head.

Next up was "She Works Hard for the Money." The two friends wailed and banged on the dashboard, with

Max howling in the background. When the song was over, they were laughing so hard, the tears were rolling down their faces. Good tears. Happy tears.

Once they reached their destination, they unloaded the groceries, Max's bed, and his bowls. Luna unwrapped the meat and salted the steaks. "Gotta let 'em rest for a half hour."

"If you say so." Gail grinned. She dug out a corkscrew and opened a bottle of pinot noir. Then she made a small platter of cheese and prosciutto. "Do you know how long I've waited for our grocery store to carry this stuff?" She waved a slice in front of Luna. "On the one hand, Sedona has gotten quite crowded since we moved here. But on the other hand, we finally have a much larger assortment of goodies."

Luna whipped the dried ham from Gail's fingers. "Never wave a slice in front of me unless you want me to steal it." Max groaned.

"Oh no, sir. You don't get any of this." Gail wagged a finger at him. She opened one of the containers and gave him a large chewy. "Here you go. This is your antipasto." He happily took the chewy and went to the door. "He likes to eat al fresco." She let him out onto the patio. "We put the stucco walls up when we started the renovation. We wanted privacy, and we didn't want to annoy the neighbors with construction noise."

"It's lovely. Don't tell me you laid all the stonework, too."

"I drew the plans and hired someone to do the groundwork. I was busy with the interior."

"What about all the plants?"

"Most of them were already here, so I just had to doll it up a bit."

Max was sitting in a shady area, enjoying his treat. "Shall we join him? The temperature should be tolerable. Unless you want to stay near the air-conditioning?"

"No. Outside is fine. I'm good." Luna picked up the tray and napkins, and Gail grabbed the wine and glasses.

They settled outside and enjoyed the sound of quiet. Luna wondered, "Does quiet have a sound?"

"Or like, if a tree falls in the forest and nobody is there to hear it, does it make a sound?" Gail tossed back.

"Well, it reverberates." Luna served herself some cheese and prosciutto. Gail poured the wine.

"To reverberating!" Gail held up her glass.

"And quiet!" Luna replied.

Gail lit the grill, while Luna made a salad and started working on the potatoes. They were bopping and weaving to the music of Earth, Wind & Fire. Max got out of the way and settled on the cool tile in a corner of the kitchen.

Gail picked up the platter of meat. "Rare?"

"Of course! It loses all its nutrients if you cook it too long."

"And this is why we're friends." Gail laughed as she returned to the patio and plopped the thick sirloins on the hot grate.

Their timing was in sync, and everything was ready within the next fifteen minutes. They decided to eat inside and watch *Jeopardy!*, each trying to outguess the other. When the question was *Known for "Boogie Wonderland,"* they both dropped their forks.

"Weren't we just dancing to that a half hour ago?" Gail flinched.

Luna chuckled. "We were, indeed. This kind of stuff

happens to me all the time. The TV talks to me. I actually keep a journal every time it happens. I'm trying to establish a pattern."

"So what do you think it means?" Gail picked up her utensils and resumed consuming the juicy beef.

"I really don't know, except I think it's a reminder to pay attention."

"Pay attention to what?" Gail asked, holding her suspended fork filled with mesclun greens.

"Pay attention to what's around you? See if it relates to anything you're doing. My ex-boyfriend Michael made fun of me. He kept saying it's just a coincidence. But my response was, 'How many coincidences can one have in a day?' A week? A year? He couldn't answer me. So I broke up with him." Luna sniggered.

"You did not. I mean you didn't break up with him because he couldn't answer your question."

"It was part of the whole 'Luna/lunatic' thing. He tried to convince me I was a bit off, and not in a funny, kind of nice way. Now, to be fair, I know I'm different, but I'm not *off*. I figured if he had no interest in pursuing the possibilities, then I was wasting my time."

"I know what you mean. It's difficult to have a debate with someone who has already made up their mind."

"Exactly. It's like trying to push a string." Luna wiped the juice from her lips. "He was an arrogant dude."

"When did you date him?"

"Right after college. I was attracted to his brilliant intellect. He may have carried a wealth of information, but I could go to the library for that. I didn't need someone to belittle what I believed in."

"Sounds manipulative." Gail took a sip of her wine.

"Very controlling. At one point, he tried to convince me I should see a therapist."

"Ha! That's funny, considering you majored in psychology."

"Well, according to him, psychology is playacting. Only psychiatrists really know how the mind works."

"I take it that was his profession?"

"Yep. He was a resident at the local hospital. That's how we met. I was working with some kids who were in the system."

"How long did that relationship last?"

"About five minutes," Luna said with a straight face. "Seriously, about three months. Even Cullen didn't like his attitude, and you know he's pretty mellow about most people."

"True. How is he doing?" Gail dug into another helping of potatoes.

"Great. He and Chi Chi have developed a nice relationship. I should say that he's in love."

"Oh, good for him," Gail cooed. "I always liked him, not as in like-like, but he's a good guy. I enjoyed it when he visited us at school and would take us out to dinner."

"He's a good sport. And he loves Chris. They're pals. They went to a car show together a couple of weeks ago. Cullen is thinking about adding classic-car restoration to his repertoire."

"I would love a classic car!" Gail squeaked.

"So would Chris. He had his eye on a 1959 red Thunderbird."

"Oooh. I like the sound of that."

"I thought you would." Luna grinned. "Personally, I prefer the robin's-egg blue."

"That's nice, too."

"He really seemed genuinely interested, so I suggested maybe it could be a project for him and Carter. Carter's twelve. It could take about five years to refurbish one, and then Carter would be able to drive it. Chris thought that would be a great motivator."

"Very good point."

"I'm full of them." Luna laughed and helped clear the table and do the dishes.

They decided to turn in early. Luna's jet lag was waning, and she wanted her body to be in the right time zone. Plus, they were scheduled to get up before the sun and head out to Bell Rock.

Chapter Sixteen

Sedona
The Pursuit

Gail tiptoed into Luna's room, carrying a mug of coffee. She whispered, "Good morning, sunshine."

Luna stretched and yawned. "What time is it?"

"Ten minutes to five." Gail handed her the coffee. "I hope it's okay. I tried using a dash of allspice and cream."

Luna took a whiff of it. "Smells good." Then she took a sip. "Not bad for an amateur."

"Ha. Come on. Shake a leg. We've got a sunrise to catch."

They put on denim shirts, long pants, and hiking boots. Gail stuffed two pairs of cotton gloves with grips on the palm side into her back pocket. "Just in case we need to grab onto something." She handed Luna a small flashlight.

Gail knew they would be back at the B&B before it got blazing hot, so their attire was appropriate for climbing the ledges early in the day.

When they arrived at the foot of the butte, several cars were already parked nearby. "Not an original idea." Luna chuckled.

They walked along a path that took them to the famous vortex and began to ascend the sandstone monument one plateau at a time. It didn't require climbing hand-over-hand, but it did require some balance.

They passed several other people nestled against the rock formation and kept moving until they found an unoccupied area. The two women settled down and waited for the landscape to come alive. It was more than watching the sunrise. The scenery changed colors, glowing gold and crimson, and the sounds of awakening birds captivated the soul. It was probably one of the most peaceful experiences anyone could ever have.

Neither woman spoke a word. They remained in a place of internal serenity for almost a half hour as the sun came into full view. Intuitively, they both stood at the same time, knowing each had been renewed. They silently walked back to the car.

Once inside, Luna sat back and let out a huge sigh. "That was incredible. How often do you do this?"

"Not often enough," Gail replied.

"I guess it's like New Yorkers who've never gone to the Empire State Building. You know it's always there, but for some reason, you never get around to it," Luna offered. "Although the energy is certainly different."

"That's for sure." Gail started the engine, and they went back to the B&B to change into lighter clothes. They had a couple more shops to visit, and then it was off to the spa.

The spa was situated next to a rapidly running creek. In the distance was another vista of red rock formations. The scent of piñon filled the air, mingling with the gentle music of a Native American flute. As soon as you entered, you could feel the stress begin to melt away.

The hostess showed them to a changing room and gave them turbans for their hair and plush robes. She showed them where they could store their personal things and gave them keys for the wooden lockers. She walked them out to the terrace, where a warm effervescent tub awaited them. "I'll leave you to your privacy."

The two disrobed, stepped into the healing waters, and rested on seats so their bodies were submerged up to their necks. Groans of delight emanated from both of them. Soft pillows were strewn around the edge so they could lie back and be surrounded by the restoring waters.

"How long do you think we can stay in here before we turn to stew?" Luna asked.

"They'll come out and get us. They don't want to have to call the coroner's office," Gail grunted.

"I suppose you don't do this very often, either?" It was only half a question.

"Same as Bell Rock. Not often enough." Gail moved her arms in rhythm with the water.

"We need a lecture in self-care." Luna sighed. "We preach it, but do we do it? Nope. At least not enough, in my book."

"I couldn't agree with you more. We are the 'always doing something for somebody else' girls," Gail noted. "Not that I'm complaining or whining, but you're right. Self-care is not being selfish."

"Let's be sure we remind each other." Luna gave her a high-five on her soon-to-be prune-like hand.

Twenty minutes later, the massage therapist appeared and signaled it was time for their massages.

"Well, I think I'm parboiled right about now anyway," Luna said, as she pulled her naked body from the bubbling water.

Luna had signed up for a ninety-minute energy balancing treatment while Gail had ordered a deep tissue massage. By the time they were both done, they were mush. The two had staggered back to the car when Gail's phone pinged. It was Robert, asking if she could stop by Whole Foods and pick up some more fruit. The musicians were on a natural sugar high. She held back from groaning and agreed. The store was on the way home, anyway.

They pulled into the parking lot, and Gail asked if Luna wanted to wait in the car. She replied, "If you don't mind."

"Be right back."

Luna leaned against the headrest, but then shot up like a jack-in-the-box. It was him! Again! The same dark-haired guy with Brendan's gait. He was wearing what looked like the same green shirt. She pulled out her phone and snapped a photo of him as he got into a truck with CANYON FARMS stenciled on the side. She enlarged the photo on her phone. It had to be him, or his twin. She started to shake. Too bad Gail wasn't in the car, or Luna would have asked her to follow him. But then again, maybe Gail would think she had totally lost her mind. She decided she wouldn't say anything to Gail for fear of starting an argument. Luna knew she was sounding like a woman obsessed. She also knew she wasn't hallucinating. If it wasn't Brendan, then she would let it go. But what if it *was* Brendan? What would she do?

Luna saw Gail exiting the supermarket and tucked her phone into her bag.

"Melons! Lots and lots of melons. That's all Robert seems to want lately." Gail shrugged. "If it makes him happy. At least he got off the chips."

Luna was trying valiantly to hide her anxiety about the mystery doppelganger. Seriously, what if it *was* Brendan? What on earth would she do? She took in several deep inhales. "Today was fabulous. Incredible. Divine."

"I don't know if I would have scheduled a day like this for myself if you hadn't come out here."

"Me either." Luna yawned. "What should we do about dinner? Takeout?"

"I have a favorite hole-in-the-wall Tex-Mex place. Husband and wife. Both have Mexican parents, but they grew up here. Great food."

"Sounds good to me." Luna's stomach growled. "Sounds good to my stomach, too." She laughed nervously.

Gail sensed something was up with Luna. Maybe it was all that relaxation. She decided to let it go. For now. Gail pushed the button for her cell phone's voice prompt. "Phone Lobo and Leela."

The mechanical voice replied: "Calling Lone Star Leaf Blowers."

"Ugh! Cancel. Cancel," Gail yelled into the center of the steering wheel. "Geez, why doesn't that woman listen?"

Luna cracked up. "I say the same thing. It's embarrassing when you can't stop the call before it rings through. Then they call you back and ask if everything is okay," Luna huffed. "I tell them my phone doesn't understand me."

"Yeah. So much for AI. That's why it's artificial. Like sweetener. It ain't the real thing," Gail pointed out.

"For sure. It's like those imitation burgers. They taste pretty good, but still not the same."

Gail handed Luna her phone. "They're in my contact list."

Luna obliged, and a cheerful voice came over the car speakers. "Hola, Gail!"

"Hola, Leela. How are you?" Gail asked in a similarly cheerful tone.

"Very good. Thank you. And you?"

"*Muy bueno*. I'm with a friend, and we want to pick up some dinner to take out. Can you give us the usual?"

"Guacamole, queso-filled peppers, smothered enchiladas, chicken with tortillas. Do you want corn bread, too?" Leela asked.

"Sure. Why not?" Gail looked at Luna and smirked. Luna licked her lips. Gail continued, "And can you pour us a batch of that spicy watermelon refresher?"

"Of course. How soon do you want it?"

"How soon can we get it?" Gail laughed.

"Twenty minutes?"

"Make that thirty," Gail replied.

"Okay."

"Perfect. See you then." Gail hit the END CALL button. She then began the five-minute drive to Airport Mesa, another well-known vortex in Sedona. "I think it's only fitting we go to one more vortex before the day is over."

"Cool."

"We don't have to get out and hike to get the vibe."

"Good, because I don't think my body is up to it. My legs feel like spaghetti. That massage was amazing. I didn't realize how out of balance my energy was." Luna chuckled.

"I didn't realize that not only do I live among the Red Rocks, but I had a few in my neck and shoulders." Gail laughed.

"Today was amazing," Luna repeated. "Thanks for arranging it."

Airport Mesa was said to have an uplifting, masculine energy field, and was considered one of the four major vortexes. If one climbed to the top, it was possible to get a 360-degree view of Sedona. But for this trip, the girls would skirt around the formation. Gail knew a back road that her Jeep could scale. It was little-known. Gail looked at Luna. "Kinda like *Fight Club*."

"Ah. You mean rule number one?"

"Precisely." Gail was referring to the movie in which members were not allowed to discuss their secret club. "You realize not everyone knows what that means."

"Yeah. Pop culture, underground lingo. It's interesting that so many expressions are from movies and TV shows."

"Imagine if you had to pay money to quote a TV show in conversation?"

"How would they be able to quantify it?"

"Don't you know about those chips they want to put in our heads?" Gail raised her eyebrows.

"You're not serious?" Luna paused. "Are you?"

"It isn't that farfetched. One celebrity billionaire's company has been given federal approval for clinical trials with humans."

"Oh, that's just swell," Luna huffed. "I heard about it, but I never delved into it. Too creepy."

"I don't know why they want to create robots and AI. Just plug *us* in, and we'll do everything automatically."

Luna shivered. "I think this is why I'm happy in my own little world of Stillwell. Sure, I interact with people, but I'm not a news junkie. I recoil when I see the same blathering faces on TV."

Gail looked over at her. "That's my girl. And I agree. Electronics and technology have taken over our lives. At least they're trying to." Her voice got louder. "No wonder people feel so dehumanized. It's really happening!"

Gail looked around for a place to park. "Can you manage to get out of the car and walk about a hundred yards?"

"That I can do." Luna unbuckled her seat belt and slithered out of the car.

They couldn't see the entire vista from their vantage point, but they could feel the energy emitted by the rocks that stood before them.

Luna placed her hand on the first spot that was within reach. "Electromagnetic energy. It's so fascinating."

"How true. Sedona is known for it, but sometimes I

wonder if half the people who live here actually align with it."

"What do you mean?" Luna asked.

"Maybe it's because a lot of people moved here because it's beautiful, and relatively accessible, but they're not necessarily interested in the spiritual aspect," Gail explained.

"I suppose a jerk is a jerk, no matter where they are."

Gail howled. "Thank you for saying that. Sometimes I think I am being unkind if I think of someone as a jerk. I should be better than that."

"You're only human." Luna smiled. They turned and walked back to the car. "Smothered enchiladas are calling my name."

It was a quick drive to the restaurant, where Leela greeted them at the door. "Your order will be out in a minute."

Luna grabbed for her wallet, pulled out a credit card, and handed it to the woman. "Do not take her money. It's counterfeit," Luna joked.

Gail shook her head. "I wish you'd stop doing that."

"Listen, girlie, you have been a wonderful hostess and tour guide. It's the least I can do."

"If you insist, but I'm buying the beer."

"Deal!"

Gail stopped at a convenience store to pick up a six-pack of Pacifico, and then they headed back to the B&B. Luna unpacked the food and beverages while Gail set the table. Max gave her a forlorn look. "Sorry, buddy. This is too spicy for you. I've got something better." She opened a can of his favorite food and put it in his big bowl. If a dog could shrug, he would have before he begrudgingly sauntered over to his dinner.

The women chatted about books, movies, and music and watched a few more episodes of *Bad Sisters* before they called it a night. It had been a long but wonderful day, and they were ready to hit the sheets.

Once Luna was in her room, she pulled out her laptop and searched for Canyon Farms. The home page declared: *Locally grown produce delivered to your door*. She wrote down the address and checked her map app. It was about twenty minutes outside of Sedona. They opened at seven a.m. Luna set her alarm for five thirty. Her plan was to leave a note telling Gail she was going for a drive and would be back soon. As exhausted as she was physically, she could not turn off her brain. The idea that she might come face to face with her friend was both alarming and exciting. She rehearsed what she was going to say over and over. "Hey, Brendan. Remember me? Remember *you*? What happened? What are you doing here?" But what if it wasn't Brendan? "Duh. My mistake." She tossed and turned and punched the pillow, the same way she had a few weeks before.

Luna didn't know how long she had been staring at the ceiling, replaying her rehearsed words in her head, when the light of day began to emerge. She shot up out of bed. She didn't want to run into Gail and have to explain where she was going. Luna quickly put on her jeans and a shirt and carried her shoes so as not to make any noise on the tile floor. She peeked out the bedroom door to make sure Max wasn't standing guard. He was nowhere in sight, so Luna figured he was in

Gail's room. She tiptoed across the living room and left a note on the dining table:

Hey, honey pie. Was up early. Went for a drive.
Be back soon.
XO

She quietly opened and closed the door, then stealthily crossed the gravel driveway in her stocking feet. As soon as she got in the driver's seat, she put on her boots and started the car. She winced, hoping the sound wouldn't wake up Max or Gail. She backed out of the driveway, keeping an eye open for any movement from inside the house.

She put the address in the GPS. The map said it would take twenty-five minutes. It was only five thirty, so she had an hour to kill. Maybe stopping at Cathedral Rock would be a good idea. It was on the way to the farm. Its aura could strengthen her resolve, especially since it was considered an uplifting energy. It was a very steep climb, and she had no intention of navigating it. Simply being near the magnificent rock formation would be enough to give her a boost of courage.

Luna parked the car and walked as close as she could before the trail began for the long climb. She sat on the stump of an old tree and meditated, asking for the courage to complete this pursuit so she could finally lay her concern to rest. A half hour passed, and she returned to her car. She still had time on her hands. It was excruciating. She decided to drive to the farm and wait there. The closer she got, the more her body trembled.

A wooden sign with the words WELCOME TO CANYON FARMS greeted her as she steered with quivering hands. She took a deep breath and began the quarter mile drive toward the building. Even though it was before seven, it looked as if there were people already working. She noticed there were three trucks similar to the one she'd spotted the day before, and everyone was wearing green shirts. What she didn't notice was another car on the property with someone inside snapping photos.

A young man walked over to Luna's vehicle after she had parked. "Morning, miss. We don't open for another few minutes. Anything I can help you with?"

She hesitated and took a deep breath. "Actually, I'm looking for an old friend from college. His name is Brendan Nelson."

The young man squinted. "Nobody by that name works here."

Luna pulled out her phone and showed him the photo she'd taken the day before.

"Oh, you mean Boyd Wilson?" the young man asked.

Luna laughed nervously. "We called him Brendan in school." She wasn't sure if that was a good recovery, but the young man didn't seem to question her. "Let me go see if Boyd is around. Be right back."

"Boyd Wilson," she whispered out loud. "Huh. Well, if it isn't Brendan, then he surely has a twin."

A few minutes later, Brendan's body double came around to the driver's side of the car. He didn't recognize her at first.

"Brendan. It's me. Luna." Tears started to well up.

He went pale. "Luna. You can't be here."

"But why? What happened?" she pleaded.

"Luna, please. Get out of here. Do not tell anyone you saw me. You have to go."

"But . . . but . . ." She was sputtering.

"Please, Luna. Just go." His voice was stern, almost harsh.

"Okay. Okay." She started her car and drove off the property, more tears streaming down her face. "Why? Why? Why?"

As she exited, she didn't notice a second car that had been parked on the other side of the entrance. When she returned to the B&B, Gail was reading a newspaper with the television on in the background. "Hey, *chica*. Where were you off to so early this morning?"

Luna looked pale. "I . . . I . . . went out to Canyon Farms."

"Canyon Farms?" Gail looked very confused. "Why?"

Luna sat down across the table and let out a long breath. "Don't be mad, but when you were in the grocery store yesterday, I thought I saw Brendan again, this time getting into a truck. I took a photo." She scrolled through her phone and showed Gail the picture of the man Luna claimed was her friend. "I just couldn't stand it. I had a feeling it was him, and it *is* him."

Gail almost dropped her coffee mug. "Holy guacamole. Wow. But why? How? What?"

"When I got to the farm, I asked if Brendan Nelson was there. A young guy said no one by that name worked at the place. Then I showed him the photo. He said the guy's name was Boyd Wilson."

"And then?" Gail's eyes were like saucers.

"And then the kid went and got Boyd. He didn't

recognize me at first, but then told me to go away, I shouldn't be there, blah, blah, blah. He was almost mean about it."

"How long did you talk to him?"

"Two minutes. Tops." Luna's eyes welled up again.

"So you didn't have a chance to ask him about the boating accident?"

"Nope." Luna twisted her mouth. "I don't know what to do."

"I think you should do nothing. Maybe he's in some kind of trouble and doesn't want to be found."

"True, but Brendan was never one for getting into trouble. I don't think he ever got a speeding ticket."

"Sweetcakes, you need to put this away. Out of your head. You can't go snooping—" Gail was cut off by a news break on the TV.

"A thirty-seven-year-old man was run off the highway just outside of Canyon Ranch. He was one of the ranch employees. By the time the police arrived on scene, the other vehicle was found abandoned, and the victim was taken to the hospital with non-life-threatening injuries. If anyone has any information regarding the accident, please contact the local police department."

Gail and Luna were frozen, holding their coffee mugs midair. Finally, Gail grabbed Luna's mug from her shaking hands. "You don't know if it was Brendan . . . Boyd . . . whatever."

"No. It was him. I just know it. We have to go to the hospital."

"Oh no, we do not," Gail insisted. "You need to leave well enough alone."

"Well enough? Well enough?" Luna's voice was at an all-time high volume. Even Max barked in response.

"Listen, if there was foul play, you don't want to go anywhere near it. There is nothing you can do except send him good vibes. If it even *is* him."

Luna began to cry. It was a waterfall of grief and relief.

"Oh, sweetie, they said it was non-life-threatening injuries. So take some comfort in knowing he's not dead."

Luna wiped her nose and face with a napkin. "I don't think I've cried this much in years."

"Old memories. Shock. Plus, you know your relationship with Chris is going to morph into something else, and not knowing what that is can bring on a lot of anxiety." Gail got up to grab a box of tissues and put a kettle on. "Tea. The Brits think it's a cure-all for everything."

Luna laughed. "That's exactly what Ellie said when I told her about Brendan's death notice."

"Tea and Brendan. Is he a Brit, by any chance?" Gail was making an effort to lighten the mood.

"Irish."

Gail laughed. "Well then, I'll make some Irish breakfast tea."

"Maybe a shot of Irish whiskey, too!" Luna joked.

"Don't tempt me. It's not even noon!" Gail laughed as she lit the gas stove. "How about we take a ride to Oak Creek Canyon, where you can walk along the river and *on* the river rocks. I don't think we did that the last time you were here."

"Sounds refreshing."

Gail served up the tea, and they watched the TV intently for any more updates on the mysterious accident. Convinced there was nothing more to be learned, they piled into the Jeep with Max in the back.

The rhythm of the briskly moving river was indeed comforting. It matched the fluid lines of the canyon rocks. Opposite in material but equal in beauty. Luna was surrounded by the nurturing layers of Mother Nature. *Everyone should have this kind of experience,* Luna thought. But despite her newfound sense of calm, she had to admit that Boyd—or whoever the heck he was—had rattled her to the bone.

Chapter Seventeen

Federal Law Enforcement Center
Glynco, Georgia
Six Hours Later

Marshal Christopher Gaines was finishing up his training for WITSEC when he got a call from his home office. "Chris, Frank here."

"Hey, Frank. I was just packing my stuff. Training went well. I'm excited about this new situation."

"Yes, I heard you did a bang-up job," Frank replied. "Listen, we have a situation. I figured it would be a good opportunity for you to get your feet wet."

"Sure. What's up?"

"The deputy director wants you to stop by his office."

"Everything alright?"

"We're not sure yet, but he has something he wants you to look into."

"Sure, boss. I'll head over right away."

Chris grabbed his gear and returned to the main office. He showed the security guard his identification.

The gate opened, and Chris drove to the visitor's parking area. It was the closest to the front of the building. By the sound of Frank's voice, it seemed to be an urgent matter.

Gaines walked down the hall to the deputy director's office. The director was standing outside, speaking to several other marshals.

"Gaines. Glad we caught you."

"Sir. What's going on?"

"We may have a breach with one of our witnesses. He was seen talking to a woman this morning, and an hour later, he was run off the road. Couple of cuts and bruises, but we have him in protective custody. His handler got word that there might have been a security breach, so he was tailing our witness to see if anyone was following him. Turns out there was another car on the premises besides the woman. He couldn't follow both of them, so he made a judgment call and shadowed the guy in a black sedan, who followed our witness. Good thing, because he was on scene when the accident happened, called it in to the local police, and the perp was apprehended." He paused to let the information sink in. "The news media is telling a slightly different story, and that's the way we want it to remain. No ID of the guy they apprehended. They're grilling him now to see how he discovered our guy.

"We don't know if they are in it together, but our agent has the person of interest in an interrogation room. We need to find this woman." He pushed a button on his laptop, and the photo of a woman's face appeared on the screen. It was a little grainy. Gaines blinked several times. He squinted and furrowed his brow. He stared at the face for several moments. *Dif-*

ferent hair. Different glasses, he thought to himself, but the resemblance was astounding. Without missing a beat, he asked, "Where did this take place?"

"Sedona, Arizona."

The words churned the bile in his stomach. He didn't want to believe it was her. *She looks so different. And why? Why would she do something like that?* He turned to the director, and without hesitating, asked, "You got a plane for me to catch?" Before he left the building, he downloaded face recognition software to his laptop. It was going to be a long flight.

Within the hour, Gaines was given instructions and who his contact person would be when he landed in Flagstaff. His mind was racing. *It's just not possible.* As soon as he got back in his Jeep, he called Luna. She answered right away.

"Hey there! What's doin'?" She sounded very chirpy.

He hadn't rehearsed what he was going to say to her. He couldn't come out and ask her if she'd been wearing a disguise earlier that day, or if she'd encountered someone in WITSEC.

"Hey, dollface. Just checking in on you." Gaines tried to sound casual.

"I'm behaving." Luna smiled. It was good to hear Chris's voice. Her encounter with Brendan had left her rattled. "Gail and I watched the sunrise yesterday at Bell Rock and then took a quick ride to Airport Mesa." She didn't dare tell him how she'd started her morning.

"Sounds energizing."

"Physically exhausting, but spiritually energizing."

Chris wasn't sure whether he should tell her he was about to board a military jet to Arizona. He decided he would wait until he got there and had more data. No sense in starting anything over the phone when he didn't have all the information. "What are you doing the rest of the day?" he asked.

"We're going to go back to the artist studios and finalize the plans for our holiday display. We found *so* many great things. I think the exhibit is going to be quite excellent."

"No doubt with you working on it." Chris thought her voice sounded normal. It couldn't be Luna in the photo, unless she was leading a double life. And wouldn't he have figured that out by now? "When are you planning on getting back?"

"Day after tomorrow. I thought I'd spend a couple more days here and enjoy more of the terrain, landscape, and the vibe. We may venture over to the Kachina Woman if we have time later. But it's a bit of a hike. What about you?"

He hesitated for a second. "I'm heading out in a little while." It wasn't a total lie. Just an omission of some very important information.

"How's Carter enjoying baseball camp?" Luna asked.

"He's loving it. I have to pick him up this weekend." Then he clenched his teeth. *What if he wasn't back in time? That meant Lucinda would have to pick him up. And the hearing was just weeks away. Swell.*

"You'll have a lot to catch up on," Luna said merrily.

"Yes, we will. You and I will, too." All sorts of things were running through his head. *Would they be catching up in a jail cell?* He shuddered. "Listen, I've gotta jump. Talk to you later tonight?"

"Sure thing. Safe travels. Love ya." With that, Luna signed off.

Chris stared at his phone. *This couldn't be happening*. The next chore was phoning Lucinda and putting her on notice that she might have to pick up Carter. Ever since she was served the papers for the custody hearing, she'd become a screaming banshee. He decided to send her a text instead. At least that way, he wouldn't have to hear her screeching voice. Not for a while, anyway. He decided to make it a group text and include Carter. She would behave much better if she knew her son was included in the communication. He texted:

Hey. I have to go out of town. Not sure if I'll be back in time. Lucinda, you might have to pick Carter up. Will keep you posted.

He could practically hear her phone exploding. Heaven forbid her schedule was tilted a bit. Not even for her son. Chris Gaines was *not* in a good mood.

Chapter Eighteen

Arizona
Face to Face

Chris boarded the military jet and settled into his seat. He dreaded opening his laptop, but he knew he had to do it. His career and his relationship were hanging in the balance. He uploaded the photo of Luna he had saved in his phone and then had it cross-referenced with the photo of the woman in the car. It took less than a minute for all the markers to match. The blood drained from his face. Think, Chris, think. There has to be a logical explanation for this.

They were the longest four hours of his life. The only upside was that Lucinda couldn't reach him. Once they landed, he was surprised to see a single text from her saying **Okay.**

Okay? Nothing was ever okay with Lucinda. She had to be up to something. His nerves were on edge, something he was not accustomed to. Another text had come in from Carter: **Okay Dad. Miss you.**

That gave him a modicum of comfort.

As Chris deplaned, he recognized the agent who was waiting for him at the gate. They gave each other a nod as Chris approached him. "Marshal Gaines? Desmond Legend. Let me grab that for you." He took charge of Chris's duffel.

"Good to meet you, Desmond. Boy, it really is hot here."

Desmond chuckled. "But it's a dry heat."

"So I've been told." Gaines grinned.

"We've got a chopper waiting to take us down to Sedona. That should get us there in about thirty minutes." The agent escorted Gaines to a golf cart that brought them to the helicopter pad on the other side of the small terminal. As soon as they boarded, the chopper was up and over the sandstone canyons. "Too bad you didn't get here early to see the scenery."

Or to stop the woman I love from getting mixed up in who-knows-what, Chris thought to himself. "Maybe on the way back," Gaines shouted above the noise of the whirring blades.

Legend gave him a thumbs-up.

Before Chris knew it, the chopper was settling down on the tarmac at the minute Sedona airfield, too tiny to accommodate anything but a small private plane. A large black SUV was waiting for them at the equally small terminal building. The driver introduced himself as Buck from the Phoenix office. "Nothing like jumping in feet first, eh?"

More like headfirst, Chris thought to himself.

"Well, now that you're fresh out of training, maybe you can finish up this job, so we can all have the weekend off." Buck shoved Chris's duffel into the back.

"That would be great. My son is getting out of base-ball camp this weekend." Chris decided to be as casual as possible. He wasn't sure if he was ready for what was ahead. In all his years of law enforcement, this was the most frightening situation he'd ever found himself in. "I don't want the ex to have to pick him up. She'll make a big stink." More idle patter.

"You too?" The driver looked up into the rearview mirror. "Must come with the job."

And a girlfriend who just might help me lose that job. Chris realized his palms were sweating. "So where are we staying?"

"Arroyo Pinion," the driver replied. "Not a spa-type resort, but not bad, either. You ever been here before?"

"Just Tucson and Phoenix. Never made it up this far."

"Wait until you see it in the daylight. It's pretty spectacular."

"So I've heard." *From my girlfriend, whom I suspect of breaching a witness.*

"You're probably hungry after your trip. I think the restaurant is still open at the hotel. We can grab somethin'," Buck suggested.

Chris's stomach was upside down. Food was the last thing he needed. "Sounds good." He had to play along. Maybe get some soup.

It was a quick drive from the airport to the hotel. The person at the front desk was an older gent with silver hair. "Welcome to Arroyo Pinion. How can I help you?"

All three men took out their fake identification. No one was to know who they really were, what they did for a living, or why they were there. Chris Gaines was now Charles Gannon, Desmond Legend was now David Lamont, and Buck was Bill Cunningham.

"I have all three of you on the same floor, as requested." The desk clerk handed them their key cards. "Enjoy your stay. If there is anything we can do to make your visit more pleasurable, please do not hesitate to ask."

Chris refrained from saying, "Can you make this nightmare go away?"

They dropped off their bags in their rooms and agreed to meet up in twenty minutes. Chris stripped off his clothes. He was in need of a shower. He smiled when he pulled out his Axe body wash and thought about taking Carter to the drugstore. He really hoped they could wrap this up in a couple of days. He missed his kid, the only stable thing in his life at the moment. And even that relationship was on shaky ground. He was in and out of the tub in less than ten minutes and then decided to give Luna another call.

"Hey! What are you doing up so late?" Luna asked, thinking he was on the East Coast, where it was midnight.

"Couldn't sleep." Gosh, how he hated to lie, but he probably wouldn't be able to sleep anyway.

"What's going on?" Luna sounded concerned.

He really didn't know what to say to her. "Just the whole custody thing," he said, which wasn't a lie.

"Is there a problem?" Luna asked.

"Not yet, but I might not be able to pick Carter up from camp, which will throw a monkey wrench into Lucinda's schedule, and she may use it against me. She'll tell the judge it illustrates what an unreliable father I am and how my job always comes first."

"I thought you were heading back today."

"I was, but something came up, and I have an assignment."

"That sounds exciting, no?"

If only. More like unnerving.

"Nah. Just some follow-up work, but it has to be done."

"Well, that's really too bad. Do you want me to get him if you can't?"

Not if you're in jail, Chris thought to himself. "Let's see how the rest of the week plays out."

"Okay, but if not you or me, than maybe Cullen," Luna said, offering up her brother's services.

"That would be good. Do you think he'd mind?"

"Cullen? Nah. He loves Carter. And they can talk about refurbishing classic cars."

"That could work." *While I find bail money and polish my résumé.* Chris was not feeling very optimistic. "Where are you now?"

"At Gail's Airbnb. I made some pasta and garlic bread."

Chris's stomach growled. Maybe he could actually eat something. "Sounds delicious."

"I've been into the lemon and herb thing lately. Gail was used to tomato sauce, but I turned her on to something a little lighter."

"You'll have to make it for me next time." *If they let inmates in the kitchen.*

"Absolutely. Not sure about the garlic bread, though. I almost burned it in the broiler. Poor Max went a little bonkers when the smoke detector started to go off."

"That bad, eh?" Chris could not fathom that this

woman he was talking to could be a double agent of some sort.

"I told Gail that while it's a good idea to have a smoke detector in the kitchen, it shouldn't be that close to the stove. She blamed Robert." Luna chuckled. There was a rap on Chris's door. "What was that?" she asked.

"Nothing. I knocked something over." Another lie. He had to get off the phone before Legend and Buck knocked louder. Chris faked a yawn. "I better go. I just might be able to sleep. I don't want to miss this window of opportunity."

"Gotcha. Sleep well. Love you." Luna signed off.

"Love you, too." And he did. Now what? He opened the door, where the two men were waiting.

"Someone smells good," Buck announced.

"I had to get the grit off me." Chris chuckled as the three men went down to the main floor.

They sat at a table far away from the smattering of people in the restaurant. Legend was the first to speak. "We have another room on the same floor that we'll set up as our workstation, since WITSEC doesn't have an office here. It's adjacent to mine so I can make sure no one else has access."

"So what do we know so far?" Chris leaned in.

"A woman named Luna Bodman was seen at Canyon Farms early this morning."

Chris thought he was going to vomit. "You have her name?" he asked as calmly as possible.

"Rental car. Either she's not involved, or she is some kind of idiot to rent a car using her real name."

"Good point." Chris knew Luna wasn't an idiot.

That was hopeful news. "Maybe she was just a friend," Chris offered. Was he supposed to tell them she was his girlfriend? If not now, when?

"It's possible. But the fact he was run off the road right after she left the farm is suspicious."

"Does anyone know her current location?" Chris asked.

"Not yet. We're checking security camera footage at the main intersections. Should have that by the a.m."

A chill went up Chris's spine. It wouldn't take long before they found out where she was. He had to get to her before anyone else did. But he still needed more information.

"What about our witness? How is he doing?" Chris queried.

"He got a little banged up. Bruised ribs. Nothing major. But he's definitely rattled."

"Do you think he'll renege?" Chris asked.

"Good question. We'll have to relocate him pronto," Legend said. "The guys in the Phoenix office are working on that now. They're going to transport him tomorrow."

"What about the guy you have in custody?" asked Chris.

"He ain't talkin'," Buck explained. "And he's here illegally, so we're trying to cut a deal with him."

"Where is he from?" Chris asked.

"Romania," Legend supplied.

"He's a tad far from home," Chris said.

"Yeah, but the Russian mob has tentacles everywhere now, between drugs, guns, and human trafficking."

"The witness. Why is he in the program to begin

with?" Chris asked. There had been no time earlier for him to be briefed. All he knew was that someone had tried to kill one of their witnesses.

"He and his wife were in the Caribbean. They rented a skiff. Out for a leisurely ride around the island. They saw something going on with another boat. One guy leaned over, and *bam*! Shot dead. The wife got a good look at the shooter. They skedaddled and notified the authorities, who were nonchalant. Evidently, this sort of thing goes on all the time. They went to the Ministry of Foreign Affairs, who put them on a plane back to Miami, where they were picked up by the U.S. Marshal Services. The wife was able to identify one of the mob's lieutenants, who was apprehended off the coast of St. Lucia. He was turned over to the FBI, where he was arraigned and faced criminal charges. With her IDing him, they were able to put him away. We, the United States Government, promised the couple they would not be in harm's way."

"Where is the wife now?" Chris asked.

"She hated the heat here and asked to be relocated to someplace where she could go snowshoeing. So we sent her to Vermont."

The waitress came over and took their order. All three ordered BLT club sandwiches. When the food arrived, Chris thought he was going to gag. He picked at his food. "Guess I wasn't as hungry as I thought. Must be jet lag." He'd blame anything at this point. Anything but Luna. At least not yet.

Chris faked another yawn and stretched his neck. "I think I need some shut eye. What time do you want to meet in the morning?"

"Eight?" suggested Legend.

"Sounds good. Room next to yours?"

"Yep. I'll order breakfast to be sent to my room. We're going to have to dig in as soon as we get the camera footage. Until we can eliminate this mystery woman, she is a prime suspect."

Chris tried to stand, but his legs were like jelly. He leaned on the table. "Long day."

"I hear ya," Legend said. "See you in the morning."

Chris managed to pull himself together before he staggered out of the restaurant. When he got to his room, he leaned against the door and slid down to the floor. He had to do something right away. He phoned Luna again.

She was half asleep. "Chris? Everything okay?"

"No. Nothing is okay. Where are you?" His voice was stern.

"I'm at Gail's. Where else would I be?" She was confounded.

"Give me the address. Please." Still stern.

"Okay." She rattled off the address. "What is this all about?"

"I'll tell you when I see you."

"When you see me? What is going on?"

"I'm in Sedona."

Luna sprang up from the bed. "You're where?"

"Sedona. The same place where you are." This was not friendly banter.

"What are you doing here?" She could hear the tension in his voice.

"I'll tell you when I get there." He realized he didn't have a car at his disposal and couldn't ask Buck; otherwise, he would arouse suspicion. After getting off the phone with Luna, Chris called the front desk.

"Hello, Mr. Gannon. How can I help you?"

"Is there a car rental agency nearby?"

"Yes. There is one about three blocks away. Shall I phone them for you?"

"No. But if you could give me the address, I would appreciate it."

"Certainly." The desk clerk gave Chris the address and phone number.

Chris called and asked if they could provide a car and could they send someone to pick him up. "One moment, sir, let me check," a pleasant voice answered him.

He looked at his watch. It was going on eleven. The woman got back on the phone. "I'm sorry, we don't have anyone to pick you up, but we do have a car. Can you get here in a half hour? We're closing shortly."

"Yes. Thanks. I'm on my way." He was grateful he was in good shape, because he had to hotfoot it ASAP. He grabbed his laptop, stashed it in a carrying case, and slung it over his shoulder. He checked the hallway and then proceeded down the four flights of stairs. When he got to the lobby floor, he peeked through the window to see if any of his colleagues were in his line of sight. All clear. He made a mad dash for the door and hightailed it to the rental agency.

He was almost out of breath when he arrived at the car rental. He made it with six minutes to spare. He pulled out his phony identification and a credit card issued to Charles Gannon. He signed the paperwork and bolted out the door. He punched in the address and tore out of the parking lot.

* * *

Luna was shaking. She had no idea what was going on. She knew this wasn't Chris surprising her. Well, it was, but not in a good way. She went into Gail's room. Her friend was still awake, reading a book. Gail looked up in surprise. "What's going on, sugar?"

"Chris is in town."

"How nice!"

"No. I don't think so." Luna looked grim.

"What do you mean?"

"He sounded rather terse on the phone. Like he was really mad about something."

"What do you think it is?" Gail sat up and shoved her reading glasses on top of her head.

"I have no idea, but he is on his way over here."

"Now?"

"Yes, now."

"Geez."

"Geez is right." Luna was pacing. "I mean he sounded horn-mad."

"And he gave you no inclination as to why?"

"Nope." Luna shook her head. "This has been some kind of a train wreck day."

"You forgot 'dumpster fire.' Come here, sweet-cakes." Gail pulled open the covers and patted the bed.

"I can't. Sorry. I have to pull it together." She continued to pace.

Several minutes later, headlights flashed across the window, and they could hear the engine of a car come to a stop. Luna was trembling uncontrollably. Gail got up and put a robe around her friend. "It's going to be okay."

"I hope so. I can't deal with any more shocking news." The two padded to the front door, with Max following close behind.

Luna opened the door. Gaines did a double take. "So it *is* you."

"Of course it's me. Who else would it be?"

He kept staring. Then she realized he hadn't seen her with her new hairstyle. "My hair!"

"And the glasses." He scrutinized her.

Gail jumped in. "Come. Let's sit down."

"Marshal Christopher Gaines." He nodded at Gail.

"Yes, I figured."

"Apologies for the intrusion, Gail, but I need to speak to Luna in private. If you don't mind." Chris's voice was steady and very official.

"Of course." Gail showed them out to the patio. The air had cooled down a bit, and it was comfortable enough for a conversation, provided the conversation didn't turn heated.

"I'll get you some water." Gail could see Chris's face was red, but she wasn't sure if it was from the heat or anger.

Luna pulled out a chair and slowly lowered herself into it. She was in flight mode. All she wanted to do was run. Run away. Run anywhere.

Chris sat across from her. He hadn't kissed her or touched her since his arrival. He was all business. They sat in silence while Gail brought a pitcher of ice water and some glasses.

When Gail was no longer within earshot, Luna asked, "Chris, what is going on?" She was almost pleading.

"Why don't *you* tell *me*?" he asked.

"Honestly, I have no idea what you are talking about. Really, Chris. Please tell me what is going on."

He pulled out the laptop and opened it. He made a

few clicks and turned it to face her. "Is this you in the photo?"

Luna's jaw dropped. She pulled the laptop closer. "Yes. It's me. Where did you get this?"

"Never mind where I got it. What were you doing there?"

"I thought I recognized someone from college."

"How did you come upon Canyon Farms?" He was interrogating her now.

"Yesterday, we were at the market. Well, actually, I thought I spotted him a couple of times these past few days. Then when I was waiting in the car, I saw him again." She got up. "Wait here. I'll be right back."

She dashed into the bedroom, grabbed her phone, and returned to where they had been sitting. "Remember when you were over at my place and you saw the Kentucky Derby program?"

"Yes, but what does that have to do with anything?"

"When I tried to reach out to my friend Brendan, he didn't respond, and none of his friends had heard from him, either. Then Anthony sent me a text with Brendan's postage stamp-sized obituary." She scrolled through her phone and showed him the announcement. "As you can see, there were no details." Then she scrolled to Eileen's obit and handed him her phone. "It was all very odd. We looked into their deaths further and found a short blurb in the *St. Kitts-Nevis Observer* about an American couple killed in a boating accident."

"You had to keep digging, didn't you?" Chris seemed more unnerved now. "Why do you always do this, Luna? Sticking your nose where it doesn't belong."

Luna snapped at him. "He was my friend, Chris! I cared about him! Why shouldn't I try to find out what happened to him? Have you ever cared for anyone and lost them? And not known what happened? You're the detective. Don't tell me you wouldn't have done the same thing!"

Gaines knew he'd struck a nerve. He also began to realize that Luna had no idea what she'd stumbled upon. "Alright. Let's start from the beginning. You were looking for information about a friend. You discovered he had been killed in an accident. Then what?"

"Then we were in Safeway three days ago, and I thought I recognized his voice, but he left before I could approach him."

"How did you end up at Canyon Farms?" He repeated the question.

Luna sighed. "When I was waiting in the car, I spotted the same guy, wearing the same shirt, and I took a photo. When I enlarged it, I knew it had to be Brendan. I saw the name of the farm on the side of the truck and took a ride out to see if it was really him."

"And that's it?" Gaines was staring her down.

"That's it. I swear. All I wanted was proof. Proof that I wasn't losing my mind." She handed him her phone. "See?"

He transferred her call log, then threw the phone on the ground and stomped on it.

Luna freaked out. "What are you doing!"

"Saving your hiney. And my job," he huffed.

Her eyes grew wide. It finally hit her. "Oh. My. Gosh."

At that point, his laptop pinged. Luna's call log came through. He looked it over several times. There were no calls out of the ordinary, in or out. He was beginning to believe her. "So what's with the hair?"

"I needed a change." She tilted her head and gave him a puppy-dog look.

"I like it." He finally smiled.

"So now what happens?" she asked.

"Now I have to corroborate your story." He picked up his phone and dialed the agent who was guarding Brendan. "Jack? Gaines here. Can you ask your person if he had any encounters with one Luna Bodman?" He paused. "I know it's late, but this is crucial to our investigation." He could hear the agent rallying his charge. Mumbled voices sounded in the background. The agent returned to the phone.

"He said they were in college together, and she stopped by the farm. He hadn't had any contact with her since before their incident. She just showed up out of nowhere, and he told her to leave."

A sense of relief flooded Gaines. "Thanks."

"Anything else I can do for you now that I'm awake?"

"No. Just get him situated to wherever he's going next."

"Will do." The agent ended the call.

"You are going to have to come to our makeshift office and explain to the other agents what happened. They're not going to take my word for it, but at least Brendan has corroborated your story, and I have your phone records. That is, provided you weren't using a burner phone." He squinted at her.

"Check the cell towers. I know you can do that." Her tone was just this side of sarcasm.

"We will do that, just as a matter of course."

"Do you believe me now?" She reached across the table to touch his hand. He pulled back.

"We have to make this a clean interview. Nothing personal."

"I get it." Luna realized she had inadvertently put someone's life in jeopardy, and she might have cost Chris his job. "I'm really sorry about all this. Truly."

His eyes softened. "I know you are." He pocketed her phone and shut his laptop. "Be at the Arroyo Pinion at nine tomorrow morning. Meet us in the lobby. Oh, and my name is Charles Gannon." He got up from his chair and went to the front door, where Max was standing guard. "It's okay, pal." Chris put his hand out, and Max gave him his paw. Luna took that as a good sign.

"See you in the morning." Chris smiled for the second time that night.

"And you owe me a new phone." Luna smirked.

As soon as the car was out of the driveway, Gail bolted out of her room. "What in Sam Hill was that all about?"

"I can't discuss it."

Gail furrowed her brow. "Is everything alright?"

"Not exactly, but it will be."

"So why is he here?"

"I can't discuss it." Luna hugged her friend. "Rule Number One."

"Ah. I get it. We don't talk about it." Gail nodded.

"Correct-o-mundo. Never. Ever." Luna clung to her friend. "Love you, pal."

"Love you more."

The two retreated to their bedrooms, but Luna knew she wasn't going to be able to sleep any time soon. It was going to be a repeat of the night before, with a whole lot of tossing and turning.

Chapter Nineteen

The Next Day
Interrogation and Explanation

Three days in a row, Luna was awake before the light of day. She wasn't sure if she'd slept at all. Reality and her whirling thoughts were intermingled, as if she were in a fugue state. At least she wasn't nervous about confronting Brendan again. Now she could be nervous about confronting the U.S. Marshal's Service. In her heart, she knew she hadn't done anything illegal. Perhaps misguided, but it wasn't due to any malice. She had all the best intentions—but as they said, the road to hell was paved with them.

She showered and decided on the cropped pants and tunic. The outfit was polished without looking as if she were going out on a date. *Some date!*

Luna skipped her morning coffee. She didn't need any more jitters than she already had. Gail offered to make her some toast, but Luna declined. Her stomach was doing somersaults.

She checked her makeup and decided to wear her

contact lenses. For some reason, they felt more natural. Gail gave her a big hug before Luna walked out the door. "Good luck, sweetcakes. I know everything is going to be alright."

Luna forced a smile. "It has to be."

At eight, Chris had a briefing with Buck and Desmond. "I was able to locate the woman in the photo. Luna Bodman."

"Impressive," Buck noted. "How did you manage that?"

Chris was trying valiantly to avoid any personal details. "I phoned the rental agency in Phoenix and got her phone number." He was half telling the truth. "That's something someone should have thought of when they identified her as the person who rented the vehicle." He looked directly at Buck.

"Good work, man," Buck snorted, ignoring Chris's offhand accusation. "You're going to make an excellent WITSEC agent."

Chris had already come to the conclusion that he was probably a better agent than Buck. Just a feeling he had. A gut feeling, as opposed to some kind of woo-woo stuff.

"I also checked with Jack, who asked the witness if he could identify her and her reason for being at the farm. According to Jack, the two went to college together, and our man had not had contact with her since the incident. He said she showed up out of nowhere, and he told her to leave and forget she ever saw him." Chris paused. "I also had her phone records dumped, and all the calls were verified to her brother and some friends. I also had the cell towers checked in this area. No unusual burner phone activity."

"So you're trying to tell us she just stumbled upon an old college pal?" Buck looked suspicious.

"I'm telling you what I know. She's meeting us in the parking lot in an hour."

"What?" Buck looked shocked. "How did you manage that?"

"I called her. Said it was of the utmost importance she meet with U.S. Marshals regarding an accident on the highway yesterday."

"And she just agreed to come here?"

"She knew about the accident. She said she had been in the area and was willing to come in and answer any questions."

Desmond put his hand on Chris's shoulder. "You are one impressive dude."

Chris grunted. "Just doing my job." *If they only knew, and I hope they never find out.*

It took ten minutes for Luna to reach the hotel. Chris and two other men were waiting in the parking lot.

"Good morning, Ms. Bodman. I'm Charles Gannon. These are my colleagues, Agent Cunningham and Agent Lamont." All three had their badges attached to their belts. "Would you mind stepping inside the SUV?"

Luna maintained a stoic demeanor. "Not at all." Desmond opened the back door, and Luna stepped up into the vehicle while the three men stood close together outside, blocking her from escaping. *As if.*

Leaving the car door open, Buck took the lead, which annoyed the heck out of Chris. "So, Ms. Bodman. Can you tell us why you went out to Canyon Farms yesterday morning?"

Luna was admirably composed. "I thought I recognized someone from college when I was at Whole Foods—or was it Safeway? Anyway, I saw him drive off in a truck with a sign for the farm. I looked up the address and drove out to see if it was him."

"How long had it been since you'd been in contact with your so-called friend?" Buck asked, with a bit of an unpleasant tone.

"It had been months. We were emailing, and then it stopped. I assumed it was because his wife was jealous." She shrugged. "Anyway, it wasn't him."

"Are you sure?" Buck peered at her intently.

She looked at Chris for a sign.

Tell the truth. He was sending telepathic thoughts to her.

She hesitated. "He told me to go away." That was the truth.

"And you said it wasn't him," Buck pushed.

"I really don't know what's going on." Another half-truth. "I don't want to get anyone in trouble, including myself."

"We already know you spoke to him."

Luna swallowed hard. "What did he tell you?"

"He said he told you to go away."

"That is correct." Luna nodded.

Chris looked at the other agents. They seemed to be inclined to believe her. There was no evidence to the contrary.

"How long are you planning on staying here?" Buck asked.

"I was going to return home the day after tomorrow." But at this point, she wanted to jump on a plane and get the heck out of Dodge, or whatever nightmare town she was in.

"You live in North Carolina?" Buck asked as he was looking at his notes.

"Yes. Just outside Asheville."

"Alright, then. Agent Gannon lives in Charlotte. If he needs any further information from you, we expect you to cooperate."

"Absolutely," Luna said convincingly. *Anything for my U.S. Marshal. If he's still my U.S. Marshal,* she thought.

Buck closed his notepad. "Thank you for your time, Ms. Bodman. If we need anything else, we will be in touch."

The three men separated, making room for her to remove herself from the car and the interrogation.

"Thank you," she replied, and walked over to her car.

"What do you think?" Gaines asked Buck.

"Everything lines up. We can cross her off the list for now," Buck said. "You all agree?"

"I got no problem," Desmond responded.

"Neither do I." Chris was more relieved than he'd thought possible. Perhaps this nightmare was over.

Luna was shaking as she put her car in drive. It appeared she'd satisfied their queries. At least she wasn't in handcuffs. She went to reach for her phone and realized she no longer had one.

Gail was pacing the floor when Luna returned. "How did it go? What did they ask you?"

"It went okay, I think. Well, I'm not in jail, so I suppose that's a good sign." Luna flopped down on the sofa.

"What can I get you?"

"How about a Bloody Mary?" Luna chuckled. "It's five o'clock somewhere."

Chapter Twenty

The Days That Followed

The three agents returned to their conference room in the hotel to wrap up the investigation. Mystery woman: Identified. Interaction: Minimal. Threat assessment: None. Witness: Relocated. Status: Situation Resolved.

The men packed their bags and checked out of the hotel. Buck shook hands and said his farewells, and Desmond drove Chris to the airfield, where a helicopter was waiting to take him to Flagstaff. A military plane would bring him back to Glynco, Georgia, where he'd left his vehicle. If there were no delays, he'd be landing in Georgia around 8:30 p.m. Once he arrived, he'd decide whether he wanted to make the four-hour drive to Charlotte. At the moment, he couldn't decide if he was jazzed or exhausted.

The chopper ride would take just over thirty minutes, but the jet wasn't going to be there for an hour and a half. Desmond instructed the pilot to "give him the tourist version."

Gaines was awestruck at the panorama below. The contrast between forest and desert and rock formations was stunning. One could only imagine the changing landscape over the centuries. Millenniums. Such a mysterious and evocative place. There was no doubt it had an inexplicable energy of its own. It came as no surprise that Luna was drawn to it.

As he gazed at the scenery, he let out a sigh of relief. At least his girlfriend wasn't a hitman. And, in his personal experience, she wasn't a liar. She wasn't one in his professional experience, either. He had to play this through. No contact until they were both back in North Carolina, unless it was about her involvement in the case, which seemed to be little. He had to admit, it was a bizarre coincidence, even for someone like Luna. *What were the odds?* he thought again. It was uncanny.

Luna and Gail sat on the patio before it became unbearably hot.

Gail let out a bit of a whine. "I wish you'd stay another day."

"Haven't I caused you enough excitement?" Luna chuckled. "It's better I get back sooner than later. I miss my pooch, and I have to give Ellie all the info, and then wait patiently to see if I still have a boyfriend." Luna sighed. "And you know how good I am at being patient." She smiled.

"Not very." Gail laughed. "First thing, we gotta get you a new phone. This way, you'll be able to answer it when your boyfriend calls you."

"You're right. I am going to remain positive. But boy, was this a huge test."

"For real. I'm sure you both passed with flying colors." Gail gathered their glasses and brought them inside. Luna and Max followed behind. "The stores should be open soon."

"I'm going to call the airline and change my ticket and start to pull my stuff together." Luna walked toward her room, opened her laptop, and checked the booking link to her flight. There was an eleven a.m. flight that would get her into Asheville at midnight with the time zone change. At least she'd be able to sleep in her own bed. *If* she could finally sleep.

She was about to send Chi-Chi and Cullen a text to let them know her travel plans when she realized she had no phone. Again. Twice in one day. *Boy, how we've come to depend on a phone being by our side all the time.* It occurred to her that she'd hardly used her phone during her stay in Sedona. She'd checked in with Chris every other day and taken the fateful photo of Brendan. But whenever they'd gone for a hike, she'd instinctively turned it off. Maybe she should try doing that more often. She thought there was an app that allowed only certain calls to come through. She would definitely look into it when she shopped for a new device.

A half hour later, Gail and Luna were on their way to a big box electronic store. "I don't remember this being here the last time," Luna remarked, as they turned into the massive parking lot.

"Yep. The rest of the world has found us," Gail said wryly. "But Sedona still hasn't lost its magic."

"You're not kidding. I wonder if I was anywhere else when all this Brendan stuff happened, whether it would have turned out the way it did."

Gail wagged her eyebrows. "Like I said—it's the magic."

While Chris was waiting for the jet in Flagstaff, he sent Carter a text, letting him know he'd be back in time to pick him up from camp. He sent a similar one to Lucinda but with much less affection. Her response was: **See you in court Tuesday.**

That answered the question he'd been going to ask Evan about the hearing. Now he had to find out the time and place. After receiving Chris's text, Evan wrote back:

2:00PM – Courthouse – Room 203 – We're ready!

This was only a preliminary hearing for the judge to listen to the complaints and then decide when the final hearing would take place with witnesses. Carter still had to see the psychiatrist for the evaluation, and Chris was expecting letters from Carter's school outlining his academic achievements and intramural activities. He had no doubt Carter would come out looking like a well-adjusted and responsible kid. If things lined up the way he anticipated, it would be Lucinda trying to prove Carter would be better off in Chicago. He also hoped the judge would ask Carter what he wanted. The rest would be a matter of scheduling. If Lucinda wanted to see her son often, there would be nothing stopping her from visiting him. It didn't have to be a one-way situation with Carter being juggled from city to city. The less disruption for him, the better.

Chris opened his duffel to find a book he wanted to read on the way back. At the bottom of the bag was Luna's crushed phone. He still hadn't decided how to get rid of it. Theoretically, it could be used as evidence to support Luna's statement, but then it would incriminate him with interfering with an investigation. Never in his life had he been faced with this kind of ethical dilemma. He pulled the microSD card and the SIM cards from the back of the crushed phone and put the fingernail-size chips in his pocket. He then made a decision. He'd wait. He'd wait until the entire case was officially closed and the witness was ensconced in his new safehold. He felt better about that idea. Once the witness was reassigned, all previous information was removed from the mainframe and stored in a highly classified facility, where there was no access from the outside via the Internet. In order to find the information, one had to physically visit the facility. It rarely happened. It was imperative that protected witnesses remain just that. Protected.

Luna and Gail browsed through all the latest phones and gadgets.

"This is just too much." Luna sighed. "I want to go back to the days when people used flip phones."

A young man with big round discs in his earlobes approached them. "Yep. We have flip phones. Lots of people are going 'old school.' Follow me."

Luna and Gail gave each other a look. Neither of them appreciated that expression. It was borderline insulting. Just because something was new didn't necessarily mean it was better. And just because something might be older, that didn't necessarily make it inferior. They followed the tattoo-covered Gen Z salesperson to a section where there were over a dozen flip phones on display. He explained the difference between a regular flip and a smartphone. Luna looked at the Samsung Galaxy Flip. It had all the bells and whistles of other Androids, but it folded in half. It was the best compromise. The salesman asked if she wanted him to transfer her data from her old phone to the new one. Her answer: "I don't have it. It fell in the river."

"Bummer," he said. "Well, you can still have the same phone number. I'll call your service provider so we can activate your new phone. But you won't have your contact list or your photos."

The word *photo* gave Luna a shiver. That photo was the singular reason she no longer had her phone. She sighed. "I guess I have my work cut out for me."

"Did you upload anything to the cloud?" he asked.

"No. I don't like the idea of my personal stuff floating in cyberspace," Luna answered.

"You'd be surprised how much is out there that we don't realize."

Again, Luna shuddered. "I guess I'll have to reset all my passwords." She was getting nervous. She had no idea what Chris had done with her old phone. She guessed she would find out eventually. That is, if they were still on speaking terms.

The clerk took down all of Luna's information and told them it would take about an hour to get her up and running. So Luna and Gail decided to grab some lunch at a local vegan restaurant.

"Do you come here often?" Luna asked Gail as she perused the menu.

"Occasionally. I like their avocado smash on millet. Their fake grilled cheese with fake bacon is pretty good, but you gotta eat it hot; otherwise, the consistency gets weird."

"There have been articles lately noting that if the world went vegan, it would reduce gas emissions by eighty percent."

"Well, you know that ain't gonna happen." Gail placed her menu back on the table. She tapped her finger on it. "Plastic. There's no getting away from it unless you live in the wilderness and eat mushrooms and leaves. Don't get me wrong, I think it's great that people are being conscious about lots of things, but to expect a complete overhaul in our lifetime is not only unreasonable, it's unrealistic."

"True. There are parts of the world where people have no access to water and very little food. Too many people live in an ideological bubble and have no idea what is happening in other places. Don't get me started." Luna smirked.

"I shan't. I know better," Gail teased. They placed their order and drank lemon water while they waited. "What do you suppose Chris is up to today?" Gail mused.

"I have no idea." Luna shook her head, then let out a big huff of air. "I wish he had called me."

"On what phone?" Gail eyed her.

"That's three times today I overlooked that important detail." Luna snickered.

The waitress brought their pretend grilled cheese and a side salad of kale.

"I'll tell you—the kale lobby has been out in full force. It's everywhere, and I don't know one person who buys it. I mean, I'll eat it, but for greens, I prefer broccoli rabe and escarole," Luna said, and then stabbed into the leafy salad.

"Your diet has become very Mediterranean," Gail noted.

"It's healthy. And delicious." Luna smiled. "Give me a plate of pasta any day."

"That dinner you made the other night was rather scrumptious. You'll have to give me the recipe."

Luna laughed. "It's not an exact science. You put some olive oil in a pan, a little vegetable stock, some herbs, lemon juice, a dash of white wine, and parmesan cheese."

"No quarter cup of this, a pinch of that?" Gail asked.

"Nope. You do it according to your own taste. That's the beauty of it." Luna squeezed one of the lemons onto her hands and wiped them with a napkin. She recalled the first time she'd done that in front of Chris. He'd laughed, because he was about to do the same thing. Luna sighed. "I miss talking to him."

"You will soon. Your phone will be ready, and you can give him a call."

"I don't know if I should. He could be mad as a hatter!" Luna cringed. "Speaking of that phrase, do you know where it comes from?"

"*Alice in Wonderland*?" Gail shrugged.

"No, silly. It was coined during the seventeenth century, when hatters were using mercuric acid to make felt. They were actually poisoning themselves with the fumes, causing them to behave erratically."

"Ha. Fascinating." Gail picked up the check from the table. "You always have a wealth of information. And to think you don't do social media!"

"I like my information to be from a sound, reliable source." She winked.

They walked back to the store, where the tattooed young man was waiting with a big grin on his face. "You're all set. Want to give it a spin?" He handed Luna the new phone. "You're gonna have to set a password or fingerprint, or both." He showed her what to do.

Gail pulled out her phone and dialed Luna's number. The ringtone was set to "Ode to Joy" from Beethoven's Ninth Symphony. Gail laughed. "Now there's irony. The piece is called 'Ode to Joy,' but ask any soprano how joyful it is to sing! We always joked that Beethoven must have hated sopranos."

"Maybe he didn't know how hard it is to hang on to all those high notes for so long."

"Nah. I just think he hated sopranos." Gail laughed again. "But it was the first symphony to incorporate vocal soloists and a chorus. Maybe you're right." She paused. "Nah. He should have known better."

The eager young salesperson was trying to further engage Luna in Cell Phone Use 101, but she graciously declined. "Just need it to send a few texts for now. I can study it when I get back home."

"It was a pleasure serving you, ma'am."

That was another thing that bugged Luna and Gail: *ma'am*. They weren't old enough to be ma'ams. When they left the store, Gail chuckled and said, "Whenever someone calls me 'Miss,' I thank them."

"Geez, we're not *that* old. Are we?" Luna's eyes bugged out. "I mean, I want a flip phone, I want social media to go away, and I want people to stop living in their parents' basements!"

Gail was howling. "I can't say I disagree with you. But that does make you sound a little, let's say, cranky?"

"I'll take cranky. You know, had any of this happened anywhere else, I probably would have had a meltdown. I truly believe the energy here helped me to stay grounded."

"Like I said. Magic."

When they got into Gail's Jeep, Luna wasn't sure if she should reach out to Chris. "What do you think?"

"He probably doesn't know you've replaced the phone. Or would he?"

"He knows I am not a techno junkie, but he also knows I have to have some way of communicating. So . . . he'll know that I'll get one but not when, although probably sooner than later."

"And your point is?" Gail gave her a sideways glance.

"He could try to call my number to see if I've bought a new phone."

"True. But you don't know who he's with, either."

"Good point," Luna huffed. "I suppose I need to wait this out, too."

"This has been a test of patience, eh?" Gail grinned.

"And my relationship." Luna sighed.

Gail reached over and patted her hand. "It's going to be okay, sweetcakes. Magic. Remember."

Luna sent her brother and Chi-Chi a group text, letting them know when she was arriving and that Cullen didn't have to pick her up because she was getting in late. She'd take a cab or Uber home.

She finished with: *Miss me?*

Chi-Chi answered: *Of course!*

Cullen answered: *Who is this?*

"Ha. My brother. Thinks he's a comedian."

Luna and Gail decided that the chaos they'd experienced required one more massage. Gail phoned the spa, and there were two available appointments, but they had to get there pronto.

It was the perfect ending to a challenging, not-so-perfect, but stimulating, exciting, fruitful, couple of days.

Chapter Twenty-one

Home Turf

Cullen brought Wylie to Luna's so he'd be there when she got in. He knew she'd want her pooch. Wylie could sense his mommy was coming home. He paced back and forth for a half hour. Cullen waited with him for another half hour until the dog finally settled down. He left Luna a note saying there was a freshly made sandwich in the fridge and that Chris had called. Chris told Cullen Luna's phone kept going straight to voicemail, and would he ask her to call him when she got back. Chris hadn't actually tried her number, but it was a good way to see if she still wanted to speak to him. It had been rather hairy the last time they were together.

Wylie began banging his tail against the floor when he heard a car pull into the driveway. He heard Luna say goodnight to the driver, and he began to howl. It sounded as if he were singing in dog language.

Luna dropped her bag at the front door and gave him the biggest, longest hug. "I am so happy to see you, pal. Boy, it was quite a trip!" She went into the kitchen to let him out and walked right past the note sitting on the counter. She dragged her luggage into the bedroom and left it in the corner. "That's for tomorrow, or whenever," she said out loud.

On her way back through the kitchen, she let Wylie in, opened the refrigerator, and spotted the sandwich. "Cullen isn't so bad after all, is he?" She patted Wylie on the head, still overlooking the piece of paper that was waiting for her. She ripped off a sheet of paper towel and brought the sandwich into the living room, with Wylie following close behind. She plopped down on the sofa and grabbed the remote. "What's been going on in town?" she asked her pup. He tilted his head this way and that. "Well, let's find out." She scrolled through the channels as she munched on the ham and brie on sourdough. "Yummy." She broke off a small piece and gave it to the waiting dog. When they were finished, she left the plate on the coffee table and went straight to her room, peeled off her clothes, freshened up, and climbed into bed. The note remained unseen. Unread.

Luna thought she would conk out when her head hit the pillow, but not unlike the previous nights, she could not fall asleep. Her relationship was hanging in the balance.

Across the state, Marshal Gaines sat at his dining room table, drumming his fingers. According to Cullen, Luna should have arrived home by now. He checked the time. It was almost one a.m. Maybe she thought it was too late to call. Maybe she'd call in the morning. Maybe she'd never speak to him again after he'd treated her like a criminal. He poured himself two fingers of bourbon. Maybe that would take some of the load off his shoulders. Maybe not. He decided maybe a hot shower would help. That didn't work, either. He was tied up in knots and decided to do some deep breathing exercises Luna had taught him.

It helped. A little.

He knew he would have to wait until morning before he could make any sort of move, but he also had to make the hour-long drive to pick up Carter. He sat up straight. The camp was halfway between Charlotte and Asheville. If Carter was up to it, maybe they'd take a detour to see Luna. Maybe not. It was a conversation they needed to have without any distractions. Actually, it was two conversations: one with Luna, and one with his son. He willed his mind to concentrate on seeing his son and hearing all his stories about camp. That did the trick, and his body relaxed. Finally.

Luna punched the pillows. She tried to calculate exactly how many total hours of sleep she'd had in the past three nights. Six? Eight? She was running on adrenaline and running on empty at the same time. She decided to make some herbal tea. Chamomile. It was supposed to help you relax. She flipped on the switch that controlled the kitchen light and the overhead fan. A single sheet of paper drifted across the counter. She squinted and picked it up. It was the note from Cullen. And it was about Chris. Her heart started to pound. He wanted to talk to her. Was this a good thing or a bad thing? The suspense had been wearing on her. She wasn't going to wait until morning. She didn't care what time it was. She dashed into her bedroom and grabbed her new phone. She punched in Chris's number.

Chris catapulted from bed. His heart was racing. No one called at that hour unless it was an emergency. He grabbed the phone and saw it was Luna. He answered right away. "Are you alright?"

"I . . . I think so. You tell me. Am I alright?" She held her breath.

Chris replied with a very long exhale. "As far as I'm concerned, you are the best."

Tears began to well up in Luna's eyes. "I've been so worried you'd never want to speak to me again."

"I was worried you wouldn't want to talk to me, either," he snorted.

"Well, you were very marshal-y with me." She could finally breathe again.

"Yeah. Sorry about that. Just doing my job." He paused. "You've got to admit, your new hair, being somewhere you shouldn't have been? Can you blame me?"

Luna thought about it for a moment. "Yes and no. Yes, because I looked like I was in disguise and someplace I shouldn't have been, but no, because you should know me by now."

"Believe me, my mind was having a tug-of-war between you and my oath."

"I guess it was a tie?" She was being cheeky.

"I think you had more points on the board." He was smiling. "It wasn't as if I doubted you personally."

"Well, then, who were you doubting?"

"Perhaps myself. But, in my defense, you didn't look like the Luna I know. It was a little unnerving."

"I get it. But you said you liked the new look." She was almost purring.

"Luna, I would like almost anything you'd do to your hair."

"What do you mean *almost*?"

"Just don't go all mohawk or mullet on me, okay?"

"Deal!"

"I think we should both try to get some rest. I have to pick up Carter tomorrow in Hickory. What if we swing by?"

"Are you sure? I mean, you haven't seen him in three weeks. Maybe he doesn't want an audience while he spends time with his dad."

"I have a confession to make," Chris said.

"Oh? What?" Luna's curiosity peaked.

"Before we both left, I told Cullen to keep an eye out for a 1959 Thunderbird that needed to be restored."

"You did what?" She was half surprised and half elated.

"Yeah. He's having it delivered tomorrow morning. I thought I'd show it to Carter and see what he thinks about our project."

"Wow. You are some quick operator." Luna chuckled.

"Why wait?" Chris laughed. "We can swing by and have lunch, and then I'll drive him back to my place. Sound okay with you?"

"Sounds close to perfect to me." Luna was smiling from ear to ear.

"Great. I'll see you around noon. Goodnight, my little lunatic. Love you, babe."

"Good night, Marshal Gaines. Love you, too."

Chapter Twenty-two

Back to Normal
Sorta

Luna slept like she was in a coma. She didn't even hear her alarm go off. But Wylie was determined to get her up so she could let him out and give him his breakfast. Luna rubbed her eyes. She was a little disoriented. *Home. Right. Got it.*

"Hey, pal. Give me a sec."

She sat up and looked at her new phone. Yes, she'd made an outbound call. Yes, it was to Chris. Then she replayed the conversation from the night before to make sure it wasn't a dream. When she was convinced it was real, she threw off the covers and bounced out of bed.

"Come on, pal! What are you waiting for?"

She let Wylie out, opened a can of his food, and set it on the floor. He must have known, because he was scratching at the door *tout suite*. Luna padded to the bathroom and went through her normal routine. *Nor-*

mal. What a nice change. She loved Sedona and was thrilled she'd had the opportunity to see her friend and the glorious surroundings. She could have used a tad less drama. On the other hand, she was happy to know Brendan was alive and well. At least she hoped he was well. Knowing he was being protected by people like Chris gave her some comfort. They were all over the situation like ants at a picnic.

Luna and Wylie piled into her SUV and headed to Stillwell. It had only been five days, but it seemed like weeks. Chi-Chi was the first to greet her with her big, beautiful smile. She was waving her hand in the air, as if she were swatting away flies. Then Luna noticed the sparkling diamond on her left hand. Luna grabbed it immediately. "*What?* When did this happen? Oh, my goodness! We're going to be related." Then she paused. "You are marrying my brother, right?"

"Who else would I marry?" Chi-Chi wrapped her arms around her future sister-in-law. "He proposed two nights ago." Chi-Chi stared at the 3k solitaire emerald-cut gem.

"Gee, maybe I should leave town more often." Luna giggled. "That is absolutely gorgeous. I guess he's doing quite well in his workshop," Luna teased.

"Your brother can be a bit sneaky. He asked Abeo to find him the stone." Chi-Chi was grinning from ear to ear. "I cannot believe he trusted him." She laughed.

Luna put her hands on her hips. "That brother of mine has become quite the operator. It would appear as if Cullen is leading a double life. Chris asked him to find a 1959 Thunderbird that needs to be restored. It's being delivered today. *Huh.* He's been quite a busy beaver." She hugged Chi-Chi again. "I am so happy for you. And for me!" She linked her arm through Chi-Chi's. "Let's go see what that rascal is up to."

The two marched into the showroom and then to the back. "Aren't you full of surprises?" Luna said, and elbowed Cullen.

"Well, hello to you, too!" He gave her a kiss on the head.

"What is with this head-kissing?"

"It's the new 'do." Cullen chuckled. "So?"

"So congratulations, you big oaf. Why didn't you tell me?" Luna whined.

"Like you would be able to keep your mouth shut."

Luna stuck out her tongue and gave him a raspberry sound as a response. She turned to Chi-Chi. "Have you picked a date?"

"We have not. We were waiting to tell you, because you and Ellie are going to plan the wedding for us."

"A-ha!" Luna was giddy. "Does Ellie know?"

"That she is planning our wedding? No. We haven't told her yet," Chi-Chi replied.

"Well, let's get crackin'." Luna grabbed Chi-Chi's arm and dragged her into the café. Luna immediately buzzed Ellie on her walkie-talkie. "Hi! I'm back! Lots to talk about. Can you come down?"

"Be right there."

Within a few minutes, Ellie was briskly walking through the atrium. Ziggy, Marley, and Wylie bounded in from the patio. When Ellie saw the ring, she squealed, the dogs barked, and Luna yelled out a "Yippee!" It was a moment of wonderful chaos.

Once everything calmed down, the three women sat down at a table. "There's so much to talk over. Where do we start?" Ellie said.

Luna took her cue. "I have all the information on the artists. They are thrilled to be part of your exhibit."

"Wonderful. I spoke with a travel agent, and she will make all the arrangements for them. When we get a little closer, she'll reach out and get their information."

"This is so exciting!" Luna said. "All of it! An atrium exhibit and a wedding! We have a lot of work to do!"

Chi-Chi said she would like to have the wedding in the fall, outside in the gardens, and the reception in the atrium.

"Easy-peasy." Luna nodded. "Got something hard for us to do?"

"Keep Jennine away from my brother!" Chi-Chi cackled.

Chris arrived at the softball camp around ten thirty. He introduced himself to the teenager, who was sitting at a table with a clipboard. "I'm Carter's dad."

"Wow! Are you really a U.S. Marshal?"

Chris smiled. "Yes, I am." He pulled his jacket aside to show the boy the badge on his belt.

"Cool!" The kid stared at the gold shiny object.

Chris interrupted the kid's gaze. "Do you know where Carter is?"

"Oh sure." He pulled out a walkie-talkie. "Do you guys use these, too?"

"Sometimes." Chris smiled.

"Marshal Gaines is here for Carter," the kid said into the device, trying to be as official as possible.

"He'll be right over," a scratchy voice replied.

"Thanks," said the teen into the walkie-talkie. Then

he turned back to Chris and asked, "So, do you have a gun, too?"

"Most law enforcement officers do."

"You got it on you now?"

"I can't say." He gave the kid a nod and leaned in. "That's classified information."

"Gotcha," the kid whispered back.

Carter came running from the barracks-style building with his backpack and a baseball bat. "Dad!"

"Hey, buddy!" Carter gave him a side hug. "How ya doing?"

"Great!"

"You ready?"

"Yes, sir."

Chris leaned over to the young man at the table and put out his hand. "Nice to meet you. Keep up the good work."

"Aye, aye, sir!" he said, and saluted.

Chris stashed Carter's gear in the back of his truck. "Listen, I have kind of a surprise for you."

"You're going to marry Luna?" Carter said, his eyes eager.

Chris laughed out loud. "I haven't asked her yet."

"Then what's the surprise?"

"Remember I went to that car show, and I told you that I'd like to get a classic car and fix it up?"

"Yep!"

"Ready to go look at our new project?"

"Heck yeah!"

Chris started the engine and began the hour-long trip to Stillwell Center. Carter chatted up a storm about camp, what he'd learned, and the new friends he'd made. He was one very happy young man. They talked about the upcoming appointment with the psychiatrist, and Chris explained about the preliminary hearing.

"Gotcha," Carter responded. "I'm ready, Dad."

Chris knew he was.

When they arrived at Stillwell, there was laughter in the air. Lots of hugs, smiles, and kisses, including a mushy one between Luna and Chris. "Get a room, Dad," Carter joked.

More laughter ensued. "Shall we take a look at your new project?" Cullen asked.

"Heck yeah!" Carter said again, and followed Cullen to the rear door. Chris lagged behind long enough to pull Luna aside.

"I missed you. And I'm sorry." He drew her close. "I don't want anything to come between us. Ever."

"Me either." She leaned her head against his chest.

"So, we're good?" He looked into her eyes.

"Couldn't be better."

Epilogue

Several weeks later, the judge decided to let Carter choose which parent he wanted to live with. As expected, he picked his father. His parents worked out the schedule and signed the agreement. Chris was certain Lucinda would never speak to him again. At least not directly, which was totally fine with him.

The following months were a flurry of wedding plans for Chi-Chi and Cullen. Members of her family were traveling from Nigeria. Luna, Chi-Chi, and Ellie incorporated Nigerian traditions into the celebration and hired a special chef to prepare authentic food. Chi-Chi wore a traditional *aso oke* outfit made of thick fabric with long sleeves that widened at the wrists. A kaftan-like skirt was tied at the waist. Luna appreciated why Chi-Chi wanted to get married in the fall. It was a lot of clothing, including the *gele* headpiece. Cullen chose a customary *agbada*, a four-piece outfit with a matching hat. He wanted to assure Chi-Chi's family he was respectful of their culture and show how much he loved her.

The garden was filled with hundreds of white orchids, white hydrangeas, and white roses, with a long red silk carpet. There were over one hundred guests. Chi-Chi's auntie acted as the *alaga*, also known as the master of ceremonies. A drummer was positioned up front. The coming together of two families commenced, with many introductions and lots and lots of dancing. And that was just the beginning.

When the festivities moved to the atrium, there were more vibrant-colored flowers throughout. The tradition of "spraying" the bride and groom with money continued through the night, with Luna collecting the stash in bags made specially for the occasion.

At the end of the evening, Chris brought Luna over to the only quiet corner of the center. "I didn't want to say or do anything to distract from Chi-Chi and Cullen's big day. But there is something Carter has been asking about."

"What?" Luna couldn't imagine what his son wanted from her, or why it was so important to have this tête-à-tête now.

"He wants me to marry you."

"He what?" Luna had had several glasses of champagne, but she knew she'd heard him right. "I guess the next question is, do *you* want to marry me?" Luna's legs were trembling.

"More than ever." Chris stared at her. "Will you?" He opened a small box with a diamond ring inside.

"More than ever."

Don't miss the fun, friendship, and romance as four lifelong friends embark on a singles cruise in a heart-warming holiday novel by #1 *New York Times* best-selling author Fern Michaels.

SANTA CRUISE

At Ridgewood High, Amy, Frankie, Rachael, and Nina formed a deep bond. Fifteen years after leaving school behind, they're back for a reunion, laughing, reminiscing, and chatting how much has changed—and how much hasn't. Nina, once the star of every school play, moved to Hollywood and landed a recurring role on a sitcom. Amy, fondly known as "the brains of the operation," is now a Silicon Valley bioengineer. Outgoing and compassionate, Frankie works for a New York publishing house. Rachael, always the most boy-crazy of the crew, married—mostly to please her parents—but is now divorced. All four are strong, successful, and somehow still looking for the right partner. But Frankie has an idea to help solve that: a singles cruise for the holidays.

In late December, Amy, Rachael, Frankie, and Nina gather in Miami, ready to board their state-of-the-art cruise ship. The entertainment options are endless, the food is to die for, and the passenger list includes hundreds of eligible men. The highlight of the week will be a magnificent New Year's Eve celebration with multiple theme parties, dancing, and fireworks. The ladies are happy to give Cupid a helping hand here and there—hanging mistletoe in elevators and cheering each other on through speed-dating events and shore excursions. Holidays—like the path of love itself—don't always go exactly as planned, but over the course of one festive, unforgettable week, all four will set sail on surprising new adventures.